LOVE HURTS

A REDCLIFFE NOVEL

Love Hurts

By

Catherine Green

MIRADOR PUBLISHING
www.miradorpublishing.com

First Published in Great Britain 2011 by Mirador Publishing

Copyright © 2011 by Catherine Green

All right reserved. No part of this publication may be reproduced or transmitted, in any form or by any means, without permission of the publishers or author. Excepting brief quotes used in reviews.

First edition: 2011

Any reference to real names and places are purely fictional and are constructs of the author. Any offence the references produce is unintentional and in no way reflect the reality of any locations or people involved.

A copy of this work is available though the British Library.

ISBN: 978-1-908200-24-2

Mirador Publishing
Mirador
Wearne Lane
Langport
Somerset
TA10 9HB

Author Biography

Catherine Green was raised on a diet of books, and her happiest memories are of school days spent in the local library on Saturday mornings, discovering the world beyond our human existence. She has finally realised her writing dream and has stories featured in both *The Mirador Fantasmagoria*, and *Devils, Demons and Werewolves* by Bridgehouse Publishing. Catherine lives in Cheshire with her husband, daughter, Staffydoodle dog, and two pet turtles. In her spare time she hunts ghosts and pursues her spiritual occult interests. Her website is -

www.catherinegreencrafts.moonfruit.com

For my sister Emily, who forced me to write this story instead of just dreaming about it.

Thank you Cheeky Monkey!

PROLOGUE

I never understood the concept of being in love. It always seems like such a big deal and yet everywhere you look you see people getting their hearts broken, scorned women and cheating men. Practically every TV show, film or novel has some sort of love theme running through it. People thrive on relationships; they chase each other for romance, for excitement, or simply to be together. They argue, fight, make up, and break up. I have seen a lot of people hurt by love and then I have seen a few people who are happy with it. The whole subject confuses me, it frightens me, and because I don't understand it, I don't miss it and I certainly don't chase it.

Don't get me wrong; love must be worth fighting for because everyone always seems to be chasing it. But not me. No, I decided after my parents died and my family abandoned me that I would look after number one before anyone else. Then I met Liz and developed love of a different kind, love for my best friend, my sister. I made an exception and vowed to always protect her no matter what. But when it came to men, not a chance. I wasn't interested. I didn't need romance, and I didn't need a relationship.

Then I met Jack Mason and his brother Danny. All of my carefully built defences came crashing down around me. Love is dangerous and painful. Love is confusing and exhausting. Love will get you killed. Yet despite everything I find myself going back for more, unable to break free of this trap. My life was normal and happy and successful before I met the Mason brothers. Then they showed me what I had been lacking and what I needed to truly be fulfilled. So let me tell you the story, about a picturesque seaside town in South Western England, and the secrets of its seemingly innocent inhabitants…

1

I was running along the cliff top in the pouring rain and it was late at night, cold and stormy. My breath caught in my throat, I could barely see where I was going and the sea was crashing against the rocks beneath me. I was terrified, running from a monster behind me. He chased me and I couldn't look back, I just couldn't. My throat felt raw from gasping, my hair soaked and cold against my neck, water dripping down my body. I shivered but I had to run. I had to escape. Then my foot caught in the rough grass and I fell to my hands and knees with a cry. I scrambled to my feet but he was there, the monster, right behind me. I screamed as he jumped and I turned to face him, to accept my fate.

I woke with a start and sat straight up in bed, covered in sweat and gasping for air. It was just a dream. It was so vivid. I even knew the cliff top location where I had been running. It wasn't far from home, out on the main road from Redcliffe to the nearby city. What was I running away from? Was it some subconscious fear of myself? Why could I feel the rain on my skin and why was I shivering in a dream? I shook my body to clear my head, looked around the dark bedroom, where I could see moonlight shining around the edges of the curtains. Everything looked normal: my clothes slung across the chair, my dressing table in its usual state of disarray, the door firmly closed and the house silent. I shivered, breathed deeply a few times, and then I lay down again, pulling the quilt up around my neck.

Maybe I should take Liz's advice and see a doctor. These dreams were getting more realistic to the point where I thought they were memories even though I had never been to this town before I moved here three years' ago, except for the odd holiday. I had started having the same recurring dream a couple of months ago but it didn't happen every night. Usually it happened once or twice a week. The dreams always had me running from some imagined monster, but it was a monster that I knew, a person who betrayed me...I drifted off to sleep again and thankfully had no more dreams that night.

I woke early the next morning, showered and went downstairs for breakfast before starting work. Although I couldn't really call running my own book shop work, I loved it. The previous owners had put up Redcliffe Books for sale when they retired and had no family to take it over. At the time I had just persuaded my best friend and now business partner Elizabeth to take the plunge and apply for a loan together so we could invest in a shop. We had been working as office administrators in Manchester and it was a huge step to move all the way down here to Cornwall but we loved it. Redcliffe is a beautiful tourist town and we get a lot of trade in the summer and during winter months we have a regular clientele who keep the place ticking over steadily.

I worked my magic on Liz, our loan was approved, and our offer on the shop accepted and now here we are. In fact Liz has me to thank for finding her husband Robert who she now lives with in a lovely little cottage across town. He is a university professor and met her when he came into the shop for some research shortly after we moved here. I now live in my own apartment above the shop, with my kitchen on the ground floor at the back. It suits me to simply wander from one room to another and be at work, so much better than all that commuting I used to do. I am certainly more suited to living in a town with lots of open space, than I am to living in a crowded city. I adore having the sea and sand right there on my doorstep. It gives me a sense of freedom that I never felt in the city.

It was 8.30am and I knew Liz had a doctor's appointment so I picked up my coffee mug and wandered through to the shop to open up for the day. At this time of year we ran it between the two of us until it got busier, then we would take on a couple of college students during the summer months to help us out. It was March and I was looking forward to the warmer weather as we had suffered a particularly cold and snowy winter. As much as I enjoyed my cosy winter evenings tucked under blankets on my sofa with a stack of books, DVDs, and my favourite wine and hot chocolate, now I was restless for some sunshine and fresh air. The sun was shining and it did feel warmer which was wonderful as I unlocked the front door of the shop and flipped the sign to 'Open'.

My first job was to check our online sales and package up anything for delivery. Then I had a few customers to deal with, and decided to have a tidy up on our sale table. The shop isn't huge but it just fits our needs. It is a square, bright room, and our counter sits to the left of the door as customers enter. Opposite there are floor to ceiling pine bookshelves built in, covering two walls and built around the window recess, framing it. Then in the middle of the room we have three large tables where we set up our promotions and special offers. We also have a picture window to the right of the front door as you face it, and here is where we set up our displays depending on the time of year and current trends. Redcliffe Books is a lovely light and airy shop, and we have a view out onto the central shopping street, which leads down to the promenade and beach.

It was 11.30am when the door burst open as Liz arrived in her usual flurry of chaos. Her dark eyes were sparkling, her short black hair glossy and sleek, and she was glowing with good health. I always envied her permanently tanned skin. She came rushing through the door grinning from ear to ear, shouted a breathless "Morning" at me and then handed me an envelope. I looked at her curiously and opened it to find a card inside, plain white. The card turned out to be a scan photograph, the 12-week image of Elizabeth's baby. My best friend was pregnant with her first child! I leaped out of my seat and flung my arms around her, almost crying with excitement as she laughed and hugged me tightly.

"What do you think, Jessica?" she gasped excitedly, "I'm going to be a Mother!"

Liz stepped back and looked at me, smiling. My own smile resembled the proverbial Cheshire cat as I replied.

"It's wonderful, Liz. I'm so happy for you." I said, "How the hell did you manage to hide this from me for three months?" I gently chided her, not the slightest bit angry of course.

"It was tough," Liz said, taking a deep breath, "You know when I had that weird sickness bug? Morning sickness! And when you kept asking me why I was quiet? We didn't want to get ahead of ourselves by telling people before we had the first scan, but here it is and the baby is perfectly healthy and you are the first person I've told, straight from the hospital."

She paused long enough to catch her breath properly, and sat down on her office chair behind the counter.

This was a huge surprise. I mean I knew that it was likely to happen, Elizabeth and Robert had been happily married for twelve months now and we were all mature enough to deal with having children. As I looked at her excited face I felt so happy but also a tiny bit jealous. I wanted my own baby. But I didn't even have a boyfriend so that wasn't going to happen for a long time yet. I would simply throw myself into being an adoptive Aunty for Liz's child.

We spent the rest of the day poring over baby books and discussing her maternity arrangements. Of course she had to telephone her parents and I heard her mother's scream of excitement from my seat beside Liz. Her parents were so lovely. They still lived in the suburbs of Manchester but visited at least two or three times a year. They had made Redcliffe their holiday town and I enjoyed their visits. Elizabeth's parents had practically adopted me when we became friends. I had been a little distant with them at first, not wanting their pity, but eventually I grew to love them and they were always there to offer support. I was so happy for them to have a grandchild to dote upon.

While Liz was speaking to her mother I let my mind wander. Perhaps I should seriously start looking for a new partner, a potential husband. I had never felt the need for anyone, and I certainly didn't have a very good track record with men. There had been one or two who wanted more from me, but I was never prepared to give myself up. I enjoyed sex of course, but when it came to heavy emotions, I got scared and ran away. It had a lot to do with me being an orphan, I knew that, but I also knew that I couldn't blame everything on that fact. Surely there were other orphans in the world that got married and settled down? I convinced myself that I just hadn't found the right man yet, and that it would happen when the time was right. Besides I would be running the business single-handedly while Liz was on maternity leave, so I had no time for a relationship now. I enjoyed my freedom, which I wouldn't get if I had a partner and a baby. No, it definitely wasn't right for me just yet.

2

That night I headed up to my local pub, the Ship Inn, to see my good friend Simon Bunce. He is the manager there and I met him soon after we moved to Redcliffe. Simon would be an ideal boyfriend if he weren't gay. He is a surfer, with a fit body and an attractive face to match. We first met when Liz and I visited the pub shortly after our move. I met Simon on the beach a few times, and made the mistake of flirting with him, until I discovered the truth.

Anyway we hit it off, finding that we shared the same sense of humour and love of the seaside, and eventually Simon and I became very close. He became my second best friend, the only other person I would let my guard down for. Simon's mother had been a single parent with schizophrenia, so his grandmother raised him. Sadly his mother had committed suicide when he was a teenager, and his grandmother died of a heart attack before I met Simon. Sometimes I thought this was why we were such good friends. We both lived in the present, and didn't have any of the usual emotional family baggage that so many other people seem to have. Simon's family were the staff at the Ship, and he was devoted to his job and to the business, just like me with my bookshop.

I wanted to share Elizabeth's news with him. She wasn't as close to Simon but we all went out regularly together socializing. It was around 8pm when I got to the pub and Simon was behind the bar when I walked in. He looked a little harassed.

"Hey, Jess how are you?" he said, his angular face flushed with heat from hurrying around, "Sorry, I know it's my night off but someone called in sick and we got busy and, look, do you want to go upstairs while I sort this out? Watch TV or something and I'll be with you as soon as possible?" he was pulling a pint while he spoke, and there was a growing queue of customers building next to me.

I smiled and leaned on the bar. I had already thought about this possibility, knowing what Simon was like and the fact that the tourist season was slowly waking up ready for the Easter school holidays.

"It's all right Simon; I brought a book with me." I said, "Just get me a glass of wine and come over when you get a minute, I have something to tell you."

I couldn't keep the excitement out of my voice. Simon grinned, made some sarcastic comment about me with my nose in a book again, and then went to serve the customers and get my wine.

I had grown to enjoy sitting in a corner of the pub with a glass of wine and my book over recent months. Since Liz and Rob got married they did more and more 'couple' things together and Simon was so conscientious about work that he was nearly always behind the bar or in the kitchen when I came to see him.

I didn't really have any other close friends here, just hadn't found anybody else that I could be relaxed with. There was Sally, who I had met through Simon, but she was a nurse at the nearby hospital and she worked practically all the time. I liked Sally though; she was like me, small and scrappy, maybe even a little more so. She was very petite but concealed a fiery temperament, and I certainly wouldn't like to get on the wrong side of her. I was used to being alone, I had been orphaned at a young age and never really felt comfortable with the foster families I was placed with. There was no surviving family that I knew of and my relationship history with men was practically non-existent; my longest relationship had lasted around four months.

I did feel lonely at home with just the television and my laptop for company, and there was only so much social networking I could handle. So I started bringing a book to the pub and chatting to Simon while he worked. Sometimes I brought my laptop and surfed the Internet. I had claimed my own table near the fireplace, which gave me a good view of the room and the bar.

Simon lived in the apartment above the pub; he managed it on behalf of its owner, a mysterious man who had apparently been working away for the last four years. Simon was very fond of the pub and I had a feeling it had something to do with this mysterious landlord, one Danny Mason. I had questioned Simon about it but he got a bit moody and changed the subject, saying it was just his boss and I shouldn't read so much into it. So I left him alone.

The Ship is a beautiful seventeenth century building and sits at the end of the promenade in Redcliffe Bay, nestled into the cliffs. It is rumoured to have been a smugglers' haunt back in the days of pirates, and there is a huge ship's wheel mounted on the wall outside which can be seen all the way down the promenade. Stories say that this wheel came from the first wreck that was looted, and the wheel is a constant reminder, a trophy from times past. I think these stories are very romantic, wild and passionate, very Daphne Du Maurier.

At the rear of the building the beer garden and smoking area lead to steps that take you right down to the beach. It even has a small enclosed children's play area, with a climbing frame, swing and slide, and I could imagine Liz and Rob bringing their child here in the future, for lazy Sunday afternoons. There is a car park at the side of the building, and the front of the pub opens onto the pavement bordering the main coastal road. Legend has it that the cellars beneath the pub have tunnels and caves leading out of it, and that it was used by smugglers in the old days. I had asked Simon about the tunnels but he laughed and said it was all talk and if there were any they had been blocked up long ago. So much for me going on an adventure!

Inside the pub there is a central hallway from front to back, from which you can enter the main bar on one side, a pool and games room on the other, and a restaurant. There is also the staircase leading to the first floor, on which there is a function room, the manager's office, and the public toilets. From the ground floor there are other doors leading from the corridor that take you into the kitchens, cellars and store rooms. I had actually been in a few of these rooms with Simon before now. From the first floor there is another staircase, which leads directly up to Simon's apartment, a place I was very familiar with since we spent a lot of time watching old films and getting drunk together.

I had just finished reading an especially intense chapter of my book and lifted my head for a minute while I had a sip of wine. It was a nice Merlot, my favourite kind, and one that Simon had started ordering in just for me. Ah the benefits of befriending a pub manager! I savoured the warmth and its fruity flavour as I swallowed.

The clock above the bar said 09:10pm and the pub was quite busy tonight. Then again it was Friday, and all the locals had come in for a bar meal and a few drinks to start the weekend. I looked around the large, square room for any familiar faces, recognizing a few people. Some were regular customers from my shop and they smiled and nodded at me when they saw me looking. Others were people I had met around the town and got talking to, just casual acquaintances. I considered joining one of the groups to be sociable, seeing a few women from the hairdresser's salon next door to my shop. They would be excited to hear Liz's news, and I knew she wouldn't mind me telling people.

My attention was distracted when I saw a man walk in that I had never met before. And yet my heart literally jumped into my throat! It was bizarre. I watched as he approached the bar, and was surprised to see Simon glaring at him as he served a pint of beer. Did he know this man? They exchanged words but I couldn't really tell what Simon said. He just looked very angry and hostile.

I watched this handsome stranger, transfixed somehow. I admired his profile; especially his firm bottom, and couldn't help but imagine him naked! Oh dear, maybe I should ease up on the wine. My stomach lurched as the man turned round to survey the room, caught my eye and approached the table, smiling. He walked casually, confident and relaxed.

"Hello," he said, in a deep and very sexy voice, "I'm

Jack. Umm, tell me if I'm being forward but do you mind if I sit here?" he ruffled his hair with his left hand and my stomach lurched. I smiled back and shook my head, fighting not to be clumsy or silly.

"No, sit down." I replied, though inwardly I was ordering myself to stay calm and not make a fool of myself.

He was gorgeous! He was tall and clearly muscular beneath the black blazer, smart grey button-through shirt, and black jeans that he was wearing. His face was all angles, manly and rugged, his short dark hair slightly curling and he had a trace of stubble as though he hadn't shaved for a day or two. In fact I noticed the envious glances from other women in the room as he sat and I couldn't help but feel proud that he wanted my attention. It was silly I know but the human ego can never be understood. No matter how independent we women like to consider ourselves, most of us are a sucker for a handsome face and a fit male body.

He introduced himself as Detective Jack Mason, recently returned from a four-year undercover job in Scotland. The surname rang a bell and I couldn't figure out why. He had the most intense blue eyes, almost hypnotic, and for some reason I found myself desperate to keep his attention and I really wanted him to kiss me. It was such a strong attraction that I could feel my body reacting to him being so close. He seemed so strong somehow, and I could imagine his crushing physical strength, but I supposed that came with the job. As we talked I could see the muscles rippling beneath his shirt when he removed his jacket. It took all my concentration just to focus on what he was saying.

Jack explained that he had returned to his hometown and was revisiting his old haunts to reconnect with people and places. He was now going to be stationed at the local police headquarters. We fell into conversation and after a while he offered me a drink when he noticed that my glass was empty. I accepted and watched him walk towards the bar with a confident, easy manner. Again I watched that nice, tight bottom in his well-fitting jeans, and just looking at him sent more shivers all through my body. It really had been too long since I had sex. Let's hope tonight I got lucky!

I watched as Simon once again served Jack behind the bar but he did not look happy. In fact he slipped me a look that plainly told me he wasn't happy with me talking to this man. What was the harm? There was clearly an attraction between Jack and me and at the very least I wanted to see what could happen, even if we just had a one-night stand. The two men seemed to be talking intently about something and then Jack shook his head and came back over to our table with a glass of wine for me and another pint of beer for himself.

"Your friend seems very concerned about your welfare, Jessica," he said, "He seems to think I will seduce you and have my wicked way."

I laughed and shook my long auburn hair back in a manner I knew would be appealing. Yes I said 'auburn!' One of my pet hates was when people referred to it as 'red hair', or 'ginger'. I blinked slowly at Jack, hoping he could see the desire in my face. I would never openly try and kiss him or anything, that wasn't my style. Besides, I didn't want to come across as desperate; I do have some standards.

I spoke in a voice that I hoped was full of promise.

"Oh don't mind Simon," I said, "he likes to pretend he's my big brother when it suits him. Anyway I'm a big girl I'm sure I can handle you." I winked and grinned.

Jack laughed and put his hand on mine where it lay on my knee. I shivered at his light touch and he fixed my eyes with his as he stroked my skin.

"I'm sure you could, Jessica." he said, "Maybe Simon should leave you to make your own decisions."

I held my breath, concentrating on keeping my body still. My god he was so sexy. I had an incredibly strong urge to throw myself at him and I had never felt like this before. In fact I was always calm and in control, never showing my feelings. He drew his hand away slowly and changed the subject but I found myself watching his lips as he talked, and imagining how it would feel to kiss him.

"Jessica?" I heard a faint accent in Jack's voice as he

eyed me curiously, "Are you all right?"

I roused myself, tossed my hair back over my shoulder, and blinked slowly.

"Sorry, what?" my voice sounded sluggish and I felt a flush of embarrassment. Jack frowned and spoke in a careful voice.

"I was asking what you do, you know, work wise?" he said, "Are you feeling ok?" his face was full of concern.

I laughed, the embarrassment rising to a flush on my cheeks. I ineffectually tried to fan my face with a hand.

"I'm fine, sorry, Jack." I said, "I think the wine's going to my head." I sat back in my chair, fighting a faint wave of nausea that suddenly overcame me.

Jack moved to stand up.

"Maybe you need a bit of air," he said, "shall we go outside?"

I nodded and shakily stood up, "Yeah ok."

3

I stood up slowly, feeling woozy. What the hell was wrong with me? I had only drunk two glasses of wine. Maybe I was getting a sick bug or something. Or maybe I was in sympathy with Liz and her morning sickness. Jack put on his jacket and led the way through the busy pub to the door at the back that led to the decked smoking area. I followed him down the steps to the car park and we moved a little away from the smell of cigarette smoke. The air out here was slightly chilly, nice and fresh and I could taste the familiar sea salt on my tongue. I leaned against the wall, hugging my cardigan around me. Jack stepped in front of me and rubbed my arms. His amazing blue eyes looked so concerned, so caring. All I wanted to do was kiss him.

"How are you feeling now, Jessica?" he asked as he gently cupped my chin and tilted my face up to him, staring into my eyes.

I half smiled, realizing I could use this situation to my advantage. I relaxed against the rough brick wall a little and shivered again.

"A bit better thanks, just a little cold," I said, my voice shaking slightly for emphasis.

Jack stepped even closer and took me in his arms, hugging me against his hard body. I tensed, but instinctively slipped my hands around his waist, inside the open jacket, accepting his unspoken invitation. His shirt was soft to the touch, possibly some sort of silk material, but all I wanted was to pull it away and run my hands over his skin. He moved back enough to look at me but kept his arms around me, and I dropped my hands to my sides. His face showed the desire he felt, and he lowered his mouth to mine. I closed my eyes and waited for the kiss, my heart pounding with delicious anticipation.

Suddenly he was pulled back and I staggered as he was

torn away from my body. I blinked and opened my eyes to see Simon standing in front of me, his face blazing with anger. He shoved Jack away from me and almost snarled. I had never seen him this angry.

"You stay away from her, Mason," he growled. "She is my friend."

Jack's face became stern, almost stony as he replied in a cold voice.

"Be careful, Simon," he warned. "I think we should allow Jessica to decide what she is doing. She seems perfectly capable of taking care of herself."

I felt a sudden rush of anger. How dare Simon interrupt something so intimate! My voice was strong and steady as I straightened up and faced the two men, glaring at Simon. He took the full force of my rage, and it surprised him.

"Simon, what the hell are you playing at?" I said angrily. "For your information I felt a bit faint inside and Jack brought me out here for some fresh air since it was so stuffy in the pub. And you don't even know him do you?" I added, the rage subsiding as quickly as it rose.

The two men looked at each other and Simon spoke through clenched teeth.

"Jack's brother is my boss, the owner of this place," he said steadily, looking from me to Jack. "So yeah, I do know him a little and I know that he should leave you alone. Come on, let me walk you home Jess." He stepped towards me but I moved to the side, angry.

"No, Simon, not until I know why you are being so moody."

I looked at Jack, who was watching Simon and me, and he swallowed, face serious as he spoke.

"I believe, Jessica, that your friend is simply concerned because he hasn't seen me or my brother in almost four years," he said, "and we had something of a reputation before we left." Jack's language was so polite, almost old-fashioned but I barely noticed at the time.

"What do you mean, a reputation?" I asked sullenly. He shrugged.

"Look, Jessica, I'll be honest with you," Jack stopped and glanced at Simon who just glared at him. Jack continued. "I have lived in Redcliffe for many years and have become known among local businesses through my police work," he paused, swallowed, and then said, "Let's just say I haven't had any long-term relationships with women." Jack stopped and I nodded, encouraging him to continue his explanation.

"Incidentally, Simon, that is none of your business!" Jack's attention switched to my angry best friend, who stood defiantly in front of me as Jack spoke again, "You report to my brother, not to me, and I would appreciate it if you gave Jessica and me a little privacy now."

I shook my head and took a deep breath. I did not understand why Simon was being so hostile with this man. Surely he should be careful of what he said to his employer's brother. Especially one who is a police detective. And besides I really didn't want to end this night and spoil my new friendship with an incredibly attractive man. Simon looked at me, his face softening slightly.

"Look, Jessica, it's getting late," he said more gently, "shall I just walk you home? I'm sorry for interrupting but I really don't think you should be alone with Jack."

That did it! Did he think he was my father or something? I blazed with anger as my quick temper flew out of control.

"Simon, what is wrong with you?" I raged, "No I do not want to go home yet, I am not some teenager with a curfew!" I shouted. I was standing upright now, my body rigid with anger.

I turned and started to walk back into the pub but Jack stopped me with a hand on my arm.

"I'm sorry, Jessica, but it is late and I understand you have work tomorrow?" he said in that gentle, slightly accented voice, "Perhaps I could walk you home instead?" he asked, smiling and fixing me with his intense gaze.

I looked at him, at his handsome face and those amazing deep blue eyes, and the butterflies in my stomach grew stronger, as did my physical desire for him. Then I glanced at Simon, stood behind him with clenched fists and an angry expression. And I felt another rush of anger. I smiled sweetly at Jack.

"Alright, Jack, you can walk me home," I said, "maybe come in for some coffee." I added, pointedly ignoring Simon.

Jack smiled and we turned to walk out of the car park. I looked at Simon over my shoulder, a level warning look.

"I will speak to you tomorrow, Simon," I said quietly.

Simon didn't try and stop us as Jack and I walked down the road along the promenade and then up into the main street where my shop was. It was only a ten-minute walk from the pub but there were people wandering about between pubs and clubs, shouting and laughing as they went.

Redcliffe is a decent sized town and of course its centre is the seafront. There are rows of houses ranging in age from seventeenth century to present day. Some of them have shops, some are residential, some are businesses, and then there are the pubs, restaurants and nightclubs. It's a nice mix, and part of the reason I love this town so much.

Jack and me walked side by side, not speaking. I couldn't understand why Simon had gone off like that. He was the most laid-back person I knew and certainly not given to being physically rough with people. In fact I couldn't remember ever seeing him so angry, and I certainly hadn't seen him act violently towards anyone. Yet Jack didn't seem surprised at his behaviour. I broke the silence as we walked.

"Jack, you don't seem surprised by Simon's behaviour," I said. "Is it because of your work, maybe you are used to it or something?" I asked, looking sideways at Jack.

He looked at me and smiled.

"No, Jessica, I'm not surprised," he said then continued, "Yes I deal with some rough people at work in my investigations but Simon was just being protective that's all. He gets like that."

That confused me.

"You sound like you know him well," I said surprised,

"how come I've never heard about you before?"

Jack shrugged and glanced at me as he answered.

"Like I said, Danny and me have lived in Redcliffe for a long time," he said, "Danny promoted Simon to bar manager just before we left on our assignment. It was all very sudden and rushed when we left. That was four years ago. Now I am back in town but my brother isn't and maybe Simon is being over-protective."

He faced forward again, seeming not to want this conversation to continue. But I wouldn't let it go.

"Ok, now I'm confused." I said, "So your brother owns the pub, why would he go on an assignment with you?"

We had reached the shop now and Jack followed me around the back of the terraces to the street behind that led to my small garden. He spoke as we walked up the path and I found my key and unlocked the door.

"My brother Danny is also a police detective and we work together as partners," he said. "He sort of acquired the pub through an old relationship but he leaves the operation to Simon and just has his name on the deeds."

Jack paused, and I nodded encouragingly.

"So their relationship is sort of business partners and friends and through that I got to know Simon," he said, "And he knows about my reputation with women and was trying to protect you."

Here Jack stopped and fixed that intense gaze on me, making my body go hot all over. He was so close and I so badly wanted to touch him again.

"Oh, ok," I said. "Well do you want to come inside for a bit?"

Suddenly his lips were on mine and we fell through the door in a tangle of arms and legs. I jumped as I felt a jolt of static electricity when his skin touched mine. I jumped back, hand to my face.

"Wow, what was that?" I cried out, surprised.

Jack looked just as surprised but his expression quickly changed and he reached for me again.

"Static I think," he said, "It must be my jacket."

He laughed as he shrugged his jacket off and dropped it to the floor, staring at me intently.

"I will leave if you want me to, Jessica," he said seriously, "just say..." his voice trailed off as he took in my eager expression and sparkling eyes.

I didn't want him to leave, especially stood in front of me with that muscular chest straining against his shirt, and his hair all tousled from our embrace. I shook my head and bit my lip in a self-conscious gesture.

"I want you to stay with me, Jack," I said quietly. "You fascinate me."

He smiled, kicked the door shut behind him, and reached for me again. I broke away from his passionate kisses just long enough to lead him up the stairs to my bedroom, kicking off shoes and losing my cardigan on the way.

In my room I sat on the end of the bed and looked at him. Jack stepped in close, grabbed my hair and crushed his lips to mine, and my body was alive with need, and with desire. I pulled at his shirt and he ripped open the buttons and flung it on the floor behind him. His body was gorgeous. He looked like a male model standing there with just his black jeans on, his boxer shorts showing over the top of the waistband. His chest was broad and muscular, with a few hairs and a slight tan. He had a tattoo on his left arm, at the top near his shoulder. It looked like some sort of Celtic design and I loved it. I saw a small, faint scar in between his right hip and his belly button.

Jack climbed onto the bed and I slid back as he crawled between my legs, a hand on my face as he kissed me again. I pulled my own t-shirt off and threw it to one side. He looked down my body with eyes full of heat and desire. He gently pushed me down so I was lying on the bed and he lay on top of me, kissing and nibbling at my skin as he moved down my body. I grabbed his hair, writhing beneath his touch, watching his body. He very carefully unfastened my jeans, as though he expected me to stop him, but I didn't. It had been so long since I'd had sex and he was just so fit! I wanted this; no I needed it.

Thank God I was wearing matching underwear tonight, even if it wasn't my sexiest. Jack pulled my jeans off and dropped them to the floor, and then he slid smoothly to his feet while he took his own jeans off. I saw his expression as he watched my body. Then I focused on his, on how tight his boxer shorts were against him, and the overwhelming urge I had for him to just fuck me now. He tormented me a little more, stroking, sucking, licking and kissing me all over until finally we were both naked and he was on top of me.

Jack smiled and kissed me on the lips as I felt him enter me, and we moved together, slowly at first and then faster, faster until I was gasping and clawing at his back. He buried his face in my neck and nipped at my skin and then his head reared back as we both reached a dizzying, ecstatic climax, crying out together.

We both fell back on the bed, Jack lying beside me, both of us gasping for air, paralysed after our passion. I turned my head to look at him and laughed, a little embarrassed at my lack of self-control. He was smiling as he turned onto his side, head propped on his arm.

"What's so funny, Jessica?" Jack asked.

I concentrated on steadying my breathing before I answered.

"Nothing," I said, gasping, "That was intense! I mean, I don't make a habit of it or anything, don't get the wrong idea." I finished, grinning.

It was Jack's turn to laugh and he reached forward and gently stroked my hair out of my face, sending more shivers coursing through me.

"Don't worry," he said, "I believe you. Wow that was some welcome home!" He let out a breath and kissed my forehead.

It felt natural to snuggle against his body, for him to wrap his arms around me, and for us to fall asleep, exhausted and happy. Jack was warm and safe and comforting, and I couldn't remember ever feeling such a sensation of contentment with another man before. I liked it, and I wanted more. Then the dream came again, but it was different this time, a new story.

I was standing on the beach watching moonlight reflecting off the gently rolling waves. This was another one of my vivid dreams I was sure, but I couldn't wake myself. I could smell the sea salt in the air, I could taste it on my tongue, and the air felt muggy as though a storm were threatening. Then I realized there was a woman standing beside me. I knew her, but I couldn't turn my head to look at her, and I didn't recognize who she was. She spoke in a gentle, clear voice.

"Hello, Jessica," she said, "Do not worry. You are safe with me. I know you are a little confused about us meeting like this."

Somehow I knew that she was tall, slim, with long dark hair, even though I still couldn't look at her. I spoke in a voice that was thankfully quite steady, no panic showing,

"Who are you?" I asked, "Why are we here?" I tried to turn my head but couldn't, and yet I remained calm.

"I am Lillian," she said, "and you will remember me when the time is right. For now I bring a message. You must heed caution with your new relationship. There are things that you cannot understand and you should not be involved with. Please remain in control of yourself and your emotion. Your life is about to change very dramatically, and it will be confusing and alien. But I will return, and I will take care of you as it is my duty to do so."

Then she was suddenly gone, and I heard the distant rumble of thunder. As the rain began to fall everything faded into blackness, true deep sleep.

LOVE HURTS

4

I woke to the sound of my alarm clock and reached out sleepily to hit the snooze button. I rolled over and stretched my arm across the bed, then as I woke more fully I realized that I was naked and Jack wasn't there. I sat up and looked around, listening for the sound of him in the bathroom or downstairs but the house was silent. His clothes had gone from the bedroom floor. Surely I hadn't dreamt him too! No, last night definitely happened, I had that slightly uncomfortable but satisfied sensation in my nether regions to prove it. Perhaps this was just his way of telling me it was a one-night stand. But as hard as I tried to forget about him, while I stood under the powerful jet of cool water in my shower, I couldn't help but feel a little upset, and quite angry that he didn't at least stay for breakfast.

Liz was knocking on the back door as I came downstairs. She had a key but had always promised to knock first so I knew she was here, and I left her to unlock the door as I filled the kettle and put bread in the toaster. We sat down together at the kitchen table once I had made the tea and buttered our toast. Then she glared at me but with a smile on her face, and spoke in a loud, clipped tone of mock disapproval. "Jessica Marie Stone, what happened last night?" she said in mock indignation.

"Nothing, why?" I asked in a meek voice.

I tried to act innocent but couldn't keep the twinkle out of my eyes, and then I got a little flushed and spilt my tea as my hands started shaking. Liz laughed at me.

"Jessica you are a terrible liar," she said, "For starters I can see a huge love bite on your neck, and for another you are bursting to tell me something."

I grinned, touched the mark on my neck, and winced as I realized it did feel quite bruised. When did Jack do that to me? It must have been during the heat of passion! Oh dear that wasn't very professional; I'd better put a scarf on before we opened the shop. Love bites were for teenagers, not mature people in their late twenties.

I proceeded to give Liz all the gory details with much laughing and pretended embarrassment on her part. But we were like sisters; we kept no secrets from each other. Admittedly she had managed to hide her pregnancy from me for three months but then I couldn't complain, as I would probably have done the same in her situation. That was just Liz's nature, very careful with everything she did. This baby meant so much to her and Rob that of course they would keep it a secret until they were sure the pregnancy was progressing safely. She was very interested in my description of Jack Mason and she refused to believe that it could just be a one-night stand.

"Jess, you know he might have been called away with work this morning," she said, "I mean surely police detectives don't work a standard nine-to-five? It's just that from your description it sounds like he was really interested, and it would be strange to just leave without even a message."

"I know, Liz," I said, "but I don't want to get overexcited. Look I had a great night and fantastic sex, let's just leave it at that. Then again I might see him again in the pub anyway..." my voice trailed off as I drifted into memories of last night.

I then told Liz about Simon's strange behaviour and she did agree that it seemed very out of character for him. She tried to suggest that he was being over-protective because I had been single for so long and I supposed that must be it. It did remind me to check my mobile phone though and see if Simon had sent me a text message, which he had. It read 'Good morning Jess, I hope you forgive me for my mood last night. Will see you in the shop later.' I showed Liz who nodded and smiled, saying that she was right and he was just being moody.

Finally I told Liz about my dream. She was quite concerned but also intrigued. "Jessica, do you think it's your subconscious trying to talk you out of things?" she said, "I mean you haven't had a relationship in such a long time. Perhaps you were so attracted to this man that you instinctively want to run away, even before anything has happened."

She stopped and watched my reaction before continuing.

"Maybe you should see a therapist," she said, "I know you don't want to, but perhaps you need closure on what has happened in your life. Or maybe you even need to find out about your real family..."

Here she stopped, seeing that I had stiffened, my body on the defensive. I spoke in a clipped, curt tone.

"No Liz." I said firmly, "I do not need to find out about any family that could abandon me at the age of six. You are right; it's probably just my subconscious. If it happens again I might consider seeing a doctor, but for now we'll just put it down to my crazy imagination."

Liz nodded and left me alone. She had tried before to persuade me to find my birth family. As far I was concerned they weren't worth chasing. I had managed this long on my own; I didn't need them, whoever they might be.

The morning passed slowly, a quiet one since the day was warm and sunny which sent most people out to the beach.

Although it was still quite cold, we Brits are a tough bunch when it comes to the weather. There would already be people sunbathing and surfing, Simon included. He surfed in all weathers, amazing me at how he never caught pneumonia or even injured himself in those treacherous seas. He thrived on the danger, and sometimes I would watch him from the beach, getting increasingly frightened when he was thrown close to the rocks or hit massive waves. But he just kept going back for more and he did have incredible strength and control when he was in the water. Actually, he was pretty strong anyway, he was always carrying heavy boxes, crates and barrels around the pub and never seemed to strain or pull a muscle.

Liz and me used this quiet time at work to restock the shelves and catch up with our Internet sales, parcelling up the books which needed dispatching. Liz decided to take them to the post office before it closed, leaving me alone in the shop for an hour. I was reading my book and sipping coffee when the bell above the door jangled and I looked up to see Simon approach the counter smiling sheepishly. His blond hair was tousled and damp and he was wearing baggy blue jeans and a yellow t-shirt, and a hooded black fleece jacket with a surf-label motif printed all over.

"Hey, Jess how are you?" he asked casually.

I half-smiled but let him see in my expression that I was still unhappy with him.

"Hi Simon." I said in a flat tone, "Yeah I'm good thanks. Liz has gone to the post office."

He nodded and crouched in front of me, leaning his arms on the edge of the counter and looking at me with his sad, grey puppy-dog eyes. I smiled in spite of myself and then laughed. It was impossible to be angry with Simon. His sad expression broke into the usual mischievous grin and he laughed.

"Look, I'm sorry I acted like that last night Jess." he said, "It was a shock seeing Jack after so long, and when he took such an interest in you I got jealous. Neither him nor Danny had told me they were back in town, not even an email, and I got upset."

Why would he be so upset? They must be friends or at least closer than just employer and employee.

"Simon, I'm confused." I said, "Were you in a relationship with this Danny or something?"

He laughed, embarrassed, but I could see the bitterness in his face. "There was no relationship Jess," he said, "When Danny took over the pub we got to be quite good friends, shared acquaintance, that sort of thing. I got to know Jack through him and then they had to go off on their assignment and no one heard from them for two years. They came back briefly at different times but were terrible at keeping in touch. I just got protective of you. Jack isn't the most reliable of men. Did he stay the night?" he asked.

I was suddenly uncomfortable under his scrutiny but

then with Simon it was never really an issue. He was the ultimate Gay Best Friend when he wanted to be and yet today he seemed old and tired. I suddenly felt sorry for him.

"Simon, I think you need a break, you look exhausted," I said sympathetically, "I mean you haven't had a night, or even a day, off work in two weeks have you? Shall we have a film night tonight? I don't mind where."

He lifted his head and wandered round the counter to sit in Liz's office chair beside me. I watched as he took a gulp of my coffee and then tipped his head back on the headrest as he looked at me from half-closed eyes, arms folded across his chest, hands clasped. Then his expression changed and he sat upright, his fingers reaching for my neck, eyes wide. My scarf must have slipped because he pulled it away, his face serious. I winced as he touched the love bite and then I stiffened and tried to move away from his touch. He was suddenly concerned.

"Jessica, that looks really painful," Simon said, "what the hell did he do to you?" he asked.

I looked down, embarrassed.

"It's nothing; we just got carried away that's all." I said, "Honestly, I didn't even notice it until this morning when Liz saw it."

I ducked my head down, put the scarf back in place, and stood up to go and refill my mug. Simon waited as I disappeared into the kitchen and came back with coffee for both of us, and a packet of biscuits. He set about eating them straight away. Simon's appetite never ceased to amaze me, he seemed able to eat all day long and he never put any weight on. He spoke after he'd munched through three biscuits at once and taken a gulp of coffee, seemingly not affected by the hot liquid, another weird trait of his.

"So, I take it he stayed the night then," he said, "Are you seeing him again?"

I glanced down, then back up to meet Simon's gaze.

"No, at least I don't think so." I said, "He wasn't there when I woke up this morning."

Simon was staring at me intently now. He put his mug

down and reached for my neck again. I sat still as he pulled the scarf away and touched the bruise, wincing only slightly as he put pressure on it.

"Are you sure this doesn't hurt, Jess?" he asked, "He almost drew blood."

"Yes I'm sure!" I snapped in a curt tone of voice.

I was getting irritated now and jerked away from him. We both looked up as the doorbell jangled and two middle-aged women walked in talking loudly to each other. I hurriedly straightened my clothes and waited while they browsed for a little, one of them bought a book after about fifteen minutes, and then the shop was empty once again. Simon had finished his drink and taken his mug out to the kitchen while I was serving the customers. He came back into the shop and headed for the door.

"Well, if you are ok I'll leave you to work, Jess." he said, "Look, don't think too much about Jack Mason. You are better off without him; believe me. He seems to attract trouble wherever he goes."

"What do you mean?" I asked, "Because of his job?"

Simon smiled wryly.

"Yeah something like that." he said.

He breathed in and out deeply and then continued.

"You are right I need a night off." he said, "Do you want to come round mine for a girly film later? I'll order some Chinese food…"

He raised his eyebrows and pulled a face at me. I smiled and nodded.

"That sounds good, I'll bring the wine," I said, "I'll see you round 8pm." Simon grinned and left, saying a cheerful hello to Liz as she returned from her errands. She was smiling as she walked in to the shop.

"So, you've forgiven him then?" she asked knowingly.

I nodded, smiling.

"Yes." I said, "he promised me a girly film and a Chinese takeaway tonight!"

5

It was almost five o'clock and Liz and I were doing our weekly routine of cleaning the shop ready for the weekend. We didn't open on a Sunday as the trade wasn't good enough and we both agreed we needed the day off. Both of us generally had a five-day working week, alternating which day off we took. When it was busy during the summer we had extra help but were both quite involved with our little shop, and didn't like leaving it. Of course now I didn't want Liz over-doing things with a baby in her belly, but she was protesting that she wasn't even that far gone yet and I should stop fussing. We were arguing over who got to dust the upper book shelves, and I was on the step ladder trying to be assertive when the bell jangled above the door and we both looked over to see who the customer was.

It was Jack Mason. He stopped just inside the door, smiling awkwardly. He was wearing dark blue jeans and a tight black t-shirt, no jacket. My heart was in my throat and I carefully stepped back onto the floor, swallowing nervously. Liz knew instinctively who this man was by my reaction. I moved towards him, smiling shyly. When he spoke his voice was so deep and husky, with a faint Irish lilt that literally made me weak at the knees. I hadn't noticed it last night, must have been too involved in other things!

"Hello, Jessica." Jack said, "I hope you aren't angry with me. I was called away on business this morning, and I hadn't got your mobile number. I didn't want to wake you."

He glanced at Liz who smiled and hurried over to the counter. I put down the duster and polish I was holding and motioned towards the back of the shop.

"Hi Jack." I said, "Um no it's fine, do you want to come into the kitchen for a minute?"

He nodded and followed me through the door. I caught Liz's eye as I went and she grinned, winked, and gave me a sneaky 'thumbs up' sign.

I led Jack into the small storeroom and then through the adjoining door into my kitchen. Once inside I turned back to Jack, trying not to throw myself at him. I crossed my arms and leaned against the cupboards in front of the window. He looked at me with those piercing blue eyes and then his gaze dropped to my neck. In a quick stride he was in front of me, gently moving my scarf and reaching out to touch the bruise with fingers that were cold. How had he seen the bruise? I was sure I had fixed the scarf properly this time, and Liz said she couldn't see anything under it. I winced, more from the coolness of his touch than from the pain.

"Jessica, I am so sorry, I didn't realize how rough I was with you," he said, voice taut with emotion.

I shook my hair back and blinked slowly, then looked into those amazing eyes.

"It's fine honestly." I said, "I didn't even feel it until this morning. So why are you here?"

Jack dropped his hand to his side and I covered my bruise again, feeling strangely self-conscious about it. Then he smiled again, looking shy and coy.

"Well first I wanted to apologize for running out like that, second I wondered if you might forgive me and come out on a proper date, and third can I have your mobile number?" he said, laughing.

I laughed in reply and nodded, reaching to get my phone from my pocket.

"Yes to all three!" I said.

We swapped numbers and agreed that he would call round for me tomorrow evening at around 7pm. Jack knew a lovely traditional seaside restaurant in a village a few miles away that he hadn't visited in a good few years. I agreed that it sounded lovely, vaguely remembering the description as a place that Liz and Rob were fond of visiting.

Jack gave me a quick kiss on the cheek, but I was sure I sensed the urge to properly kiss me vibrating through his body. Apparently he had decided to act as though we were simply going on a first date and hadn't already slept together. No problem, I could play along. I followed him back out into the shop where I introduced him to Liz.

Rob had arrived to meet her from work and I introduced him to Jack. He surprised me by saying, "Yes, I know Detective Mason. How've you been, Jack? Your brother ok?"

Jack nodded and smiled, reaching out to shake Rob's hand and pat him on the shoulder.

"Hello, Rob." he said, "Yes we are both well thank you. So you got married. Congratulations!"

Here he looked at Liz who smiled proudly at her beloved husband. Rob spoke in response to my puzzled expression.

"I met Jack quite a few years ago now, when the police needed help on an investigation involving some students at the university." he said, "We found a shared interest and kept a casual acquaintance, mainly professional. You remember I said I help out with legal things occasionally?" He motioned towards Jack and I nodded. Liz exclaimed about what a strange coincidence it was and then Jack left, giving me another kiss on the way out and leaving me with butterflies in my tummy.

I locked the front door and flipped the sign to say 'Closed' then turned to face Liz and Rob who were both smiling at me with that sickening expression that couples sometimes have for their single friends. It's a look which says 'I hope you can be happy like we are' when you meet a potential new love interest.

"Stop it you two, we are just going on a date alright?" I said sulkily. They both laughed and Rob replied.

"Sorry, Jess," he said, "He's a decent bloke you should get on well. Just don't get too involved, he's not the commitment type and the Mason brothers notoriously stick together above all else. You know what I mean?"

I nodded.

"Don't worry Rob I just want a bit of fun." I replied, "And it can't be a bad thing to make new friends who are police officers surely?"

"Not just officers, detectives Jessica." Rob said, "They are devoted to their jobs, don't expect too much."

"I won't." I said, "Now don't you two have some lovey-dovey husband and wife stuff to do? I have a date with my Gay Best Friend and a Chinese takeaway."

6

An hour or so later I was walking into the Ship with my overnight bag slung over my shoulder. I wasn't surprised to see Simon once again behind the bar giving instructions to a young barmaid. She seemed quite frightened of him and I felt sorry for her. I leaned on the bar and called over to him.

"Hey, Simon I thought you were taking the night off!" I shouted, "Stop terrorizing your staff and focus on me."

He looked up and grinned at me, and the young barmaid hurried off, relieved to escape him as he walked round from behind the bar.

"Yes I am off Jess thank you." he said, "Come on, food's on its way."

Sure enough the Chinese takeaway deliveryman sauntered into the pub, recognized his regular customer, and handed over the food to me as Simon paid.

I followed him upstairs and then up another level into his self-titled 'penthouse' apartment. It was a good-sized place, with two bedrooms, a bathroom, a small square kitchen, a little hallway and a large living/dining room overlooking the sea. Instead of a window he had French doors that led onto a neat, square balcony on which Simon had a bistro table and two chairs. I often borrowed this balcony during the summer months; I loved sitting out with my book listening to people on the beach, and the sounds of waves and birds. Simon's décor was simplistic and clean, monochrome I think is the official name. His apartment was very modern and chic compared to mine, which had mismatched furniture and brightly coloured throws and cushions everywhere.

We were both relaxing in Simon's living room watching our all-time favourite girly film *To Wong Foo, Thanks For Everything, Julie Newmar*. It was a strange choice I know but one that Simon and me could watch time and again and never get bored of. We were on our second glass of Rose wine; I was lying with my legs slung across the arm of the comfy chair while Simon was stretched out on the sofa on his back. He caught my attention when I saw him literally gnawing on the bones of the spare ribs he had ordered. He was intent on them, licking and nibbling almost like a dog and I giggled. He looked up, surprised

"What?" he said.

"Nothing," I replied, "Is there any meat left on those ribs? I think you chewed them clean."

Simon grinned sheepishly and dropped the bone onto his plate on the floor.

"What can I say, I love spare ribs," he said, "You don't know what you're missing."

I smiled and said, "It's alright I'm quite happy with my egg fried rice and Vegetarian spring rolls thank you very much."

Simon pulled a face then rolled off the sofa in one smooth movement and fetched the wine bottle to refill our glasses. I watched his body as he moved. He had changed into what he called pyjamas – just a pair of dark purple boxer shorts and nothing else. They left very little to the imagination and yet he didn't seem embarrassed that I could see his body. In fact he seemed oblivious to my staring. Then again he had a perfect six-pack and washboard abs so he really should be proud of his muscle building efforts I suppose. And I was quite happy to watch! It never ceased to amaze me how he got such a perfect body when I never knew him go to the gym, or at least not very often. Oh well, one of life's mysteries I suppose.

What the hell was wrong with me? This was Simon, my second best friend and a gay man. I hadn't thought of him in a sexual way since I first met him and I knew for certain that he didn't think about me that way. It was as though all of a sudden I was sex-crazed. Jack Mason must have woken some sleeping demon inside me.

I roused from my musings at the sound of my mobile phone bleeping to announce a text message and I reached for it. The message was from Jack and read 'Hey Jessica

I'm looking forward to our date tomorrow, Jack'. I suddenly felt like a giddy teenager again and couldn't keep the smile from my face. Then I looked up to see Simon watching me as he topped up the wine.

"That's from Jack, isn't it?" he said.

His expression was blank, careful. I nodded, smiling.

"Yes it is." I said. "We are going on a date tomorrow night. He came in the shop this afternoon to see me."

I watched Simon but he just nodded and gulped his wine. That was another thing I noticed – he never seemed to get drunk no matter how much alcohol he consumed. He answered in a voice blank of emotion, no tone of anger or reprimand. "Well I'm not going to act all protective of you again; I know you'll just get angry." he said. "Look I do like Jack Mason don't get me wrong. But he's not like other men, he has a history of trouble, and he isn't the relationship type. I just don't want you to get hurt."

"It's fine Simon." I said, "I'm not expecting anything from him. We had a great time together last night and I'm happy to be going on a date with him. If it's just a casual fling I'll be quite content. Now can we get back to watching the film please?"

He nodded and turned back to the television. But for a while my mind was racing. Simon was making a very big deal about Jack Mason. Surely he couldn't be that bad? And why was everyone so concerned with me getting hurt? They should know by now that I wasn't that type of person. No way would I get so emotionally involved with a man that I ended up heartbroken and abandoned. I would never get that close to anyone. It just wasn't worth the pain.

7

The next evening I was dressed and ready for my date in good time, having spent the day in excited anticipation. I was wearing my favourite dress, a pretty short-sleeved button-through ditsy-print style in a pale green colour with delicate pink roses all over. It brought out the unusual green colour of my eyes and I had my long auburn hair brushed out straight and sleek over my shoulders. I had to admit I looked very sexy in an English Country Rose kind of way. I looked delicate and appealing. Of course I liked to believe I was strong and brave but time would tell. I slipped into my silver high-heeled sandals and was just applying lipstick when I heard a knock on the door downstairs. I grabbed my jacket and handbag and hurried down, careful not to trip on the stairs. I never did manage well in heels; I'm clumsy enough at the best of times.

Jack was standing in the doorway looking so sexy I could have happily jumped into his arms as soon as I saw him. He was wearing black jeans and a fashionable button-through shirt that was black with a silver pinstripe. He had his black blazer on and his hair was slightly ruffled. He was clean-shaven and his aftershave smelt wonderful, musky and masculine. Jack smiled and looked at me appreciatively as I carefully stepped onto the pathway and turned to lock the door behind me.

"Wow, Jessica you look beautiful!" he exclaimed.

"Thank you Jack." I replied, ducking my head modestly.

He walked with me down the path and onto the street behind where he walked over to a large black BMW four-wheel drive car. I laughed at the sight of it, dwarfing my tiny red Fiesta parked in front.

"Whoa, that's a large vehicle!" I said.

He laughed, unlocked it using the button on his key fob, and opened the passenger door for me.

LOVE HURTS

"It's a company vehicle, very practical." He said, "Hop in."

I climbed into the passenger seat as carefully as possible, trying to be dignified and ladylike, smoothing my skirt and glad that it was a longer length than the ones I used to wear, which would most definitely have flashed my bottom! This was one very fancy car. Jack jumped easily in on the driver's side and we set off. I looked around me and saw that the central console wasn't like on ordinary cars. It had what looked like a radio set-up and some switches that I couldn't identify. Jack saw where I was looking.

"It's a police radio," he said, "and I have flashing lights and a siren installed." I nodded. He must be quite high up in the force structure to have his own car. I was impressed.

The restaurant was perched on the cliff top just on the outskirts of a village about five miles away from Redcliffe. It was a beautiful quaint building, decorated inside with traditional Cornish Blue pottery on shelves, a wooden ship's wheel above the open fireplace, and old-fashioned solid wooden tables and chairs. The waiter smiled politely when we entered and Jack gave his name for the reservation. The waiter faltered at the name Mason and then quickly showed us to a corner table that was secluded from the main restaurant by a couple of large potted plants. It gave a nice illusion of privacy but we could see people around the room quite easily. We sat down and the waiter took our jackets and disappeared. He returned almost straight away with menus and wine lists.

I was determined to stay sober and not embarrass myself but Jack persuaded me to order a bottle of wine saying he would have a glass with me. I couldn't resist; I do love my wine. So I chose a nice Merlot, which Jack seemed to agree with. We ordered our food and were served the drinks, and then we were alone. I looked around me and then at Jack.

"Are you always on duty, Jack?" I asked him.

I was smiling and he looked puzzled.

"What do you mean?" he said.

I motioned to the room; "Well I take it you chose this table so you could keep an eye on people." I said.

Jack smiled and looked down, embarrassed. He laughed self-consciously and ruffled a hand through his hair.

"Yes, sorry," he said, "I've pretty much done nothing but work for the last four years. It will take me a while to get back in a normal routine."

Still smiling I replied. "Don't worry I think it's very admirable. We like to see a good police force in this country. So can you tell me about this mysterious assignment you were on or is it top secret?"

Jack's expression became serious.

"I can't tell you too much," He said, "It's still ongoing and involves a serious organized crime unit. Basically I would be putting you in physical danger if I gave you any details. Suffice to say it was tough and it will take a while to tie up the loose ends."

My heart was pounding. I had never been involved with anyone like this before and I had to admit it was a little unnerving. Yet at the same time it was exciting, a promise of adventure. I took a sip of wine and changed the subject.

"So, what about this brother that I've heard about?" I asked, "Tell me about him, and your family."

Jack smiled; relieved I think.

"There's not much to tell," he said, "Danny is my identical twin brother."

Here he paused and looked at me for a reaction. I nodded encouragingly, thinking nothing of it, and Jack continued.

"We work together as police detectives, partners," he said, "Danny is still in Glasgow finishing up some paperwork before returning home sometime in the next few weeks. We share a house in Redcliffe and our parents are both dead. We have no other family. What about you?"

I told Jack about being orphaned at the age of six. He seemed surprised that I had no surviving family members to take me in but realized that I was a bit sensitive about it.

"If I had any family they never came forward to adopt me so as far as I'm concerned they can suit themselves." I said grimly, "I got used to being on my own anyway. Until I met Liz of course."

I told Jack a little about the two foster families I was placed with and then about how I met Liz and what brought us to Redcliffe. Jack seemed just as reluctant to talk about his own family. He simply said that both his parents were dead and it was just he and his brother. I didn't ask any more questions as I felt that would be rude and a little too inquisitive on a first date. Before I knew it we had finished our meal and were drinking coffee. Jack called over the waiter and paid the bill.

I was feeling very slightly giddy from the wine and concentrated on not tripping over when we were outside in the car park. The fresh sea air hit me, and actually helped sober me a little, which I was grateful for. I turned my face up to the cool breeze, enjoying the sensation on my skin, and inhaling deeply.

Jack helped me into the car, his hands lingering on my body before he moved round to the driver's side. He had had one glass of wine and then drank lemonade during our meal. He looked at me as I fastened my seatbelt and then slowly he leaned across and kissed me very gently on the lips. I tensed, my heart in my throat, and then relaxed into the kiss and the sensation of his soft lips on mine. When he drew back his eyes were hazy and he spoke in a low, husky voice.

"Would you like to come back to my place, Jessica?" he asked.

I nodded and smiled.

"That would be lovely Jack." I said.

Jack's house was set back on the coastal road on the outskirts of Redcliffe, not far from the Ship. It was well concealed from the main road behind thick shrubs and trees and he drove through a pair of large wrought iron gates into a spacious driveway. The house looked like a beautiful old grey stone cottage, the kind that would come with its own resident ghosts in storybooks. I instantly fell in love with it, appealing to my romantic imagination. There was a detached double garage to one side of the house but Jack left his car on the drive and led me to the front door. We entered into a hallway that seemed to follow the length of the house, and I could see the stairs to my left, just past another door, which could be a downstairs bathroom or a cupboard.

I followed Jack into the living room to the right of the front door, and sat down at his invitation. He went through to the kitchen to make coffee and I looked around. The room was large; I was sitting on a two-seater sofa that was made of a dark red fabric, soft and comfortable. There was a matching three-seater sofa on the adjacent wall and an armchair in the window recess. Next to this was a large flat screen television on a stand with what looked like a Sky digibox, a Blu-Ray player and an X-Box set out on the shelves underneath. This was definitely a man's house. All I had was standard Freeview and a DVD player.

The walls were painted a soft mocha colour, simple and un-fussy, and the carpet was a darker shade of chocolate brown. It was a deep pile and I could imagine it would feel silky-soft under bare feet. There was a shag-pile rug in front of the fireplace, in a contrasting shade of coffee cream.

Behind me was a freestanding bookshelf of dark wood, possibly oak, set against the wall and it contained a few obscure titles relating to police work and forensics. They were books I hadn't come across and I guessed they were official textbooks of some kind. Then there were a few modern detective novels and crime thrillers, which told me just how involved in their work these men were. I wondered if just one or both of them read those books. I couldn't see any family photographs or ornaments. The only other furniture in the room was a square coffee table in the middle of the floor which was bare except for a couple of drinks coasters and the local daily newspaper. The fire was a modern square gas one, very simple with no mantelpiece, just a square wooden-framed mirror above it.

Jack entered the room carrying two mugs of coffee, and he handed one to me. He sat down on the adjacent sofa and looked at me with eyes full of passion. I looked around the room again and then back at him.

"This is a very manly living room, Jack." I said, "You have no ornaments at all!"

He laughed.

"We don't need ornaments." he said, "Don't forget we have lived away for a few years now, we are essentially still moving in."

"Did you have this house before you moved away?" I asked.

He nodded.

"Yes we have had it for some years now." he replied, "We just had a housekeeper to look after it."

Suddenly he seemed unable to contain himself and he leaped off the sofa, gently took my mug from me and placed it on the coffee table, and kissed me passionately on the lips. He moved down my face to my neck, and my chest, undoing the buttons of my dress as he went. There was some giggling on my part as we fell over the furniture, and then I let myself go and just enjoyed being with him. I had never been with anyone so passionate before, and I loved the freedom of ripping each other's clothes off and chasing each other up the stairs. We ended up in his bed and I had yet another night of amazing raw sex.

8

I woke slowly the next morning to feel Jack gently stroking my hair, my head resting on his chest. I had had that strange dream again, with the woman, Lillian. Again she warned me to be careful, and not to throw myself into anything. I dismissed it as my subconscious mind playing games with me. I stirred and lifted my head. Jack smiled down at me from where he lay on his back, half propped against the headboard.

"Good morning, Sleepyhead," he said, "How are you?"

I yawned and rolled over, then caught sight of the bedside clock and sat bolt upright. It was 8am on a Monday morning!

"Shit I need to get to work! Sorry!" I said, flustered.

He laughed at my expression.

"You are your own boss," he said, "surely Elizabeth can manage on her own for an hour?"

I smiled.

"Yes you are right but I can't be too late." I said, "I'll just text her so she doesn't worry. Anyway don't you have work to go to?"

He shrugged.

"They owe me a lot of lieu time; I think I'll start cashing it in." he said, and leaned forward to kiss my neck.

We leisurely made love again before getting up and showering together. It was such a strange experience, to be sharing my morning routine with a man. I only had my date clothes from the night before but that didn't matter. Jack made me some toast for breakfast along with a cup of tea and then I reluctantly decided I had to go. I couldn't leave Liz any longer. Jack dropped me off at the shop with more kisses and a promise to see me that evening, and then I finally made it to work and to an interrogation from Liz.

So began one of the happiest times of my life. Over the

next few weeks Jack and me spent almost every night together and it was as though we had known each other forever. We played pool in the Ship and Simon acted very civilly with him. I noticed a tension between the two men at first, but they gradually seemed to relax around each other, which I was relieved about because it was important to me that Simon accepted my new relationship. Jack and I went to the cinema a few times, discovered a shared interest in classic horror films, and Jack took me on cliff top walks and out in the forest behind his house. He told me more stories about Redcliffe.

The town apparently got its name when the locals saw the setting sunlight reflecting from the side of the cliffs in the bay. I have seen the magnificent sunsets, and the colour when the cliffs turn red is truly spectacular. Sometimes they even look like they are on fire. But I hadn't heard that story before, so I was fascinated. This town is steeped in history, and I love visiting the local museum and heritage centre. I was even more impressed when Jack came with me, and when he took me to the art gallery in the nearby city. Liz's belly was slowly filling out and she and Rob seemed charmed by Jack. Of course Rob already knew him and they seemed to enjoy catching up. The four of us met up in the pub a few times and they accompanied us on a cinema date, and to a few restaurant meals. Before I knew it a month had passed and Jack and me were getting closer and closer.

But the dreams persisted. It was strange, sometimes the monster chased me, but I always woke just at the point when he attacked. Luckily I never had those dreams when I stayed with Jack, only when I was alone. It would have been embarrassing to explain that to him, because I always woke up sweating and confused, and sometimes with tears on my face. But I met Lillian a few more times, and she intrigued me. She seemed so real, and so familiar. We would always be standing on Redcliffe beach when I dreamt about her, and we were always staring out to sea, unable to look directly at each other. At first she warned me about my relationship, but over the weeks she seemed to accept it. Or maybe I was accepting it. Maybe I was growing up at last, and settling down.

9

It was a Sunday morning and I had stayed over at Jack's house. He had got up early as was his habit and I sat up in bed, looking around me. There was sunlight showing around the curtains, and the air felt warm, which was great. Jack's bedroom was very cosy. He had a king-size bed, and the wardrobe and chest of drawers were antique pine. His walls were painted a neutral shade of pale grey, and he had dark red curtains and coordinating bedding. There was also an en-suite bathroom, which apparently Danny had leading from his room also. The men had two more bedrooms and a central bathroom upstairs. One of the bedrooms was used as a home gym, and I had enjoyed watching Jack working out a few times, which inevitably led to more passionate sex. He was an intense lover, and showed me things that I had never experienced before. He always left me wanting more, aching for his touch and his body.

I crawled out of bed and slipped on my red satin chemise before wandering downstairs to find him. The radio was switched on in the kitchen and I sung along quietly to a pop song as I walked over to the kettle, filled it up and switched it on. "Jack?" I called out, "Where are you? Do you want a drink?"

I turned round and jumped as I saw him leaning in the doorway, his arms crossed, grinning at me. He was wearing a pair of black baggy skater shorts that I hadn't seen before. I smiled and sauntered over to him, swaying my hips. I put my arms around his neck and he rested his hands on my hips, his expression playful. There was something different about him though.

Then I heard Jack reply from inside his office further down the hall, and I froze as I realized I had my arms around another man!

"Jess?" Jack called, "Oh…" his voice trailed off as he

approached the open doorway.

I jumped back to stare at the man I *thought* was Jack, and the man who *was* Jack as he came to stand beside his brother.

"Holy shit, you're Danny!" I cried to the stranger in front of me.

My legs went weak and I sat down suddenly on the chair at the kitchen table behind me. Danny laughed.

"Hello, Jessica," he said, "I'm sorry but I couldn't resist then. No harm done?"

Jack frowned at his brother and moved over to crouch beside me where I sat with my head in my hands. I turned and looked at him, at his familiar face, at those intense blue eyes, that slightly curly black hair, and then I looked at Danny and saw the exact same features. The only difference was that Danny's expression was playful and teasing while Jack's was thoughtful and serious. He put his arm around my shoulder.

"I am sorry about that, Jessica." he said, "My brother returned late last night without warning and didn't stop to think that you might be staying over. I did tell you we were identical," he reproached.

I looked at him and laughed.

"I know but I didn't think you meant quite literally." I said, "I mean don't all twins have some small difference?"

He shrugged.

"Not us I'm afraid." Jack said, "Except for a few odd scars we are completely alike."

Danny walked over to the kettle and proceeded to make coffee for us all. Although I'd have preferred tea I accepted the drink, my head spinning as I watched the two men. I slowly recovered from my embarrassment and listened to the brothers talking about things that had been happening. I didn't take in much of their conversation, was too busy comparing their physical appearances.

Danny had quite a prominent scar on his stomach; I hadn't noticed it the first time. But he even had the same tattoo as Jack on his shoulder, and the designs were identical. Strangely I didn't feel uncomfortable with Danny even though I knew nothing about him. But I found him very sexually attractive and guessed that it was only natural since he looked just like his brother who I was attracted to. Eventually I excused myself to go and have a shower and get dressed.

When I walked downstairs I overheard part of their conversation in the kitchen.

"You have to tell her the truth or stop seeing her, Jack, it's going to get dangerous." Danny said, "Seamus is probably here already waiting to attack and you know he'll use her against you. I have to get the Inn secured as it is, we can do without the extra stress."

I heard Jack sigh.

"I know, Dan but I can't just dump her." he said, "She means a lot to me already, it's like we are old friends or something. Please just support me on this ok? I had enough trouble convincing Simon to let me date her."

"Simon?" Danny replied, "What's he got to do with it?"

"It seems they are friends." Jack said, "They met when she moved here three years ago. You really should have kept a closer eye on your people Danny."

Heart pounding, I moved closer to the kitchen as quietly as possible but jumped when I heard the scrape of a chair and Danny appeared in the doorway. I walked in smiling brightly.

"So, what are we doing today Boys?" I asked.

10

Danny said he wanted to visit the Ship and check up on the business, so I suggested we all have lunch there and then Jack and me would leave him to it. I wanted to know more about him. The two of them fascinated me together. We all walked through the town to the seafront and I was quiet, just watching Jack and Danny.

Their accents sounded the same, both with that very faint Irish lilt. I had asked Jack about that and he said he was born and raised in Dublin but the accent had faded during years of undercover police work. How they could both do the same thing to their voices amazed me. Danny had added a red t-shirt to his surfer shorts, while Jack was wearing his usual jeans and a dark grey t-shirt today. I was in my standard weekend wear: dark blue cropped jeans, trainers and a skinny pale pink t-shirt with my favourite black velour jacket over the top.

The pub was bustling as usual with the sound of families laughing and chattering, people playing pool and darts, and the rattle of crockery and cutlery. It smelt delicious and my stomach rumbled as soon as we stepped inside and found a table in the restaurant area.

Danny looked around him with an expression of contentment, as though he was happy to be home. I wondered what had happened up in Scotland but it was none of my business. For some reason Danny thought it was hilarious that I was vegetarian when we chose our meals. I couldn't understand it and Jack quietly told him to leave me alone. Then he calmed down again and decided to go and fetch us some drinks from the bar. We gave him our order and he wandered off.

I looked at Jack across the table. He was smiling but waiting for me to speak. I couldn't help myself.

"So, what is the deal with Danny owning this place?" I

asked, "How come you don't? I just think it's a bit strange if he's never even worked here."

Jack nodded and spoke quietly.

"My brother was in a relationship with the woman who owned this place several years ago," he said, "back when your friend Simon worked as a barman. She was in love with Danny but she was also a bit eccentric and slightly unstable in her mind. He tried to take care of her but eventually she died in an accident. We then found that she had a will, and in it she had left Danny in charge of the Ship. He kept it on sort of in her memory I suppose, and Simon took over as manager because he was capable and he knew her as well. But please don't ask Danny, at least not yet. I don't think he ever quite got over it."

I nodded and sat back in my chair, feeling quite sorry for Danny actually. How terrible it must have been to lose someone you loved like that. Fair enough, I wouldn't poke my nose in any further. It wasn't my business.

Danny came back with our drinks, handed me a glass of Diet Coke as requested, and put down a pint of beer each for him and Jack. He sat beside his brother.

"Food's ordered, shouldn't be long." he announced. "So, Jessica, tell me about yourself."

Danny turned that intense blue gaze on me as he continued.

"My brother here has been very secretive about you while I was out of the country." he said.

I laughed and smiled at Jack.

"I find that hard to believe, Danny." I said, winking at him with mock-seriousness and he laughed as well.

"So you've picked up on Jack's serious nature then." Danny said, "What a shame for you."

He grinned at Jack as he scowled at his brother and I couldn't help but laugh again. Danny seemed so easy-going. I knew we would be good friends.

A young waitress came over with our food and put the plates down where we motioned. I noticed that she seemed hostile towards Danny, slamming his plate down in front of him and scowling. He looked up at her and spoke in a quiet, stern voice, which seemed quite out of character.

"There is no need for that behaviour, Holly." he said in a tone which sent chills down my spine, "I understand it is a shock to see me after so long but I will be here to speak with you and the staff after your shift." He continued, "Please remember to show respect for your superiors."

The girl, Holly, looked surprised and stepped back. She answered quietly but there was defiance in her voice.

"I cannot show respect for someone who would abandon us like that." she retorted, "Simon is my Master, not you."

She turned to walk away but Danny gripped her wrist, turning her back to face him. He didn't speak but something in his expression affected her. She mumbled an apology, broke away and hurried back towards the kitchens.

I looked at Danny in surprise. What was all that about? He glanced at Jack, whose face was serious, and then he smiled at me apologetically.

"I am sorry about that, Jessica." Danny said, "This town is a bit old-fashioned sometimes, and Holly has been on my staff for several years, she is a local girl. I need to spend some time here I think to reassure everyone that I didn't just abandon them. Anyway, forget about that, let's eat."

I nodded and focused on my dinner, my mind whirling with what had happened.

The brothers changed the subject and eventually I decided to forget the whole incident. It was obviously something that Danny had to deal with and I shouldn't concern myself with it. After lunch Jack and me went for a walk, leaving Danny in the pub. I didn't see Simon while we were there but someone said he was in his office, so Danny went to see him and we left.

11

Later that week I had arranged for Liz and Rob to meet us in the Ship on the Friday night. I wanted them to meet Danny. Well, Liz anyway, Rob already knew him of course. Jack and Danny were meeting me there and I walked in feeling very excited at the prospect of bringing my new friends together. It finally felt like things were falling into place. Simon was working behind the bar and gave me his usual grin. Jack and Danny were leaning against the bar with a pint each and they waited while I ordered my drink, then we moved over to my favourite table in the corner. When Liz and Rob arrived everyone seemed to be quite happy together and we fell into conversation.

I couldn't help but notice that Simon kept glancing over but his eyes were following Danny. He clearly had romantic feelings for his boss and I felt a little sorry for his unrequited love. I was even happier when Sally wandered in to the pub. I hadn't seen her for a while because she was always at work, but apparently she knew Jack and Danny, and so she came to see them. It became obvious that she adored Danny and he seemed quite happy to be affectionate with her in front of everyone. I wondered what Simon would make of this, but if Danny was straight, as he seemed to be, there wasn't much that Simon could do about it.

The pub was heaving with both tourists and locals and there was something of a dance floor set up in a corner of the room. Simon had hired a DJ and people were strutting their stuff, mainly women. I was feeling a little drunk and very happy, and Sally seemed the same so we both got up and started dancing to some Disco tunes. After forty-five minutes of solid dancing we needed a break and I headed for the bar where I could see Jack. There was a man standing with him who I hadn't seen before.

Jack introduced me to Marcus Scott, an old friend who

he hadn't seen in years. Marcus smiled and gently kissed the back of my hand in a very old fashioned gesture. I was instantly charmed.

Marcus was tall but slightly shorter than Jack. He had short blond hair and intelligent pale blue eyes. I guessed he was around twenty-five but he seemed so much older and wiser. It turned out that he was something of an entrepreneur and businessman working in IT. He owned a large telecommunications company and had shares in several smaller ones. I had no idea how he had managed that at such a young age. Yet he seemed fascinated by me for some reason.

I knocked back another glass of wine and instantly regretted it as the room started to swim around me. Sally and Jack had disappeared, Liz and Rob were smooching on the dance floor, and Simon was busy behind the bar. I staggered a little and looked around for Jack but all I saw was Marcus' concerned face before me. He shouted above the music.

"Are you feeling alright, Jessica?" he asked, "Do you want some air?"

Suddenly I felt sick and rushed past him and outside. I hurried round the side of the building away from the smokers' area and leaned against the rough brick wall, waiting for my head and stomach to settle. Why do I do this to myself?

"Jessica?" said a male voice that was tentative and unfamiliar. I opened my eyes to see Marcus standing in front of me. I moved and tried to straighten my hair and focus my eyes but he stepped closer, effectively trapping me against the wall. I was suddenly very aware of his firm body against me and alarm bells started to ring.

"I'm fine, thank you Marcus." I said, "Where's Jack? I should get back to him."

Marcus reached up to stroke my hair and I was suddenly alert, sobered by this inappropriate behaviour. I tried to push him away.

"Marcus please, I'm with Jack," I said in a shaking voice, "I don't know what you are expecting."

"Shush Jessica." he replied, "Jack won't mind. Trust me."

He leaned his face in against me, and his body was firm and heavy. He was too strong for me to move. I tried to struggle but he pinned my arms at my sides. Now I was starting to panic. I raised my voice but was suddenly hoarse, maybe from the alcohol.

"Marcus stop!" I cried, "Please stop, you're hurting me!"

I was suddenly in a blind panic as he lifted his head, his face pale, and his eyes wild. He opened his mouth and I tried to scream. He was going to bite me!

Suddenly he was flung away and slammed into the ground across the car park. I saw Danny standing before me. He glared at Marcus.

"What did we tell you?" he yelled, "She is with Jack; she is not yours to take. Leave us!"

Marcus smoothly stood and put a hand to his mouth where he was bleeding from Danny's punch. He smiled and sauntered away without a word. Danny turned back to me.

"Are you alright, Jessica?" he asked, "Did he hurt you?"

Tears sprang to my eyes. I felt so foolish, so stupid. If I hadn't gotten drunk I could have stopped this from happening. Danny's expression was full of concern.

"Hey it's all right." he said softly, "Look, come inside and I'll get you some water and find Jack."

Danny put his arm around my shoulder and led me back into the pub and upstairs to the Manager's office.

It was cool in this room. Danny switched the light on and led me over to the sofa. He disappeared and came back with a glass of water moments later. I sank into the large fabric sofa, and sipped at the cold liquid, holding the glass against my face to sooth my hot skin. Danny leaned against the desk, watching me.

"Did he hurt you?" he asked.

I shook my head and answered with a shaky voice.

"No, you got there in time." I said, "I think he was going to bite me or something, what's his problem?"

Danny shook his head.

"Marcus is a little different compared to most people." he said, "I'm sorry he did that to you. He should have left you alone. I will have words tomorrow."

I nodded but stopped when my head hurt.

"Where's Jack?" I asked, "I think I should go home."

Danny inclined his head, running a hand through his hair.

"He got a phone call," he replied, " he had to go and take care of some business. I'll take you home; are you staying at our place?"

I had sobered up by now and walked slowly down the stairs with Danny, gripping the banister. A couple of younger women tripped past us, smiling at Danny and giggling to each other as they went to the Ladies' toilets. I concentrated on fighting back the nausea and not fainting, while Danny stayed close to me. Simon met us at the bottom of the stairs, face full of concern.

"Jessica, are you ok?" he said, panicked, "Do you want to stay here?"

He held my arms gently, trying to look into my eyes, and I shook my head carefully, trying not to jar it. I must have hit it on the wall when Marcus pinned me.

"I'm fine Simon, honestly." I said with a watery smile, "Danny's taking me back to his place, Jack should be home soon."

Although he seemed reluctant, Simon left Danny to walk me home. We were silent most of the way. I stumbled a little in my high heels and Danny put his arm around my shoulder to support me. It felt strangely intimate and I had to remind myself that this was Danny, not Jack. Things were suddenly getting very confusing in my head.

12

Back at the house Danny helped me up the stairs and left me to get undressed while he went to fetch a drink. I was completely sober now and trembling slightly from the shock of my ordeal. I had never been attacked before and although I had no physical wounds my head hurt and I felt nauseas. When Danny returned with a cup of hot chocolate I was huddled under the covers wearing my pink cotton pyjamas, still shivering. He knocked quietly before entering the room and then handed me the mug very carefully and sat down on the bed beside me.

I sipped tentatively at the hot drink and felt it warm my throat as I swallowed. Then I looked at Danny. He was watching me intently with those familiar bright blue eyes and again my body responded to his presence. It was so confusing. He broke the silence.

"How are you feeling now, Jessica?" he asked.

I carefully placed the mug on the bedside table and glanced at the clock, which said 12:35.

"I'm ok thanks," I said, "just cold and my head hurts. Where's Jack?"

"He got called away on police business." Danny replied, "He asked me to bring you home when you were ready because he couldn't find you and it was urgent. That's when I found you with Marcus. Did he hurt you?"

"No." I said, "You got there in time."

I shivered violently and Danny instinctively moved closer to hug me against his warm body. I rested my head on his shoulder, comforted by the warmth. I spoke in a quiet voice, still a little croaky with shock.

"No he didn't hurt me, just frightened me," I said, "I thought he was your friend."

"He is our friend." Danny said, "I'm very angry that he treated you that way, especially since Jack made it perfectly clear that you are with him."

"Well shouldn't you arrest him or something?" I said in a voice that was growing stronger as my anger returned, "I mean he assaulted me, what if he does that with other women?"

Here Danny drew away from me so he could look at my face. His expression was very careful, his voice low.

"Do you want me to arrest him?" he asked "I will of course, it's my job, but I really don't think it will do you any good." Danny paused, "I mean, Marcus has one hell of a good lawyer on his staff and you have no physical proof of an attack. It would just make things more awkward for you."

I thought about that for a minute and knew Danny was right. But now I was angry.

"So what, he just gets away with it?" I retorted angrily, "He has no respect for women!"

"No." Danny said, "I will speak with him tomorrow and I know Jack will be extremely angry when he finds out. Marcus is a good friend to us Jessica; he just misunderstood your intentions. He was attracted to you and, I know this sounds silly, but he's not used to being refused by any woman."

I laughed at that and then stopped abruptly as I felt a shooting pain in my head. I winced and touched the back of my skull, feeling a bump where I had hit the wall earlier. Danny's face was suddenly concerned and he moved round to inspect my head, gently parting my hair to look for the wound.

"There's no cut but you have a bit of a lump," he said, "Did you hit the wall?"

"Yes." I answered.

"Ah." Danny said, "Well in that case you have evidence of assault. What do you want to do?"

I thought about it for a few minutes. Danny watched me with a careful expression on his face, trying not to show any emotion. Eventually I answered, speaking slowly as I voiced my thoughts.

"Well, I had been drinking and therefore it could be argued that I misinterpreted Marcus' intentions." I said, "I also appreciate that he is your friend and I believe you when you say this a rare occurrence. I would rather forget the whole incident and just take it as a learning curve, ok?"

"Ok." Danny said, "Will you tell Jack about it?"

"Yes." I replied, "Otherwise he might wonder why I dislike your friend. Where did Jack go anyway?"

"He got an urgent call out on police business, something that I couldn't deal with." Danny said, "He asked me to get you home safely when you were ready. I suppose I failed at that task."

I had to smile at his stricken face, and I reached out instinctively to touch his arm in a comforting gesture. He suddenly fixed those intense blue eyes on me and I was transfixed. Again I had to remember that this was Danny, not Jack. But there was a tension in the air that wasn't there a moment earlier. It took all of my self-control not to reach out to his face, Jack's face, Danny's face. This was a confusing mess. Was it like this for other people dating an identical twin? Or was I just reckless?

Danny moved away from me slowly, reluctantly. He stood up.

"I should let you get some sleep, Jessica." he said, "Jack should be home soon, are you alright on your own?"

I nodded and let out a breath I didn't know I was holding. Danny ran a hand through his hair and hesitated, and then he bent down just as I turned my face up to look at him, and our lips met in a chaste kiss. We both jerked back and stared at each other and he backed away to the door.

"Ok," he said, faltering, " Well um, I'll be in my room if you need me. Goodnight."

He shut the door carefully and I flopped back on to the bed with a huge sigh and then cursed as the pain shot through my skull from the bump on my head. What the hell happened? Why was I attracted to Danny? And did he feel the same way? It certainly seemed like it. I would have to be very careful and make sure I didn't get the brothers mixed up again. I was overcome by exhaustion after a long and confusing night. I welcomed sleep as it enveloped me, deep and dreamless for once.

13

I woke to the sound of bird song in the garden outside and I yawned, stretched and opened my eyes. Jack was next to me in bed, fast asleep lying on his front with his head turned to the side away from me. I smiled at the sight of his body, half naked, with the duvet down around his waist. It felt warmer this morning and I desperately needed a shower to rid myself of what had happened the night before. I carefully slid out of bed and went into the en suite bathroom for a hot, steamy shower.

I stood in front of the sink looking at my reflection in the mirror. My face was pale and I felt exhausted. How would I tell Jack what had happened? Somehow I felt stupid. If I hadn't got so drunk, if I had gone to the toilets instead of outside, that whole incident wouldn't have happened. But it did happen and I would have to deal with it. Jack would understand. I just wanted him to hold me in his arms, comfort me and reassure me. How had I ended up so dependent on a man? I shrugged, sighed, and climbed into the shower, enjoying the hot blast of water on my skin.

When I finished and came back into the bedroom to get dressed Jack was still fast asleep. He must have got home in the early hours; I had never even stirred from my sleep. In fact I felt strangely refreshed after the shower and my head didn't hurt this morning, which surprised me. Jack's clothes were strewn across the floor and I tidied the room up a bit while I waited for my body moisturizer to soak in. I picked up his jacket and was surprised to feel a weight in the pocket. Curious, I put my hand inside the folds of material and closed my fist around something metal and smooth. I had a shock when I drew my hand out to find I was holding a gun. It was slightly too big for me to hold comfortably and I panicked, stopped myself from dropping it, and carefully placed it on the cabinet beside the bed.

The gun clunked slightly as I put it down and as I stepped back Jack suddenly woke, sat bolt upright in bed, and before I could blink he was out of bed and had me pushed against the bedroom wall, his arm across my throat. I shouted at him in the split second before he pinned me, my heart racing. I was terrified. He was crazed!

"Jack it's me, it's Jessica!" I cried, "You're hurting me!"

He focused those blazing eyes on me, and his expression changed into one of bewilderment. He released me and stepped back, his Irish accent suddenly far more pronounced than usual.

"Jessica!" he gasped, "Jesus I'm so sorry. Did I hurt you?"

He reached out to touch my face and I jerked away from him, tears stinging my eyes. This was too much. I fought back the urge to cry and dragged some anger out instead as I pulled my jeans and t-shirt from my bag and hastily got dressed.

"Yes you hurt me Jack!" I cried again, "What the hell was that? Were you sleepwalking? Did you think I was some kind of criminal?"

I was almost hysterical, my words pouring out in an angry jumble.

"Why the hell do you have a gun hidden in your pocket?"

I gestured towards the cabinet and he followed my hand. I hurriedly shoved my things into the bag and pulled my shoes on, going for the door. The tears were welling up and I would not let him see me cry.

"I suggest you calm down, and then explain yourself Jack Mason." I said through gritted teeth.

I stormed out of the bedroom onto the landing and down the stairs with Jack following me. He grabbed my arm but I shook him away roughly and opened the front door.

"Jessica please, wait," he cried, "I can explain!"

But I didn't want to hear it. I unlocked my car and sped out of the drive just as Danny came round the side of the house from the back garden. It was only when I shut my kitchen door behind me that I let the tears flow. I fell to the floor, my head in my arms, and cried.

14

I hadn't answered the phone to Jack all day, had ignored his text messages and was huddled on my sofa trying to watch a film on TV to take my mind off the events of the past 24 hours. Elizabeth had phoned earlier, not knowing what had happened to me, but I didn't want to worry her. Apparently she and Rob were still in the pub when I disappeared, and then Danny had told them I was going home, not feeling too well. Liz hadn't believed him, but he had insisted, and then Simon had backed him up. I just said I'd had an argument with Jack and would explain everything to her at work the next day. She was obviously concerned but I didn't want her to come round. I needed to be alone for a while, or so I told myself.

It was early evening and I heard someone knocking on the back door. My heart raced as I walked slowly down the stairs, hesitating, with a faint feeling of nausea in my stomach at the thought of confronting Jack again. But I found Simon on the doorstep, not Jack. He was smiling but it faded as he saw my pale face and tearful eyes. I was suddenly so pleased to see him that I threw myself into his arms and sobbed.

Simon didn't ask questions, he led me further into the kitchen and rubbed my back gently while I cried, making soothing sounds and resting his chin on the top of my head. He was so warm, so familiar and comforting. Eventually I calmed down enough to sit at the kitchen table while Simon made tea for us both. He put the mug in front of me and then sat down opposite with his own.

"Tell me what happened," he said, "I know this isn't just about last night."

I told him everything, starting with how Marcus had charmed me and then terrified me, how Danny had been such a comfort and support when he took me home. Simon nodded when I told him about my confusion over my feelings for Danny but he didn't interrupt. Finally I told him about what had happened that morning when I discovered Jack's gun, and then how Jack had almost assaulted me and how he had frightened me. When I finished speaking, Simon let out a breath, thinking carefully before he spoke.

"Perhaps you would be wise to take a breather in your relationship." Simon said, "I knew that Jack was licensed for firearms; it's part of his job, and Danny's. But I would've expected him to tell you if he was carrying to prevent something like this happening." He continued, "To be honest I'm almost as angry as you. Please Jessica, believe me when I say that the Mason brothers are trouble. They don't mean to be, but they will cause you more grief if you continue this relationship with Jack. It will be worse now that Danny is back in town. And I'm not just saying that to get you away from them. As your friend I am concerned for you, I don't like seeing you upset."

We talked for a few hours about the state of my relationship. Simon finally confessed to me that yes he was attracted to Danny Mason, and yes he did wish that something could happen between them. But he knew that Danny was not interested in him romantically and so he was trying to forget about him. We ordered a take-away for tea and spent the rest of the night bitching about men and cheering each other up, and by the time Simon left me to return home I felt a lot happier.

The happiness faded slightly when I listened to my answer phone messages on my mobile. Jack had left three messages throughout the day, begging me to call him back. By the third message he said he would visit me at work the next day to make me speak to him. I switched my phone to silent mode and went to bed.

I had the dream again. I was running along the cliff top towards Redcliffe. It was raining, my skin and hair were soaked, fear coursed through my body, and I was being chased by a monster. The monster knew me and I knew him, and that's why I didn't want to turn around. But then I slowed, realizing I couldn't outrun him. I should just face up to it instead. So I turned slowly, and drew in a sharp breath as I saw Marcus Scott advancing upon me, with his face hideously distorted and his eyes glowing silver. That surprised me. Then I woke up.

15

"Jessica, are you all right?" Liz asked in a concerned voice, "You look really pale and you've barely spoken all morning. Is it Jack?"

I was roused from my thoughts by Elizabeth standing in front of the counter, hands on her hips, staring at me.

"What?" I asked in a croaky voice.

I lifted my head, blinking to focus on the shop, and on Liz. She moved round to sit beside me.

"What happened over the weekend Jess?" she asked gently, "Tell me."

So I told her. I told her about Marcus and what he did, about how Danny took me home, and then how I found Jack's gun in his pocket. Her expression changed from horror to anger and finally she got that expression that meant she had a plan and she was about to tell me.

"Why didn't you get this Marcus guy arrested?" she said angrily, "He sounds dangerous and you are dating a police detective for goodness' sake! I don't care if he is their friend he shouldn't be allowed to get away with it."

She spoke in an increasingly agitated tone, "And as for Jack, he should be ashamed. He can't blame that behaviour on a bad dream, I mean who else would be in his room with him? And to carry guns around and not even tell you. I am shocked!"

"Liz, please calm down." I said, "First of all I don't want to even see Marcus again for as long as possible and he didn't do anything physically to me. If I got him arrested I would just end up with more grief and stress." I paused, "And second, yes I am angry with Jack but I am also confused. I want to know why he needs to carry a gun round in this part of the country, and who he thought I was when he pinned me against the wall. But mostly I'm concerned. He's obviously got some stress-related condition probably caused by his work."

Liz's expression softened slightly but she was still stern.

"Yes but Jessica he cannot use that as an excuse for what he did." she said, "Surely there are counsellors he can see if he has a problem."

"I know." I said, "But I will at least listen to what he has to say before I take any action."

I felt that lump in my throat again, and the hot tears stinging my eyes.

"Liz I don't want to break up with him." I said.

Her expression was all concern suddenly and she put her arms around me and hugged me close. When she drew away to look at my face her eyes were gentle. "Jessica, do you think you are falling in love with him?" she asked.

My heart lurched and I nodded, blinking away those tears that threatened again. What the hell was wrong with me? I never cried. I was always in control, strong and secure. And now this man had reduced me to a quivering wreck. I swallowed twice before I managed to speak, and my voice was hoarse.

"Liz I think you are right." I said, "I do love him. I have never felt like this about anyone before. And it's horrible!"

Now she was smiling.

"Yep, love really does hurt!" she said, "It isn't just a cheesy power ballad song."

Liz left me to my reverie for the next hour. She made us each a cup of hot chocolate and a toasted sandwich for lunch, while I served customers and stayed behind the counter. I remembered an incident between her and Rob when they had only recently been dating. He had disappeared at short notice on a research trip to Prague with some academics from the university. Liz had been very upset that he didn't tell her about it, and when he returned at first he didn't see what the problem was. To be honest, I hadn't really understood either. I had thought Liz was overreacting. But now I understood. When you love someone and you want to spend time with them, it physically hurts to think that they don't feel the same way about you. I distinctly felt that Jack was keeping a huge, life-shattering secret from me, and I was beginning to feel like I had a right to demand that he tell me what it was. It was either that or we broke up, and I really did not want to do that. I actually couldn't be without him, and I hated admitting it to myself.

16

It was late afternoon when Jack walked into our shop. I was on the stepladder restocking some shelves when I heard the bell above the door jangle. Then I heard Liz speak in a clipped, curt tone.

"Hello, Jack," she said, "I understand you need to speak with Jessica."

I fought to remain calm; my body tense, butterflies in my stomach, and then I turned and climbed carefully down the ladder.

"Hello." I said quietly.

Jack moved towards me, his face serious.

"Hello Jessica. Hello Elizabeth." he said.

I looked at Liz and she nodded.

"You two go in the back," she said, "I can lock up here. You need to talk."

I walked through the small stock room and into my kitchen, heart thudding in my throat, my hands shaking. Jack followed with a brief nod and a 'Thank You' to Liz. He stopped in front of me as I leaned against the kitchen cabinet, my arms crossed over my chest, defensive. I would not cry again.

Jack looked at me with those blazing eyes, like blue flame, so intense. The line of his jaw was so sharp yet so sensual and it was all I could do to stop from reaching out and touching him. I was not going to give in so easily. My voice was hard and sharp.

"Well, what do you have to say for yourself?" I asked.

He swallowed nervously.

"Jessica I am so sorry." he said, "I should never have done that to you. I should have told you about the gun before, I just didn't want to frighten you."

Now I was angry and I welcomed it.

"Well you did a pretty damn good job!" I said, "You

don't need a gun to frighten me Jack, your physical strength and that raw look in your eyes did enough damage yesterday. I thought you were going to strangle me."

My voice was rising and I choked back those tears and turned away from him, leaning my hands on the worktop. I took a few deep breaths and then spoke again, channelling the anger, gripping the smooth hard edge of the work surface. My teeth were clenched, and my voice was low and dangerous as I spoke over my shoulder.

"Did Danny tell you about your dear friend Marcus and what he did to me?" I asked, "He almost raped me Jack! And it was only because Danny found us and stopped him that I was saved. Before I met you my life was safe!"

I flinched as he tentatively touched my shoulder.

"Jessica, please." he said, "I am so sorry, please believe me. I would never harm you, it was an instinctive reaction, and I forgot it was you momentarily. You have to believe me!"

He dropped his hand and I turned round slowly to face him again. Now his face was angry but it wasn't directed at me.

"Yes Danny told me about Marcus." Jack said, "I have been to see him today. He will not harm you again. Please, please forgive me. I cannot lose you."

He stared at me with those bright blue eyes, imploring me to soften. It started to work on me.

"Why were you carrying a gun Jack?" I asked in a quieter voice, "You didn't have it when we were in the pub, I had my arms around you, I would have known. So where did you get it from and why take it afterwards? And why leave it somewhere I would find it?"

"I didn't mean for you to find it Jessica." he said, "Both Danny and me are licensed for firearms and are trained to use them if necessary. The business I was called away on was potentially dangerous and I needed the gun for self-defence."

He paused and looked at me again, then continued.

"It was in my car," he said, "I was exhausted when I got

home, and when I heard the metal hit my bedside cabinet it was instinct when I jumped out of bed. I thought you were an intruder. But I understand if you want me to leave."

He dropped his head and stepped back, and I moved towards him without thinking, my temper softening slightly.

"Jack, I do not want to break up with you," I said quietly, "It hurts me that you would keep secrets like that. We may have only been dating for a few months but I feel really close to you, and I did think I could trust you. Now I'm not so sure."

He nodded. "I understand." he said, "Jessica I do not want to lose you. I care very deeply for you already and that confuses me. For the past four years all I have done is work. I worked on the case in Scotland and the only person I had to look out for was my brother. Now I find that I want to take care of you but you are so bloody stubborn you won't let me! Please give me another chance."

I looked into his eyes again, and that handsome face, and again I felt those butterflies and that ache of longing deep in my belly.

"You call that taking care of me?" I asked, "You need some lessons in being gentle with people Jack. And I am not some soft little girl; I can handle the truth." I said, "Just trust me, and let me into your life, please! Tell me what these secrets are that you are hiding, because I know it will involve me eventually."

We were staring at each other and suddenly he closed the distance between us and took me in his arms. As his mouth found mine I tried to resist but I couldn't, and I returned his kisses hungrily, my body feverish for him. He pushed me against the cabinet, pressing his body against me, and the roughness excited me, made my body tighten with lust and desire.

"Well, it seems you two have kissed and made up," Elizabeth said loudly, clearing her throat for emphasis, "Don't mind us we will sneak out the back door and you will never know we were here!"

We both jumped and turned to see Liz and Rob stood in

the door to the shop, grinning at us. Liz took Rob's hand and led him to the back door.

"Come on darling, I think Jessica and Jack need some alone time." she said. Rob laughed and followed her.

"Hi Jess, hi Jack, goodbye!" he said

Jack and me both laughed, embarrassed, as we said goodbye. I noticed that Rob gave Jack a very direct look as he left, as though he were warning him. But I forgot about it once the door shut and Jack took me in his arms again.

We ran upstairs and he pushed me against the wall on the landing to kiss and caress me again. But as my head impacted with the wall memories of the weekend flooded back and I panicked. I pushed at Jack.

"No," I said, "I can't do this, stop!"

He stepped back, confused, and I hurried into the living room, arms crossed in front of me defensively. I turned to face him as he stood in the doorway, looking so deliciously attractive it physically hurt low in my belly.

"Jack, I can't just let you sleep with me and pretend nothing happened." I said, "You clearly have problems, and we have been together long enough that I have to believe you can trust me. Please, tell me what it is that made you behave like that yesterday. And why do you keep disappearing on mysterious police jobs that apparently Danny or your other colleagues can't do?"

Jack's expression turned to one of sorrow, then seriousness. He spoke carefully, thinking about his words.

"I am sorry, Jessica." he said, "I understand you cannot just move on. There are a lot of things about me and the nature of my work that I cannot explain to you at the moment. It is too dangerous. Please believe me when I say that you are better off not knowing anything."

Now I felt the anger again, the frustration with his behaviour. I refused to believe that he could keep such terrible secrets from me just to keep me safe. I mean, this was real life, not some Hollywood film. What could possibly happen in Redcliffe? It was a safe, quiet, holiday town full of happy tourists.

"Jack why are you so secretive?" I asked. "It really is starting to get to me. If you care about me so much, and about our relationship, then trust me. Let me into your life properly."

"I am sorry Jessica," he said again, "I cannot be completely open with you at this time."

He looked down, and when he looked back at me there was moisture in his deep blue eyes.

"Please understand Jessica, I am trying to keep you safe." he said, "I care so much for you, and it has been such a long time since I was close to a woman. All I need is a little more time to take care of business."

I wanted to believe him, but I wasn't ready to give in. He obviously didn't trust me, and he couldn't be serious about our relationship if he kept secrets from me. I fought back the tears, swallowed the lump in my throat, and managed to keep my voice steady.

"Then we have nothing to talk about Jack." I said, "We have been together long enough now that I would hope we could move the relationship on a step."

I sighed.

"If you are not ready, perhaps we should call it a day. I do not want to break up with you. But I do not trust you at the moment. Please come back to me when you are ready to talk properly."

He nodded, and I thought he was going to speak again, but he seemed to change his mind. Those words went unspoken once again. I wanted to say, "I love you" to him, but I would not say it first. That would make me even more vulnerable, and I was not enjoying these feelings as it was. Jack approached me and I stood my ground as he touched my cheek and kissed me gently.

"Very well Jessica," he said tenderly, "I will leave you alone for now. Please do not give up on me. I will speak with you during the week if you are willing."

After he left I stood for several minutes just staring at the door blankly. Then I let the tears flow once again, and this time I phoned Elizabeth. She came round straight away and

LOVE HURTS

hugged me while I cried, soothing me. She insisted on preparing some food for me, telling me I must eat, and eventually she returned home when I said I wanted to go to bed and she should get home to Rob before he started to worry. But I was so grateful to have such a wonderful friend, and I knew that Liz would never let me down.

17

That night I dreamed again. The monster was chasing me, running along the cliff top in the rain. Part of me knew it was a dream, but some other part of me said it was real, and I had to wake up. I was confused and terrified, trying to escape. When I stumbled and hit the wet ground, I scrambled round to face the monster, not knowing what to expect.

It was Jack. He was just as he usually is, wearing black t-shirt and jeans, rain water dripping from his slightly curling hair. But his face was hideous in the moonlight. His eyes were glowing silver and he had fangs. His cheekbones seemed to stand out starkly on his face, making him inhuman. I screamed and tried to stand up, to run away. He pursued me, and just as he grabbed me against his stone cold body, I woke up, sweating.

I was in bed, alone. I was safe. It was only 2:00am when I looked at the bedside clock, and I remembered our argument earlier that day. That must be why I was dreaming he was a monster. What a confusing mess.

I fell back to sleep again but it would not be an easy night. I was once again standing on the beach in Redcliffe Bay, staring out to sea. The waves were rolling in gently, and the sun was setting. It was a beautiful scene, and I felt calm and relaxed. The woman was beside me again, Lillian. She spoke in a gentle voice.

"Hello, Jessica." she said, "I am sorry you have suffered so much over the last few days."

I was surprised. How could this imaginary woman know about my life? I tried to look at her again, and almost managed it. I sensed that she smiled.

"Do not be alarmed, child." she said, "I am always here to watch over you. I will always try to protect you as much as I can."

"Who are you Lillian?" I asked, "How do you know

what has been happening? This is a dream. I don't understand…"

Then I woke again, the dream fading just as quickly as it had started. I felt exhausted, confused, and all I wanted was to sleep, just sleep. Eventually I drifted into the blackness, and thankfully didn't wake or dream until my alarm went off the next morning.

18

The next two days at work were long and tedious. Liz didn't question me about Jack, or push too much for me to talk about my feelings. She knew how upset I was, and tried to distract me by talking about the baby and the business. I was glad to have something else to occupy myself with, and so I avoided the Ship and tried to ignore my mobile phone as much as possible. But it was so hard.

I badly wanted to phone Jack or send him a text message, but I wouldn't allow myself to give in. For some strange reason every song I heard on the radio reminded me of him, and every TV program made some sort of reference to my relationship. It was horrible. No wonder people wrote about love in such a heartrendingly miserable way. It made perfect sense suddenly, now that I was experiencing it for myself. I spent a couple of evenings lying on my sofa shovelling chocolate chip ice-cream into my mouth, knocking back the wine, and watching my favourite DVDs, the ones that made me cry. And I wallowed in self-pity.

Simon phoned me a couple of times and I told him what had happened. He came to see me after work, listened while I spoke about how I couldn't just give up on Jack, on our relationship. Simon didn't judge or offer advice; he simply accepted what I said. Even Danny sent me a few text messages in those first couple of days. He said if I needed to talk he was there as my friend. He also said that Jack was missing me but was giving me the space I needed. I suddenly realized how close I had become to both these brothers in a short space of time. I valued my friendship with Danny, it was important to me. We had lots in common, and we could teach each other about new interests as well. I did not want to lose that.

It was my day off mid-week and I had decided to go shopping in the nearby city. Some retail therapy was just what I needed to take my mind off things. Sally had met me in the morning for a few hours but had left to go to work. We had enjoyed spending time together recently, what with her dating Danny and us sharing interests in books and films. I liked Sally, she was down-to-earth yet fun at the same time. Her work was very important to her, and if ever I was in hospital, I hoped she would be the one to look after me.

I had asked her tentatively about her feelings for Danny, and her expression became dreamy as she replied.

"I don't think we will ever be serious, Jess." she said, "Danny's great and everything, but he's not interested in a relationship. No woman can tame him!"

I had laughed at that and suggested that Sally might meet another man, one who might be interested in a more serious relationship.

"Oh no Jessica," she said in pretend horror, "Once you've had a Mason brother you cannot leave him. Don't you feel it with Jack? It's so intense!"

Then she had stopped herself.

"Sorry," she faltered, "I didn't think. Oh Jess, just ignore me!"

I smiled, ignoring the way my body was suddenly trembling.

"It's fine Sally, honest." I said, "Jack and me are just taking a break. Something happened over the weekend and I felt a bit suffocated. I'm sure it'll be fine. We haven't broken up."

I paused, thought for a minute, and then continued, "I just can't handle all the secrecy around him, with his work and everything."

Sally had seemed to understand, and hadn't probed further. That's what I like about her, she knows when to keep quiet.

After Sally left I stopped in a small coffee shop for my favourite Mocha with extra cream, and a large chocolate muffin. The place was bustling with couples, families and friends, and I quite enjoyed people watching while I sipped my drink and demolished my muffin. I hadn't spent much time alone recently and was actually relishing the opportunity for once.

It was strange to think how much things had changed in a few months. I was determined not to dwell on the situation with Jack. Today I needed 'me' time, to remember who I was as a single, independent woman.

My heart sank as a familiar man walked into the shop and approached my table. I stiffened and fought to keep a calm composure when Marcus Scott stood before me. He was dressed in a very smart grey business suit and he did look incredibly handsome, sort of a mixture between an olden-day gentleman, and a modern-day playboy, if such a thing were possible. I looked up at him with a stony expression, and his was solemn as he spoke.

"Good afternoon, Jessica." he said, "May I sit down? We need to talk."

Not wanting to make a scene in public I nodded reluctantly. But I did not want to be here all of a sudden.

Marcus sat down slowly opposite me. I noticed that the waitress had spotted him and was hurrying to the table. I couldn't help but smile, and then I quickly suppressed it. Marcus ordered himself a black coffee and the waitress went away, disappointed that he wouldn't speak with her, even though she was doing her best to flirt and be appealing. I waited for him to speak.

"Jessica, I want to formally apologize for my behaviour on our last meeting." he said, "It was unacceptable, and I am terribly sorry that I upset you in such a way. It was not my intention."

His language was so formal it took me by surprise. The waitress returned with Marcus' coffee and when she left I spoke.

"It certainly seemed as though your intentions were pretty clear that night." I said, "Did Jack come and see you?"

Marcus nodded.

"Yes, he visited me at work and we had words." he said.

Something in his tone made me frown.

"Did he hit you?" I asked curiously.

Marcus nodded again and sipped his coffee. His manner was very calm, very civil, and I found it hard to be angry with him. The thought of Jack defending my honour stirred a feeling of excitement, and a little unease, especially knowing so little about his apparently violent work history. Who exactly was this man that I was in love with? And what sort of trouble was I getting myself into? I thought about all the news stories I had heard over the years about domestic violence. Wasn't that a version of what I had just experienced with Jack? Yet I wouldn't say he was violent with me, because that sounded too serious, and made him sound dangerous, and me weak.

I sipped my own coffee and spoke quietly.

"Well, I think it's best that we forget the whole incident." I said, "Maybe I gave you the wrong impression, I know I can be a little flirty after a few drinks. And perhaps I over-dramatized what happened between us. There was no serious harm done, so I suppose we can be civil."

Marcus smiled suddenly and it was dazzling, infectious.

"Thank you Jessica." he said, "You truly are special!"

Now I was embarrassed.

"I wouldn't go that far Marcus." I said, "Perhaps mature is a better word."

He nodded, still smiling.

"Alright, mature then." he said, "I hope we can put this behind us."

I began to relax a little. There was something calming about Marcus. I found that I didn't want to be angry with him. But a voice in the back of my mind still urged me to be cautious. Marcus became serious suddenly.

"Now we have dealt with that issue, I would like to ask about something else," he said.

He reached into his jacket pocket and handed me a small business card. "These are my personal contact details," he said, "I understand that living with Jack and Danny can be confusing sometimes; their behaviour might seem strange. I am their oldest friend. If you need to speak with me about anything, or ask me anything, please do not hesitate to phone. And you are welcome at my home anytime."

I frowned again. Why would he say this?

"Marcus, what are you talking about?" I asked, "Why would I be concerned about their behaviour?"

He gave me a level look, one that said I knew exactly what he meant.

"You need not be concerned Jessica," he said, "but if they seem a little odd, or different, I may be able to help. But I can see this is upsetting you, so I will leave." He stood gracefully, finishing his coffee, and left a £10 note on the table.

"Marcus, that's too much, let me get you some change." I said.

He smiled, "It is no matter, my treat, my apology to you." he said, "Remember Jessica, if you feel confused about anything please speak to me and I will try to help."

And with that he was gone, walking swiftly out of the coffee shop and into the busy street. I turned and watched him leave before I even realized. He was such a strange man! I still felt uneasy about him, but curiously I was no longer afraid. Actually I was intrigued, I wanted to know more about him. So much for forgetting my problems. I finished my muffin and coffee and headed home, thoughts and confusion whirling through my mind.

19

I parked my car in the road behind our shop, and let myself in through the kitchen door. Normally I would go through and see Liz in the shop but suddenly I was exhausted. On the drive home I had thought about what Marcus had said, and then what Sally had said about the Mason brothers being intense. She was right, they were. And I couldn't explain it.

I had never been in love before but now I was certain this was it, even though I wouldn't admit it to Jack. But I kept remembering odd little things that had made me wonder. Jack would often disappear at night, apparently called out on business that Danny couldn't attend to. And then there was the whole thing with Danny owning the Ship. I could not understand how a police detective came to own a pub simply through a past relationship. It was just too strange. And then of course there were my dreams, which I was increasingly starting to believe. But why was Jack a monster in them?

I dropped my shopping bags on the living room floor and kicked off my shoes. Then I flopped down onto the sofa, turned on my side, and promptly fell asleep. Once again I dreamed. I was on the beach again, with Lillian stood beside me. Now I wanted answers. This had gone on long enough and I was angry and frustrated. I stared out to sea again as I spoke.

"Hello, Lillian." I said, "Why do you keep appearing in my dreams? And why am I conscious of them now? They seem too real, too solid."

Her voice was gentle as she replied.

"Hello Jessica." she said, "I am here to guide you. You are finally seeing that there is more than meets the eye with Jack Mason and his brother. It is my job to protect you, and to offer advice if you will take it."

Here I gasped.

"How do you know about Jack?" I asked.

I tried to turn towards her but was stopped again by that invisible force. The wind was rising, whipping my hair around my face and I shook it back impatiently.

Lillian replied.

"I have always been here with you Jessica." she said, "You simply weren't ready to see me yet. But Jack has awakened your power, and now I am able to freely communicate."

Who was she? I knew her! That was it. I had to face her. I turned and this time there was no invisible barrier. And I gasped with shock. There stood an older version of me! Although she had black hair, it was long and straight like mine, and she had my green eyes, and my pale face with freckles across her nose.

"Lillian, you are my mother!" I cried, "How are you here? How can we speak like this?"

She smiled and held her arms out to me, and I rushed into her embrace. My beloved mother was not lost! She was right here, on the beach, comforting me! I was crying as she hugged me, kissed my head, and whispered soothing words.

When I drew away from her, she spoke quietly.

"I have always watched over you, Jessica." she said, "It is only now that you give me strength to communicate. We are born of an ancient line of witches, and your abilities have lain dormant all these years. Jack Mason has awakened your natural energies, and now I can cross that bridge between the Spirit plane and the Earth plane, and we can finally speak. But I grow weak now, and your dream may fade. Rest assured, I will be with you again soon. I love you, my daughter."

Everything faded around me, and although I cried out for her, she was gone again. I woke slowly to find myself on the sofa in my living room, with tears on my cheeks. Then I jumped and sat bolt upright as I realized someone was sitting in the chair watching me.

"Jack!" I cried, "What the hell are you doing here? You

frightened the life out of me!"

He smiled but it was careful, cautious.

"Sorry Jessica." he said, "I went in through the shop and Liz let me in. She said she heard you come home and she thought you might want to see me. Are you alright?"

He rose and came to perch on the sofa beside me, frowning as he tentatively reached out to touch my face with his fingertips.

"You were crying." he said, "Was it a dream?"

I blinked away the moisture and wiped my eyes with my sleeve. This was too personal to share at the moment.

"I'm fine Jack." I said, "Yes it was a dream, but it's nothing, honestly."

He nodded but he didn't seem convinced. I felt awkward, remembering our last meeting. My body was tense and I fought not to show it. So I changed the subject, my voice growing stronger as my body calmed down from the sudden fright. "I saw your friend Marcus earlier today." I said.

Jack was suddenly alert, face serious.

"Did he speak to you?" he asked.

I nodded.

"Yes." I said, "He saw me in a coffee shop and came to apologize for what happened at the weekend. He said you 'had words' and when I asked, he admitted that you hit him."

Jack looked down, then up at me with those intense blue eyes.

"Are you alright? Did he behave?" he asked.

I smiled.

"Yes of course he did," I said, "Actually he was very polite and I just said we might as well be civil. He seems genuinely sorry and I'm happy with that. Don't worry, you've no need to defend me or anything."

I told Jack about Marcus giving me his phone numbers, and about how he kept talking about Jack and Danny acting strangely. At first Jack seemed annoyed, then he relaxed.

"Yes I suppose Marcus does know us the best out of all

our friends." he said, "But he also likes to tell stories Jessica so don't take him too seriously."

I promised not to but my mind was left whirling. Jack was clearly hiding something that Marcus knew about, and I wanted to find out what it was. Then there was the whole thing with my mother. I would keep that a secret for now, at least until I knew more about what it meant, and what I was able to talk about to other people. Liz might think I was crazy, and Jack would probably just give up on me. No, this would be my secret until Lillian told me more about my family, about our history, and what it meant to me. I was certain she would return to my dreams very soon.

20

For the rest of that week I slept dreamlessly. It was strange, I felt bereft, abandoned by my mother all over again. I was actually quite upset that Lillian hadn't visited me. Now I knew that my mother could still speak to me, I needed her. I had to know what she meant by us being witches, and how Jack fit into it. But something told me that all would be answered in time, and I should simply be patient. I kept a distance with Jack that week. He stayed with me for a few hours on the Wednesday evening but I sent him home, telling him we needed some space. I would not allow him to kiss me again, even though he tried.

I worked over the weekend, and spent the Sunday with Simon at the pub. Danny came in while I was there but he simply acted as normal, which I appreciated. Jack dutifully gave me the space I asked for, and even though it hurt to be apart from him, I knew it was necessary. My mind was still whirring over the possibilities of what these mysterious secrets could be. I thought maybe Jack and Danny had secret identities, sort of like James Bond characters, but that just seemed too ridiculous. Then I considered what Lillian had said about me being a witch. I found myself picking out books from our Mind, Body and Spirit section in the shop. These had never interested me before, but somehow I felt they would offer some answers. But all they said was that there were possibilities beyond physical human life, and I became frustrated and gave up on that train of thought. Surely Jack couldn't really be some sort of mythical monster? It was too bizarre.

It was Monday, and I was worried about Liz. Her bump was growing fast and she seemed unwell, even though she told me to stop fussing. She was pale and kept getting breathless. I made her sit down with a glass of water late on in the morning but she insisted there was nothing wrong and it was a natural part of pregnancy. I wasn't convinced, and sent Rob a text message asking him to keep an eye on her that night. He was at work finishing up the summer term at university, and he promised to make her rest. But that wasn't to happen.

Just before midday I came back into the shop from the stock room to find Liz leaning on one of the book tables. She was gasping for breath and I dropped the box I was carrying and hurried over to her.

"Liz!" I cried, "Liz what's happening? Sit down, I'll call the doctor."

She tried to speak but couldn't, and when she turned towards me her face was deathly white. Then she collapsed on the floor in a faint, too fast for me to catch her. "Elizabeth," I cried again, "Oh my god."

I grabbed my mobile phone from my trouser pocket and dialled 999. The female operator answered. I tried to keep my voice calm, choking back tears.

"Send an ambulance, quickly," I said frantically, "My friend has collapsed, she's twenty-two weeks' pregnant. I don't know what's up with her."

The operator calmly asked for the address and advised me to put Liz in the recovery position. I was shaking so much I could barely function, but Liz had woken up and was trying to move. I managed to rest her head on my knee while I phoned Rob, and the ambulance arrived within ten minutes.

I hurriedly locked the shop up while the paramedics put Liz in the ambulance. I jumped in with them, trying to reassure her even though my voice was shaking and I was trembling all over. She was crying now, worrying about her baby. The paramedics were wonderful, assuring her that everything would be fine, and we were rushed through to the antenatal section of the hospital's A&E department. Doctors were quick to establish that the baby was healthy, they knew what the problem was and would just run some routine tests, and keep Liz in overnight for observation. Rob came running into the hospital about twenty minutes after we arrived, and when he found us I left the two of them alone while I went in search of the café. I suddenly realized how thirsty I was, and that I should at least have a sandwich as I was starting to feel faint myself.

After a strong coffee and a cheese toasty I was walking back to the antenatal ward, getting lost in the maze of corridors. Hospitals were very confusing places. I had never liked them, because they reminded me of the car crash when my parents died. I had been carried in on a trolley much like Liz today, but my memories were hazy because I was so young. I just remember crying for my mum and dad, and the nurses telling me everything would be all right. But of course it wasn't. I fought to repress these memories as I headed back to see Liz, and then stopped as I turned a corner and saw Danny and Sally further down the corridor. It was quiet here, the hustle and bustle coming from rooms along the way, and for some reason I stepped back and peeped around the corner, not wanting them to see me.

Danny was standing close to Sally, and he looked quite angry and intimidating. In fact he looked different, more frightening, very like Jack had on that morning when he pinned me in the bedroom. Sally seemed to be acting submissively to him, as though she had done something wrong, but I couldn't imagine what. Surely they must be a couple and they were having an argument. But why would Danny be in the hospital when Sally was working? He should be at work today I knew that. Actually he was dressed in jeans and a smart shirt rather than his usual surfer clothes. I knew enough to see that these were his work clothes. Maybe he was on an investigation or something.

As I watched he leaned in closer to Sally, and appeared to sniff her neck, his lips turning up in a snarl. It seemed so inhuman, and my heart skipped a beat, a pang of fear washing over me. I should not be watching this; it was none of my business. But somehow I was transfixed. There was a faint voice in my head, telling me to watch, that it was important for me to realize the truth. I didn't understand what that truth could be, but I stood transfixed, wishing I could be closer to hear their conversation. Then Sally opened a door behind her and led Danny into the room beyond, and they were gone from sight.

I shook my head, blinking to focus my thoughts. Never mind Danny and Sally, I had to check on Liz. I finally found my way back to the ward, where Rob was sitting beside Liz's bed, holding her hand and stroking her hair. They both looked up as I approached the bed. Liz smiled, looking more like her old self, although she was still pale.

"Hey, Jess, sorry to frighten you like that." she said.

I laughed.

"You couldn't frighten me Liz," I replied, "But I did tell you to take a rest."

I put my hands on my hips and tutted at her, and Rob smiled.

Liz spoke again.

"The doctors are keeping me in overnight," she said, "and apparently I need to rest for the next few days."

I nodded in agreement.

Liz continued, "So shouldn't you get back to the shop? It can't be closed all afternoon."

I laughed again.

"You never stop do you Elizabeth," I said indignantly, "Fine, I know when I'm not wanted, I'll go."

I looked at Rob.

"Phone me when you have an update from the doctors." I said. Then I looked at Liz.

"And you," I said, "behave, listen to the doctors, and get some rest."

They both nodded and saluted me in mock-obedience, and I left them alone.

I walked out to the front reception area and remembered I didn't have my car. The hospital was on the outskirts of the city, some twenty miles from Redcliffe. I walked out into the bright June sunshine, squinting without my sunglasses, and pulled out my mobile phone. I had a taxi number stored in it for emergencies. As I switched my phone back on and watched the screen light up, I became aware of someone approaching me. I looked up to find Danny smiling in front of me.

"Hi, Jess what are you doing here?" He asked.

I told him about Liz, and he said he was here on business, something to do with an injured suspect.

"So I take it you need a lift home then?" he said.

I nodded, and accepted Danny's offer. We walked across the car park to his large black 4x4; almost identical to the one Jack drove.

Once we were on the main road Danny spoke.

"Jack misses you, Jessica." he said, "Are you ready to give him a second chance yet?"

I stiffened, not wanting to discuss my relationship at this time. But Danny was only concerned for his brother and I knew that. I looked at him as he concentrated on the road. His features were so perfect, so like Jack's.

"I don't know what to do with him Danny." I said helplessly, "You are both so secretive and it's getting to me now. It was easier to ignore at first, but Jack and me are supposed to be getting more serious. We aren't teenagers, we are mature adults, but I can't continue a relationship with him if he keeps all of these secrets from me."

"So am I part of the problem?" Danny asked.

I smiled, amused at his sense of self-importance. But it was true. He and Jack were so wrapped up in each other; he couldn't help but be involved. And then there was that mysterious business with Sally I had just witnessed.

"Yes, I suppose you are Danny." I said, "I don't know how to behave with both of you. It's like you are in some exclusive club that I'm not a part of, and sometimes it seems that Simon is as well. I feel left out, and that makes me feel stupid."

"You are not stupid Jessica." Danny said, "We both care very deeply for you."

He risked a glance at me as he stopped at traffic lights, and the look in his eyes made my heart skip a beat. It was affection, but it was also something more. I knew that he was telling the truth, and suddenly I felt slightly sick with nerves and unease. I fought to get my emotions under control before I spoke again.

"You keep saying this and so does Jack," I said, "but that doesn't change anything. Until he can properly speak to me about his life, and your life, I can't be a part of it. You know what I mean."

Danny did seem to understand. He came into the shop with me for a little while when we returned, but we didn't say much. I asked him if he had to return to work and he said he was on field duty, which meant he had no real restrictions. Again I felt that strange intimacy between us, and it made me tense. He really seemed to be lingering here, asking if I needed anything doing. I said no, the shop was fine and I would just have a quiet afternoon.

Danny made us some coffee and sat with me behind the counter, making polite conversation, cautiously asking whether I was ready to see Jack again or not. I answered him, saying that no I still needed some time alone. And now I needed to focus on Liz, to ensure she took a step back from work while she was carrying the baby and it was taking a toll on her body. I was actually glad when Danny got a phone call and had to leave.

21

For the rest of that week I ran the shop alone, struggling when it started to get busier. I decided it was time to call our summer staff back to help out, since the holidays were about to start anyway. Liz agreed, so I spoke to the regular students that we kept on record, and managed to get one of them in later that week. Her name was Marie, she was studying to be a barrister at the university, and she enjoyed working in the bookshop because we allowed her to read her law books in between serving customers.

Liz kept in touch by phone but Rob dutifully kept her at home on bed rest, under doctors' orders, for one week. Simon came to see me and we had a few evenings at the Ship together playing pool and having a few drinks. He didn't question me about Jack, and we simply pretended that everything was as normal. I was glad about that, I felt that my life was starting to spiral out of control, and I desperately needed to rein it in before things became too frightening.

Jack and Danny met us one night, and while it was awkward, I felt better for it. Jack was very careful not to put pressure on me, and I appreciated that. I wanted nothing more than to invite him home, or to stay at his house. I ached for his body, for his kiss and caress, but I could not allow myself more pain. Even standing close to him at the pool table sent my body into shivers of anticipation. I would normally use the opportunity to tease and torment him, but now I felt stiff and awkward, and I resented him for putting me in this situation.

It was made worse when a young woman in the pub started flirting with him; oblivious to the way we were acting together. He watched me cautiously as he tried to avoid her, but she seemed to know him and wouldn't give up. I couldn't help but feel a crazed kind of jealousy and possessiveness, and I felt horribly aggressive to this woman, this stranger. I had to remind myself that she didn't know about Jack and me, and that it was up to him to tell her to leave him alone. Eventually she gave up and wandered off, and I felt the tension ease slightly from my body.

Then I witnessed another strange occurrence. I had been to the Ladies' toilets in the pub, and when I walked back out onto the landing I noticed that the door to the Manager's office was open, and there was someone inside. I had left Jack, Danny and Simon downstairs in the poolroom, so I wondered if maybe a customer had wandered in to the room being nosy. I strode over and pushed open the door, then gasped as I saw Simon leaning against the desk with Danny right in front of him, apparently kissing him. Danny jumped back, embarrassed, and I stuttered an apology.

"Oh, I'm sorry," I said, "I thought you were downstairs. I'll, umm, get back to Jack…"

I hurried back down to the poolroom. Did this mean Danny was bisexual? I knew for a fact that Sally had been staying in his room and I was sure they were having sex. Wow, maybe Simon did stand a chance after all. Jack asked what was wrong and I said it was nothing, just that I had seen something unusual but it wasn't important. He seemed concerned and intrigued but he dutifully stayed quiet. For some reason I didn't want to talk about seeing Danny and Simon together. After a short time they returned, looking at me warily, but when I didn't react they seemed to relax and the rest of the evening passed without incident.

I didn't have any more dreams. I was desperate to speak to Lillian again, to see if she really was my mother. I believed it, even though my rational mind told me to grow up and stop being silly. I continued to read the self-help books, and did some Internet research about witches. Instinct told me that I was on the right path, but I still couldn't get over that last hurdle, the one in which society told me there was no such thing as monsters.

Nothing strange had ever really happened to me before, not that I could recall. In fact I was probably a very ordinary and boring individual really, who just enjoyed socializing with my close friends and running my business. Yet I knew instinctively that something big was about to happen, and it had nothing to do with Liz having a baby, and everything to do with Jack and Danny. I was restless, confused, even anxious, although I didn't know why. Perhaps it was time to resume relations with Jack properly and give him a chance to explain himself.

Although I had made that decision it was now Friday afternoon and I hadn't actually spoken to Jack properly. I had sent him a few text messages saying we should meet over the weekend, and he had phoned me back to say yes of course, whatever I wanted. There had been an unspoken weight of emotion in our conversation. I knew he wanted to say 'I love you' and I wanted to say it too, but we were both holding back, both stubborn and afraid.

That afternoon I had set Marie the task of helping me to clean the shop. We had dusters and polish and were working our way through the shelves, tables and display stands. Liz was due to return on Monday and I knew she would start fussing. I did not want her over-exerting herself again. Marie was working on one of the tall built-in bookshelves, on her hands and knees dusting the bottom rows. I was wedged awkwardly in the window, cleaning round the display and rearranging some of the books. People were walking up and down outside, wandering between the beach and the shops, eating ice creams, enjoying their holidays.

Then I saw Marcus walk up the street toward the shop, smiling as he saw me in the window. I became all flustered as I scrambled back out of the display, trying not to stumble as he came into the shop. He was dressed in dark blue designer jeans and a long-sleeved button-through shirt that looked a sort of purple colour with a diagonal black print on it. It was clearly an expensive designer brand, as were the black sunglasses he wore. His hair was softly spiked, inviting me to run my hands through it, and his aftershave smelled delicious. It was musky and heady, but not heavy. I felt my body react to him in spite of me trying not to see him that way.

"Hello, Jessica," he said, removing the glasses and winking, "I was wondering if you fancied coming out for dinner this evening? Perhaps a night away from everything would do you some good."

I smoothed down my clothes and patted my hair, which I had tied back in a ponytail. I felt scruffy and self-conscious. Marie had stood up and was gazing at Marcus, clearly in awe. He seemed not to notice, focusing his attention on me. I replied, and managed to sound halfway coherent which was good.

"Hi, Marcus," I said brightly, "Yes that sounds good. Did you not have plans tonight?"

His smile was dazzling.

"Yes," he said, "I want to spend the evening with you, offer myself as your friend. If that is all right with you."

I nodded, and then looked at my watch.

"Marie," I said, turning to face the younger girl, "you might as well go home now, it's almost closing time. Thank you for today, you have done a great job."

Marie smiled and thanked me, then went to retrieve her bag from the stock room. She gushed at Marcus as she walked past him out of the shop, and he smiled politely, held the door open, and said goodbye to her. I put away my duster and polish and turned back to Marcus.

"Right," I said, "well, I'll just lock up and get a quick change of clothes if you don't mind?"

He shook his head, waited while I locked the front door, logged off the computer and locked the cash register away in our safe in the storeroom. Then I led him through to my kitchen, locking the connecting door behind us.

"Do you want a drink or anything?" I asked.

Again he shook his head, looking at me with that intense stare, so similar to Jack, but Marcus' eyes were pale blue where Jack's were bright.

"No, thank you Jessica." he said, "I will wait while you freshen up. Take your time, we have all night."

I led him upstairs to the living room and left him there

while I went to the bathroom. I splashed cold water on my face and applied some light make-up for the evening. I didn't want to overdo it, reminding myself that this wasn't a date, but somehow I needed to be smart next to Marcus and his designer clothes. I applied some powder foundation, a little bronzer to brighten my white skin, some bronze eye shadow and black mascara, which accented my eyes nicely. I added a little gold glitter eyeliner, since it was Friday night and I liked wearing it. Then I finished the look with some dark red lipstick, and I had to admit I cleaned up pretty well.

I went through to my bedroom and looked through the wardrobe. I settled for a pretty brown silk dress that had a pink and green rose flower print all over. It had been a sale bargain, and made me feel chic and sophisticated when I wore it, which wasn't very often. The dress had short sleeves that were flared, and it came just above my knees, not too short. It had a v-neck and delicate buttons down the front. I slipped into my brown patent high-heeled shoes and picked up the matching brown clutch bag. The dress needed simple jewellery so I wore my delicate gold necklace with a small pearl pendant, and matching earrings. They had been a present from Liz for a birthday a few years ago. I added a delicate gold bracelet on one wrist, and my watch on the other. My hair was brushed out and lay sleek and smooth over my shoulders. I looked in the full-length mirror and had to admire my reflection. I really was an attractive woman when I made the effort. I decided to be brave and not take a jacket. After all it was summer and had been a beautiful day.

Marcus was stood in front of the bookcase behind my TV, inspecting some of the titles on the shelves. He turned when I entered the room, and couldn't disguise the desire on his face.

"Wow, Jessica you look beautiful." he said with wide eyes.

I smiled and ducked my head.

"Thank you Marcus," I replied, "Are you ready to go?"

He moved towards me, keeping eye contact, his movement smooth and graceful yet totally masculine, the smell of his aftershave deliciously overpowering. I led him downstairs and out through the back door, feeling slightly nervous and excited. This was not a date. We were just friends. I had to remember that. Besides, I had to remember our first meeting, and to take things slowly with this man.

We walked round the building and onto the cobbled shopping street, walking past the shop front. Instinctively I glanced through the window to make sure I had turned all the lights off. I noticed that the window display still needed some tidying, and made a mental note to do that tomorrow. Then I became aware of Marcus watching me. I looked up to see him smiling indulgently.

"You care very deeply for your business, don't you Jessica?" he said.

I smiled and nodded.

"Yes of course I do," I replied, "Without it me and Liz wouldn't be here." Marcus nodded and we continued walking onto the promenade. It was bustling with tourists and local people. There were families trouping back from the beach, children covered in sand, parents laden with beach towels, bags and other sunbathing paraphernalia. They would be heading back to their apartments and caravans to freshen up and go out for the evening entertainment no doubt. Then there were the couples, young and old, and groups of younger men and women, all dressed up and on their way to the pubs. I even spotted a few groups in fancy dress, obviously birthday parties, and hen and stag parties. The atmosphere was happy, excited, and I loved it.

Marcus broke the comfortable silence.

"I thought, perhaps we could try the harbour end of the town for a change," he said, "Give the Ship a miss tonight, since we are keeping your mind off certain matters."

I smiled and agreed with him. The harbour front housed lots of little Cornish local restaurants and old pubs, as well as a few nightclubs and a big amusement arcade. It was especially fun at this time of year, when it was filled with holidaymakers. We walked slowly along the promenade, watching the people around us, and I inhaled the fresh sea air, enjoying the taste of salt on my tongue. I was aware of Marcus walking close to me, but he kept a respectful distance.

We chose a quaint seafront restaurant that specialized in freshly caught fish dishes. The waiter seated us at a table in the window recess, so we got a good view out to sea, where the fishing boats and pleasure cruisers were bobbing gently at their moorings, and I could vaguely make out the shapes of larger freight ships on the horizon. The restaurant was filling up fast, and we only just managed to get our table in time. Ironically, I chose the vegetarian lasagne for my meal, and Marcus chose a steak, cooked rare. My stomach turned at the thought of it, with all that blood and raw meat, but I would just avoid looking. I had grown used to sharing my mealtimes with meat eaters anyway.

Marcus asked if I would like to share a bottle of wine, to which I agreed of course. He chose a nice rich Merlot, a more expensive variety I noticed. The waiter poured a little in my glass for me to taste, and naturally I agreed that it was delicious. The waiter filled both our large glasses halfway, set the bottle on the table, and left us alone.

I sipped at the wine, savouring its rich, fruity taste. This wasn't too heavy or dry; it was just right, and I enjoyed it. Marcus sipped his wine before speaking.

"Do you enjoy red wine, Jessica?" he asked.

I nodded, smiling.

"Yes, this one is delicious," I said, "So are you a connoisseur yourself Marcus?"

It was his turn to smile as he took another large sip.

"Yes I do have a weakness for the drink." he said, "I only drink red wine though; I enjoy its rich and earthy flavour. You should come and sample my wine rack at home sometime, I will invite you to my next social party."

We fell into conversation and I soon relaxed. Marcus had topped our glasses up by the time our meals arrived, and I started to get that familiar warm feeling as the alcohol soothed my mind. Sometimes it felt like I needed wine just to stop me over-analysing everything. Did that mean I had a drink problem? No, I just needed to calm down and relax a little. I did drink a few glasses of water with my meal, just to balance it out.

During the meal I asked Marcus about his business. I was intrigued about how he could run a large global company at such a young age. He told me that his father had set up the company and raised him to follow in his footsteps. His father had died of a heart attack two years ago, and his mother apparently died before that of some long-term illness. Marcus was very matter-of-fact about it and I wondered if perhaps he hadn't been close to his parents. But he seemed happy enough with his business. "So, Jessica," he said, "how did you end up in Redcliffe? I know you are not local, your accent gives it away."

I laughed at that. Apparently I would never lose my 'Northern twang.' I took a sip of wine from our second bottle and then replied.

"Well," I said, "me and Liz worked as office administrators in Manchester. It was ok work but there was no career progression for us. So I persuaded her that we should set up our own business. We had been here on a holiday and I fell in love with the town, and when I found out that the bookshop was for sale, I persuaded Liz to join me."

"So you forced your best friend to leave her family and move all the way down here?" Marcus asked.

He was smiling and I flushed, embarrassed.

"Not exactly," I said defensively, "She wanted to move, and she was bored. Anyway if we hadn't moved down here she wouldn't have found Rob." I added. Marcus nodded.

"This is true." he said, "Well I for one am glad that you moved here. I might have met you sooner, but I have spent a lot of time away on business over the last few years. Perhaps I could have met you before Jack. What a shame."

I looked at him sharply. His expression was playful, and I could see he was flirting. I went hot all over, and then tried to regain my composure.

"It obviously wasn't meant to be Marcus." I said lightly.

He shook his head in mock regret; at least I thought it was. We finished the meal with coffee. I had a strong filter coffee; Marcus had a liqueur one with Whiskey. He insisted on paying for the meal, saying that he was out to cheer me up and that I shouldn't worry about it. So I left him to it.

We walked out of the restaurant to a cooler evening, and the fresh air felt good on my face and across my arms. I stopped outside the restaurant.

"Do you want to go to a pub Marcus?" I asked, "I don't want to go home yet." He nodded in agreement and we walked along the street and into a pub named the Smugglers. It was another old, seventeenth century building, much smaller than the Ship. This pub had white stone walls, exposed timber beams, and was decorated with rows of beer mats above the bar, and those old brass medallion-type ornaments that are common in Old-World English pubs. I loved its quaintness.

Marcus led me to a small table and upholstered bench in one corner near the front window. The place was crowded, with a group of younger men and women stood near the darts board, all talking and laughing loudly as they knocked back their drinks. There were a few groups of older people seated at the adjacent tables, and I noticed a few admiring glances in our direction from some of the men and women in the room.

Marcus went to the bar and returned with another bottle of red wine, similar to what we had drunk in the restaurant. He set it on the table with two glasses, and sat down beside me. I looked at his pale blue eyes and spoke in a sharp tone, pretending to reprimand.

"Marcus," I said, "are you trying to get me drunk?"

He looked sharply at me, alarmed I think, but then he saw my smile and he relaxed.

"Of course not," he said, "I know you are enjoying this, and so am I."

I giggled at his embarrassment, and poured two generous helpings, then picked up my glass in a salute to him.

"Well, thank you Marcus." I said, "I really am enjoying

tonight, it is so nice to have a break."

He nodded and clinked his glass to mine. We each took a generous sip before putting our glasses back on the table, and then he fixed that piercing pale blue stare on me.

"Jessica I am really enjoying your company this evening." he said, "I know I promised you that I am simply here as your friend, and I stand by that promise. But friendship can mean many different things."

I jumped as he placed his hand on mine where it lay on my leg. He gently squeezed my fingers, brushing his fingers against my skin, sending shivers of excitement coursing through me.

I should push him away. This wasn't right. But I didn't. I enjoyed his attention. I wanted more.

"Marcus," I said, "I can't give you what you want. I am still with Jack no matter what problems we have. We can't forget that."

He nodded, and continued to stroke my leg very gently. I still didn't stop him. Marcus spoke in a gentle voice, keeping eye contact with me.

"I know you are loyal to Jack." he said, "I understand completely. That doesn't mean that you and I can't be good friends. Things aren't always black and white Jessica, especially human emotions and relationships."

I shook my head and changed the subject, hoping he would forget about it. We spoke about safe things like books and television shows, and I talked about Liz and her baby. Marcus humoured me and drew his hand away, but he sat close and gave me his full attention. Somehow I knew this had nothing to do with alcohol. He didn't strike me as the type that would get drunk, and, thanks to me drinking water and coffee I had dulled the effects of my indulgence. Eventually we finished the bottle, and I said perhaps it was time to go home. Marcus agreed, and said he would walk me back to my place.

I was quiet on the way home, and Marcus didn't try and push me. He knew I was confused, and I was thankful that he at least understood when to stop. However I was intrigued by his words. He had said that friendship could mean many different things. I was certain that he was just as messed up as Jack and Danny, which would not help me in my current situation. Yet he enthralled me, and I couldn't just leave him.

We reached my door and I unlocked it, hesitating. I wanted to invite him in but that would cause more trouble. I turned to face him and he was suddenly there, right in front of me. He stepped in close and gently kissed my lips, and when I didn't pull away he grew more passionate, wrapping his arms around me and pushing his tongue against mine. I wanted him, my body screamed for his touch, but I couldn't do this. I broke away, pushing him back.

"Marcus, please," I gasped, "We cannot do this. I am trying to sort out my relationship with Jack. You are supposed to be my friend. This is wrong!"

His eyes were blazing with that heat that men get when they want sex, but he subdued it with great effort. His voice was quiet when he spoke.

"Very well Jessica." he said, "I am sorry. I will leave you alone now."

I watched him turn and walk back down the path, and then I closed the door, locked it, and leaned against it for a minute. My heart was racing. I had come so close to betraying Jack. I found Marcus incredibly attractive, not just physically but intellectually, and he had charmed me. But in all honesty I had done my best to encourage him because I enjoyed his attention. Who was I? How could I do that to the man I loved, after all my complaining about him keeping secrets? I had to resolve things with Jack, and decided to phone him the very next day.

22

It was actually a relief that Liz was off for another day. If she had been in work she would have known there was something bothering me, and she would have made me talk. I didn't want to talk. I felt ashamed that I could so easily have cheated on Jack with his friend. I didn't blame Marcus. After all, he had said he would just be my friend. Although he had made it clear what he wanted from me, he had stressed that it would simply be a friendship. Yes I found that strange, but then Jack and Danny were strange as well, so why would I expect their friend to be anything different.

Marcus sent me a text message that morning. It read 'Sorry for my indiscretion last night. I had a really enjoyable evening with you, hope we can do it again sometime.' I replied saying I had enjoyed it too and he needn't apologize, I did feel partly responsible.

Marie was continuing the cleaning that she had started the previous afternoon, and I finished tidying the window display. There wasn't much left to do, and we were finished by lunchtime. It was a quiet day because all the holidaymakers were on the beach. We had a few customers looking for holiday reads, some children buying activity books and spending their pocket money on the latest hit novels, and one or two regular customers collecting orders. By early afternoon we were both sat behind the counter. I had updated our online sales and Marie was reading a book for her university research. She really was a serious young woman, and I hoped she did well in her career.

Finally I plucked up the courage to send Jack a text message. I didn't want to phone him while I had Marie in the shop with me, so I asked him to come round and see me that night if he was free. He replied almost immediately to say yes of course, he would be there when I closed the shop. I felt butterflies in my stomach, and I also felt excited and giddy.

I was ready to resolve my relationship. Jack needed to be honest with me, but if it was related to his work, and if he really was serious about being with me, then I supposed I could give him a little more time. My experience with Marcus last night had made me realize that perhaps I was being a little too sensitive. It was so easy to make mistakes. Perhaps I should ease off with Jack and just enjoy being with him. He would open up to me in time, I was certain of that.

Marie had gone home, I had locked the shop and closed everything down for the weekend, and walked through to my kitchen, locking the central door behind me. I felt tired, perhaps because of last night and because of all the thoughts racing through my head. But I really wanted to see Jack, and couldn't wait for him to arrive. I walked slowly up the stairs and into my bedroom to change out of my work clothes. My trousers and sensible shirt were restrictive, and somehow I wanted to look more appealing for Jack. If I could make an effort for Marcus then surely I could make an effort for the man I was in love with. But I wasn't going to apply make-up since we weren't planning to go out anywhere.

All I wanted this evening was to resolve our relationship, relax in front of the TV, and probably have great make-up sex, because I really needed it. All of these incredibly attractive men that had recently appeared in my life seemed to have woken the sex demon within, and I loved it!

I settled for one of my favourite gypsy skirts. This one was blue, in a broderie anglais material, and ended just below my knee. I wore a white vest top with no bra, and decided to go without underwear altogether because I was more comfortable that way. It was a cool evening so I slipped a lightweight cardigan on, a nice soft off-white one that I called my 'slobbing-out' jumper. I brushed out my hair, which I had worn in a tight ponytail for the day, and I enjoyed the silky feel of it on my shoulders. I knew Jack preferred it loose; he liked to play with it, which excited me all the more. Then I heard the doorbell ring, and skipped downstairs barefoot to answer it.

Jack stood on the doorstep looking irresistible as always, dressed in dark blue jeans and a white long-sleeved shirt, with his favourite black blazer, and my heart lurched into my throat with sheer emotion at seeing him again. I wanted to throw myself into his arms, but he was holding a pizza box, and smiling.

"I bought some tea," he said, "cheese pizza and a bag of chips, is that all right?"

I laughed, nodded, and he walked into the kitchen, placing the box and bag on the table. I pulled two bottles of chilled beer out of the fridge and opened them for us, fetched myself some ketchup from the cupboard, then sat down opposite Jack and tucked in, suddenly remembering I was starving. It was a complete contrast to my meal with Marcus last night, and yet I thoroughly enjoyed it. Jack knew exactly what I liked; that had to count for something.

We ate in companionable silence and eventually I sat back, stuffed and defeated. Jack finished the pizza then closed the box and moved it to one side. He stared at me with those gorgeous, intense blue eyes, and I didn't know what to say. Jack spoke first.

"I've missed you, Jessica." he said, "The house seems empty without you there. I know that sounds silly, but it's true, even Danny feels it."

I smiled, touched by his sincerity.

"Marcus told me about last night." he said.

My heart lurched, panic shot through my body, and I sat up straighter.

Jack continued, "Don't worry, I know nothing happened between you. He said you were intent on reminding him that you and I are still a couple, and he told me I should stop being stupid, and that I should do what it takes to win back your trust."

I thought about what he had said before I replied.

"I appreciate that you have given me some space over the last few weeks Jack." I said, "And I'm glad that you have come tonight. We need to patch things up." I hesitated, wanting to say those words, but not quite ready. Instead I gave him eye contact and kept my voice steady.

"I care very deeply for you Jack," I said slowly, "and I have never felt this for another man before. Obviously there is something worth saving. Whatever secrets you are keeping from me, I trust you enough to tell me in time, when you are ready. But for now I just need to know that you are serious about us as a couple."

Suddenly he leaped up from his chair and was in front of me, making me jump. He crushed his lips to mine and I responded hungrily. I needed his touch again. He pulled me to my feet, wrapping his arms around me as we kissed passionately. I broke away to gasp for air, and looked at his intense eyes, hazy with lust.

There were no more words. I smiled seductively and tugged at his arm, leading him upstairs. Halfway up he stopped me with more kisses, pulling my cardigan and top off and caressing my breasts, while I ripped open his shirt and pushed it off him. Then I giggled and ran up to my bedroom, with Jack in pursuit.

He pushed me back on to the bed, pressing his body to me, and kissed my face, my neck, down my breasts to my stomach. I moaned and watched him, wanting more, as he tugged at my skirt and pulled it off. Then I stopped him, returning the favour, until he knelt before me naked and gorgeous. We fell back onto the bed in a tangle of limbs, kissing and nibbling, caressing and touching, until finally he was inside me, moving against me slowly at first and then faster and faster, until we climaxed together in a crescendo of pent up sexual repression and lust. It was perfect.

We spent the night exploring each other's bodies again, making love, and talking about trivial things that had been happening. It was so blissful, so right that I should be here with this man. Finally I didn't care about being vulnerable. I realized that sometimes you had to be vulnerable in order to be happy. And I was bad enough in my own way, having come so close to being unfaithful to Jack with his friend. We all had our demons, and maybe I should be grateful to have this man's attention and affection, and just let events unfold naturally instead of trying to force everything. I fell asleep in his arms, and slept deeply and peacefully for the first time in weeks. I didn't need my dreams, and my mind could finally relax.

The next day we went for a long walk over the cliff tops around Redcliffe Bay. We did what young couples in love do. We walked hand-in-hand, kissing and touching each other as much as possible. We lay in the grass together, listening to the waves rolling against the cliffs below, kissing and cuddling and teasing each other. We had lunch at the Ship, and saw Danny and Simon in there. They seemed very pleased to see us together again, and Sally even joined us at the bar later on when her shift finished. I was intrigued to see her and Danny flirting, kissing and cuddling together publicly, even in front of Simon. Maybe I had imagined what I saw the other night. I dismissed it, simply enjoying my reunion with Jack, and too exhausted to be getting involved with other people's relationships for now. If Simon wanted to talk about it he would. Otherwise I would just keep out of their business.

It felt normal and happy to be sat here with my friends, and I was so glad that we could move on from this. So we hadn't actually said 'I Love You.' So Jack hadn't told me about any of his secrets. That didn't matter. I knew that he loved me, I just knew it, and he would tell me everything soon enough. In the back of my mind I knew that Lillian was there, and that she agreed with me, she wanted me to continue my relationship. It felt perfectly natural and I knew that I was finally maturing.

23

I spent Sunday night at Jack's house, relaxing, watching television with him, cuddling on the sofa, and making love. Danny saw us during the day but stayed away that night, I thought to give us some time alone, and I appreciated that. He had been spending a lot of time at the Ship anyway, and I knew that sometimes he stayed at Simon's apartment. Now I idly wondered if there was something more to their relationship, but again I dismissed it as none of my business, especially after seeing Danny with Sally last night. It would be nice for Simon though if it were true. He deserved a good partner, and I already knew how he felt about Danny. But again it was just another secret that I would discover the truth of in time.

The next morning Liz was at work before I got there. She met me at the back door, smiling and happy, having heard the news from me, and claiming that she felt much better and was ready to get stuck in to work again. We had breakfast together as usual, and caught up on the gossip of the previous week.

She was concerned when I told her about my evening with Marcus, believing that he was simply trying to manipulate me. But I assured her that he had actually proved to be a perfect gentleman and that maybe I had over-reacted to our encounter that night in the pub. I didn't tell her about our kiss, or even that we had been flirting with each other. I knew that was wrong, and Liz would be deeply upset if she knew the truth. I kidded myself that what she didn't know wouldn't hurt her, and I ignored the stabbing guilt in my chest. Liz grudgingly accepted what I said, and agreed to be civil if and when we met Marcus socially again.

I tried to persuade her to take it easy at work because I did not want her collapsing again, and she agreed to a compromise. Rob had now finished for his summer holidays, and had offered to help out in the shop if we needed it. But for this first few days Liz and me were happy on our own, catching up with each other. Of course we had Marie for extra help, but she could only work three days a week.

Those next few days passed slowly and without incident. Jack and me spent every night together at his house. For some reason I needed a change of scenery, and I liked it at his house, it felt comfortable. I played computer games with Danny and Simon, we all watched films together, and everything was normal and happy.

Sally came round one night and stayed over, and we enjoyed chatting about 'girlie' things that the men just couldn't understand. I relaxed and let my guard down, feeling that I had finally taken a step in the right direction with my friendships and relationships.

It was mid-week and I was trying to be assertive with Liz at work. She was still trying to lift and carry piles of books and heavy boxes, despite the health scare, and it was worrying me. I had resorted to telling her that she could just go ahead, end up back in hospital, and see if I care. She was about to retort to my tone when the doorbell jangled and two women walked in.

One was older, probably in her late thirties, and she was tall and carried herself in a very confidant way, quite intimidating. She had long blond hair pulled back in a severe ponytail, her skin was very tanned, and her eyes seemed cold and severe. The other woman was short, looked very young, early twenties at most, and seemed in awe of the older woman. This one was all soft angles, long black hair that fell straight down her back, and an innocent face, but her dark eyes were scathing. They were both dressed in black clothes, what I would call the 'classic rock chick' look, and they both looked very attractive in their own way.

I felt uneasy somehow, as though there was a strange atmosphere, and I glanced at Liz to see if she could feel it too. The women browsed for a few minutes and then the older woman approached the counter, the younger one following. They took their time, as though they were enjoying the moment, which confused me.

The older woman looked at Liz and me, and then settled her gaze on me, and I went hot all over at her direct stare. She smiled but it was cold and very formal. "Hello," she said, "You must be Ms Stone?"

I nodded, confused, and then smiled politely as I replied.

"Yes." I said, "I am sorry, do I know you?"

Again she smiled and the younger woman laughed quietly as though at some private joke. I did not like these two at all and I glanced at Liz who gave me a sideways nod of agreement. The woman spoke again in a very pronounced American accent.

"You don't know me." she said, "I am an old acquaintance of Detective Danny Mason, or rather, my friend Celine is."

Here she motioned over her shoulder at the other woman who nodded and smiled sweetly. She continued in a slightly less formal tone.

"Don't worry Honey," she said, "I'm only passing on a message. Tell Danny that LuAnn Moor and Celine Toulouse are in town and we want to see him. In fact we want to see him tonight, 9pm in the old cemetery just out of town. He knows where that is." she paused, "Tell him to come alone," she said curtly, "We do not need his interfering brother, or his pack. Tell him if he brings back-up, everyone he cares about will die."

She stared right at me, inferring her meaning until I went hot and then cold as I realized what she meant. Then she turned and stalked out of the shop, Celine following like a faithful puppy. They shut the door loudly behind them and I turned to Liz, shaking.

"Oh my god," I said, "what was wrong with them? Are you alright Liz?"

She nodded.

"Yeah I'm fine but that was weird," she said, "I think you should speak to Jack and Danny straight away. It sounds pretty serious, must be related to that job in Scotland or something."

I nodded. Something was wrong here, very wrong, and I instinctively knew somehow that things were about to get worse. I tried to phone Jack but his mobile kept ringing out and I couldn't get hold of Danny either. Eventually I left a message at their office for one of them to phone back as soon as possible, along with messages on both their mobile phones, and I waited anxiously for a response. Liz tried to carry on as normal for the rest of the day, but I knew she was nervous too. There was something frightening about both of those women, and I knew that they were telling the truth. I considered calling the police, but instinct told me to wait until I spoke to Jack and Danny, and to let them handle it.

24

It was getting on for 5.30pm and I had put my foot down and sent Liz home. She was looking tired and the shop was quiet anyway, there was no need for her to be there. She had protested after our encounter with the strange American woman but I had argued that we would surely be fine, Jack and Danny would take care of it and I had my mobile phone if there was an emergency. Plus I had the next day off work and told her she would have enough to deal with on her own then. So she left, grudgingly. Personally I think Elizabeth wanted some gossip when I finally got hold of Jack.

I was moving some stock around and trying unsuccessfully to shift the table we had in the middle of the room. It contained our latest special offers, sale items, promotional features, that kind of thing, but I needed to make room for a cardboard book stand next to it ready for a new bestseller we were having delivered later in the week.

The door opened and I looked up to see Danny stride in looking very purposeful. He saw me trying to shift the table, walked over and leaned his weight against it.

"Where do you want this, Jess?" he asked.

I stepped back, blowing hair out of my face, huffed a little with impatience, and then directed him to where I wanted the table.

"Thanks Danny." I said, "How did we ever survive without you."

He laughed at my sarcastic tone and playfully punched my arm.

"Ha ha very funny." he said, "You know women are by genetics, physically weaker than men. There's no ego involved."

Then he laughed as I crossed my arms, raised my eyebrow and tapped my foot with impatience.

"Ok maybe there is some ego involved." he said, "Come

on, you like watching me work, admit it."

He winked at me, flexed his arm muscles, and my heart lurched. What was happening to me? I ignored it because now there were more important things to worry about. Instead I gave in and laughed.

"Fine," I said, "whatever, you are the big strong male, all hail you."

Danny moved away from the table and pushed his hair out of his eyes, a gesture identical to his brother. How could I tell them apart? I don't know; it was a subtle knowledge, something different in their tone of voice, the way they dressed, and their attitude. Whatever it was, I knew this was Danny standing in front of me. His face became serious suddenly as he spoke.

"I got a message on the mobile from you," he said, "and the office said you had been phoning. Is everything alright?"

I told him about the strange women that had visited today and when I said their names he went pale and his body went very still. He spoke in a calm, careful voice. "They said meet them at 9pm in the Old Cemetery?" he asked.

I nodded, my heart pounding.

"Yes," I replied, "and the American woman, LuAnn, said she wants to see you again. And she said to go alone; this doesn't concern your brother or your pack." Here I paused, wondering how to tell him the rest of the message, but I knew it was important. He waited patiently for me to continue.

"Danny," I faltered, "she said you must not take back-up, because if you do she will kill the people you care about. And she was very clear on that message. What did she mean by that?" I paused, "She was a bit scary Danny, what kind of acquaintance is she?" I asked.

He was very serious as he replied.

"She is connected to the job in Scotland; they both are." he said, "I'm sorry Jessica; it looks like we have inadvertently drawn you into our mess. I need to find Jack and go sort this out. Please promise me you will stay home, don't answer the door unless you know who it is, and phone Jack or me if you get worried about anything, no matter how small or trivial. Will you do that?"

He grabbed my shoulders, staring directly into my eyes, and I gasped, shocked at his forcefulness. I nodded, feeling sick with nerves.

"Yes of course." I said, "Am I in danger? What about Liz?"

He relaxed slightly and eased his grip on me.

"Liz will be fine," he said, "she is of no concern to them. But they seem to have found out about you and your relationship with Jack and me. You don't need to be overly concerned just yet; hopefully we can settle this tonight. Please just stay home and keep all your doors locked and your mobile phone handy, ok?"

I nodded and Danny left, saying he would call Jack on the way.

25

It was late; just after 10:00pm, and I found myself pacing up and down the living room unable to settle. I had heard nothing all night from Jack or Danny and had tried to call their mobile phones several times in the last half hour, but they just rang out and then switched to answer phone. I knew I should leave them to deal with their police business but I was worried about both of them. I couldn't help it.

Liz had phoned earlier and I told her what Danny had said. She had offered to come round with Robert but I said no, I was all right on my own. If anything happened to me I didn't want my pregnant best friend to get hurt. I almost phoned Simon but what could I say, that I might be involved in some shady police business with criminal dealings? It sounded absurd and not something a pub landlord could do anything about anyway. I considered calling Marcus, but again, what could he do? So I waited anxiously.

Eventually I flopped down onto the sofa and tried to watch TV to take my mind off things. I must have fallen asleep, because gradually I realized I was stood on the cliff tops overlooking Redcliffe Bay again. It was dark, there was a storm brewing, the wind was whipping my hair around my face, and the rain was pouring down but I barely noticed. This was the point when the monster would attack, I knew it. I had to run away. As the fear coursed through me I was suddenly stopped by my mother's voice, calling to me.

"Jessica," she called, "Jessica, wait! It is Lillian."

I hesitated and half-turned around. It was my mother. I relaxed, forgetting about the storm, not feeling the cold or the rain, simply thankful that I was safe for now.

She approached me, her hair soaking wet from the rain, and her beautiful green eyes full of sorrow and pain.

"Jessica, my darling child." she said, "I cannot protect

you in the physical world. There are revelations that you are about to discover, and you need to know them. I cannot stop that. But I can warn you to be prepared. Please, please listen to what the Mason brothers say. You can trust them, even if you doubt your own emotion. They will try to protect you, and you are strong enough to withstand the trauma."

She gripped my shoulders and I shook my head.

"What do you mean, Mum?" I asked, "How do you know what is happening in my life? Is it to do with those women today, this job that Jack and Danny have been working on? I'm scared."

She nodded, tears in her eyes.

"Remember your heritage," she said, "You are strong, and you are a survivor. The human world will throw challenges at you, but you can handle them. Be vigilant, accept what you hear, and trust your instincts."

Then she turned her head, apparently listening to something.

"I must go," she said, "our time here is up. I am watching over you Jessica. I love you."

And she faded into blackness, leaving me panicking and confused. I heard a crack of thunder up above, loud and clear, and then I woke with a start.

It wasn't thunder of course; it was someone knocking at the back door. I sat bolt upright on the sofa, listening. The knock came again, insistent but growing weaker as though the person was losing strength. I had to see who it was. It must be Jack, or Danny.

I jumped off the sofa and ran downstairs, hesitating just inside the kitchen. What if it was the bad guys? Oh come on, this wasn't some cheesy Hollywood film; this was Redcliffe, a sleepy old Cornish town. Who would come banging on the door for me at this time of night? Besides it wasn't like I was a witness to anything criminal. I should stop being stupid and just answer the door.

I was barefoot, and almost slipped down the stairs in my haste. I stood on tiptoes, looked through the peephole and saw the top of Jack's head. He must be looking down for some reason. I flung open the door, and then gasped in horror. He was leaning against the doorframe; his face covered in blood from what looked liked a large gash above his right eye, and several scratches and cuts on his cheeks and chin. His clothes were dirty, torn, and bloody, and he fell through the door into my arms. Instinctively I tried to catch him, and fell to the floor with a cry, trying to support his weight.

"Jack," I cried, "Jack can you hear me? Speak to me!"

Shit. I fumbled for my mobile phone in the pocket of my jeans, and then he opened his eyes and mumbled something. I tried to keep my voice steady, speaking as clearly as I could without it shaking.

"Jack," I said tentatively, "I'm going to call an ambulance, stay with me." He seemed to wake up, making me jump.

"No!" he cried.

He tried to grab my hand, his face wild, and he struggled to stand up, leaning heavily on the table, using the back of a chair for support. He spoke through gritted teeth, his face hideously distorted under the blood and dirt. His appearance reminded me of something from a horror film or a gory action thriller.

"I don't need an ambulance," he said firmly, "They took Danny. Please, phone Simon, tell him Danny needs him."

I looked at Jack in surprise as I stood and moved closer to him.

"Simon?" I asked, "What can he do? Don't tell me he's a police officer too."

Jack collapsed to the floor and I tried to catch him, jarring my arms with his weight. I ended up back on the floor with his head in my lap, my legs straight out in front of me, my bottom taking most of the impact of his weight, jarring my back as well. But I barely noticed at the time. He struggled to speak, his eyes were rolling in his head, and I panicked.

"Jack, please let me phone an ambulance, you are bleeding and hurt." I implored him.

He stopped me again, his hand on my arm.

"No Jessica," he said, "I'll be fine. Please phone Simon immediately."

His eyes were blazing and I was terrified. I did what he asked and dialled Simon's number. Jack managed to sit up stiffly, clearly in pain, and leaning against me heavily. He took the phone from me with a shaking hand and spoke in a croaky voice.

"Simon," he said, "It's Jack."

He paused to catch his breath.

"They are here. They took Danny. You have to find him," he paused again, his breathing shallow, "Take Sally and get to the Old Cemetery now. Alert the pack, tell them it's an emergency; they are all under threat. Then meet me at Marcus' house."

He fell back against me, his eyes closed, and I cried out.

"Jack," I cried, "Wake up, please."

I caught the phone as it fell from his hand, checked the call had ended, and then put the phone on the floor beside me. Jack half-opened his eyes and smiled but it was eerie, frightening. His eyes were blazing with a strange blue flame, and his face was white underneath the drying dark red blood.

"Jessica," he said softly, "You are so beautiful. Such lovely skin. And your blood smells so sweet."

He reached out stiffly with one arm and touched my face with ice-cold fingers, making me shiver with fear and confusion. My heart was pounding, and I was frightened, suddenly remembering that morning a couple of weeks ago.

"Jack," I said again, my voice shaking, "What can I do? Please, I need to help you."

He seemed to come round again, and spoke more clearly, struggling to focus on his words.

"Call...Marcus." he said slowly, "Please, call Marcus. He can help me. Do it now!" his voice grew strong suddenly and I jumped.

"Marcus?" I asked, "What about the police, the back-up, your colleagues?"

Jack laughed and shook his head, then winced and

moaned in pain.

"The human police can't help us now." he said, "Marcus will help. You have to phone him. Please Jessica, trust me."

Jack tried to pick my phone up again, struggling with the effort, his fingers refusing to grip the small instrument. I gently took it from him and dialled Marcus' number, feeling sick with worry and fear.

"Hello, Jessica what can I do for you?" Marcus said in a voice that was bright and cheerful.

I fought to keep my voice steady as memories of the other evening flooded into my mind, and I looked down at the barely conscious man lying in my arms.

"Marcus," I said, "I need your help. Jack came to my house and he's covered in blood, he won't let me call an ambulance, he says you can help him," I spoke in a voice growing frantic and hysterical, "Please, I don't know what to do."

There was a momentary silence and then Marcus spoke in a clipped, efficient tone.

"Jessica I will be there in ten minutes." he said, "Please do not move him, I know what he needs. Try not to worry. I will take care of it."

Before I could answer Jack took the phone from me.

"Marcus," he said weakly, "Yes I'm alright but I can't hold it together. You must hurry. Jessica must know the truth."

He swallowed and took a few breaths, then continued, "They took Danny, he isn't dead but he's close, I can feel it. Simon and Sally have gone to find him, they will bring him to your house. We must be there to heal him." He listened to Marcus and then replied, "Yes the pack is on full alert, and the Ship is being secured."

Jack cried out in pain, his body went limp as he seemed to faint in my arms again, and I caught the phone as it fell.

I pressed the 'call end' button, fumbled to put the phone in my pocket, and then turned my attention to Jack. He seemed barely conscious, barely breathing, a lead weight in my arms. I had to try and clean up his wounds at least.

LOVE HURTS

"Jack," I asked, "Can you stand? I can't lift you."

He roused as I tentatively tried to stand up and we rose slowly to our feet, Jack holding on to the back of a kitchen chair. He slowly straightened up and looked at me and what I saw in his eyes terrified me. They were not human eyes. They were burning with a blue flame, his face was white except for the blood and he was staring at me intently, like a hunter. His cheekbones seemed to stand out in stark contrast to his face. I froze. Then I hurriedly remembered that this was Jack, the love of my life. He wouldn't hurt me. But I backed up slowly, unable to convince myself of that fact as I remembered the feel of his strangling grip across my neck so recently.

I spoke carefully, my tone cautious, and my voice shaking ever so slightly. "Jack," I said, "I'll get some water and a cloth and clean your face, alright? You sit down here."

He nodded slowly, blinking, and he started to look more normal, although his skin was deathly white. I edged round him carefully, wary not to make any sudden moves. Then I ran up the stairs and grabbed a clean flannel from the bathroom, and my first aid kit from the cabinet. I ran back downstairs, heart racing. Jack was sitting in a kitchen chair with his head tipped back, eyes closed. I went to the sink and picked up a spare plastic bowl, hurriedly filling it with warm water.

When I turned around Jack was watching me with half-closed eyes. I put the bowl down carefully on the table, soaked the flannel and wrung it out.

"Jack, can you hear me?" I asked, "I'm going to try and clean your face a little."

He nodded slightly and I very gently dabbed at the cuts and grazes. He winced and drew in his breath sharply when I moved to the cut above his eye, but it actually looked worse than it was. It seemed to have stopped bleeding at least. My heart skipped a beat when I saw his intense gaze on my face.

"Jack, are you alright?" I asked fearfully.

He smiled, but it was sinister, and it frightened me.

When he spoke his voice didn't sound normal, its tone was darker somehow, and it sent shivers through my body.

"You are so beautiful, my delicate human," he said.

He reached up and gently touched my face with his left hand, stroking my cheek with fingers that were icy cold. I smiled but was still frightened. He wasn't well, I knew that, and something instinctively told me to run away, to escape before I got hurt. But I didn't. I couldn't leave him. I dropped the flannel onto the table, transfixed somehow, though I couldn't explain it.

Suddenly he was on his feet, so fast I didn't see. He lunged at me and I screamed, jumping back as he grabbed for my neck. He fell to the floor and I backed up, finding myself pressed against the wall, staring at him in horror. He had tried to bite me! He wasn't human. I couldn't move; my body was frozen in fear as I watched Jack gather himself and stand up slowly. It wasn't Jack that looked at me from those beautiful blue eyes. It was the monster from my dreams and I screamed as he lunged at me again. I called his name, trying desperately to bring him back.

Suddenly in a blur of movement someone pushed me away from Jack and put himself between us. It was Marcus. His eyes were glowing silver, his face white, and then he turned to Jack, restraining him, whispering to him. Jack went still in his arms and Marcus turned his head to me, looking very human again.

"Are you alright, Jessica?" he asked gently.

I nodded, unable to speak, swallowed and spoke in a low voice, my throat dry.

"Yes, I think so." I said, "What is wrong with him? Who are you people?" Marcus' expression was tragic; full of sorrow but his attention was mainly for Jack.

"I am sorry Jessica," he said, "but explanations must be kept for later. Danny is at my house, he is dying, and only Jack can save him. Please follow me; you are not safe here alone."

He turned and led Jack out of the house and down the path. I had to follow them. What else could I do? I shoved my feet into a pair of black pumps I had left by the door, grabbed my house keys and hastily locked up as I left.

Marcus opened the rear passenger door of a large silver Mercedes that was parked in the road behind my house. He helped Jack into the car and then looked at me.

"Please sit in the front, Jessica," he said, "I will take care of Jack."

His tone was calm, authoritative, and I climbed into the front seat, glad to have some help at last. There was a woman in the driver's seat. She had short blond hair cut in a classic bob, and her face was pale but carefully made-up from what I saw in the light from the streetlamps. She was wearing a smart black business suit. She turned to me with a serious face.

"Hello, Jessica." she said, "I am Alice; Marcus' personal assistant. I am sorry we have to meet under such circumstances."

Then she put the car in gear and drove off very carefully but very quickly. I twisted round to look at Jack. His head was resting on the back of the seat and Marcus was very still beside him, ready to restrain him if needed. Their faces looked eerily inhuman in the electric lights bordering the roads. I said nothing, turned back and closed my eyes, not quite sure what was happening or even if I was awake. The car gave us a smooth ride and I was grateful, as I felt nauseas; ready to throw up if we hit the slightest bump. There was too much happening this evening, and I knew it was about to get worse.

26

I opened my eyes properly as we pulled up on the driveway of a large modern house. I had vaguely seen that we drove out along the coastal road, past the Ship, towards the city. Alice had turned into a side road and then into a narrow lane, which led to this driveway. Marcus slid out of the car and helped Jack who seemed to be struggling, but was slowly coming round, and Alice motioned for me to follow her. We all moved toward the house, me walking slowly, in a daze. Jack was leaning heavily on Marcus. He really needed medical attention, why wouldn't he let me call an ambulance? And why was Marcus so calm about all of this?

We walked into the large, square hallway and I could hear a man's voice upstairs, crying out in pain. Jack suddenly straightened up, shouted "Danny!" and ran up the stairs, Marcus right behind him. They moved so quickly that it shocked me and I looked at Alice. She eyed me warily, apparently not sure what to say. Danny cried out again and that was it. He was clearly in a great deal of pain; I had to try and help. I ran up the wide, curving staircase after them and stopped just inside the doorway of a bedroom, standing beside Marcus. He tried to restrain me but I shook his hands off, my eyes fixed on the occupants of the room.

Danny was lying on a large bed, on his back, his body convulsing, and he was moaning and crying in pain. His chest was bare and I could see a huge open wound near his heart, bleeding profusely. The metallic smell of blood was thick in the air, choking me, making me cough and heave. It was horrendous; why had no one called an ambulance? Danny's head was thrashing from side to side but he seemed unable to move, paralysed, his body twitching and spasming involuntarily.

Jack moved slowly towards the bed, eyes on his brother. I watched in horror as he climbed onto the bed, straddling

Danny's body. I looked at Marcus but he was watching the brothers, oblivious to me now. There were two other people at the foot of the bed but I took no notice; my eyes were on Jack and Danny, my mind blank with shock and confusion.

Jack cradled his brother's face with both hands, holding him still, whispering something I couldn't hear. Danny calmed down, became still, watching Jack. Then Jack lowered his face to the wound and licked the blood on Danny's chest. He proceeded to suck the blood, drinking it deeply, and my legs buckled beneath me, my heart lurched, and the room swam. I fell to the floor on my knees, transfixed in horror, wanting to look away but desperate to see what was happening.

Jack drank the blood, his throat convulsing as he swallowed, and his mouth making a wet noise that made me feel sick. I choked back the nausea, forcing myself to watch this horrific scene before me.

Jack raised his head, lifted his arm, and bit his own wrist until the blood welled up thick and dark. He lowered his wrist to Danny's mouth, and I saw Danny's throat convulse as he swallowed the blood but he seemed barely conscious. Then he lifted his head and fixed his mouth over the wound, sucking hungrily until Jack broke away with a cry. Jack pulled away from Danny and fell onto his back beside him, unconscious. They both lay still, covered in blood. I thought they were dead. The stench of blood was thick, metallic, nauseating. I had never experienced it before and I felt suffocated.

A silence fell over the room and I looked around wildly and scrambled to my feet. I saw that the two other people were Simon and Sally; I had no idea what they were doing there, I had forgotten Jack's phone call to Simon earlier. They looked at me with serious faces, and then I turned and ran out of the room in a blind panic. They were monsters, all of them! I had to escape.

I heard Marcus call my name but I carried on running, knowing that I wasn't safe. They would kill me. I ran out of the house, down the drive, and onto the cliff road, stumbling and crying, gasping for breath but determined to keep going until I was safe. It was dark, the rain was pouring, the wind whipped my hair around my face painfully, and I slowed, as my recurring dream suddenly became terrifyingly real.

This was it. My dream, my nightmare, had finally become a reality. I was running on this stretch of road back towards Redcliffe, it was raining and dark. A monster was chasing me. This time it wasn't Jack, or Marcus, or even Danny. It was all of them. They were all out to get me, and I had to escape. But all I heard was Marcus' voice calling my name, shouting at me to stop, please stop.

The rain was lashing down, soaking my hair, skin and clothes, and the wind whipped around me in a crescendo of a storm. I don't know if it was real or part of my imagination. In my terror I called out for my mother, for Lillian to rescue me from this nightmare. I wanted to be back on the beach with her, safe and warm in her arms. But she wasn't there. She was lost once again, and this was real life, no dream, not even a nightmare. I screamed, my foot caught in the rough grass, and I fell to the ground, finally succumbing to the nausea, and then I fainted with shock and terror.

27

I woke slowly in a warm room, lying in a large comfortable bed. I was lying on my back under a duvet, and someone had taken off my clothes. I was in my underwear. I sat bolt upright with a gasp, clutching the duvet around me, and then saw Marcus sitting in a chair beside the bed. There was a lamp on the bedside cabinet beside me, casting a soft light to the room. Marcus sat up straight, his pale blue eyes serious and concerned.

"Jessica," he said, "are you alright? Please, I mean you no harm, you are safe now."

I caught my breath, closed my eyes and breathed carefully in and out, in and out, the duvet clutched up to my neck. This was real. I wasn't dreaming. It was a solid, real room, and Marcus was right there sat in the chair. Then I sank back against the headboard, my body aching all over though I didn't know why. Then I remembered. My voice was croaky, throat dry as I spoke.

"Where am I Marcus?" I asked, "Did I just have some crazy nightmare?"

"You are in my guest bedroom." he replied, "You were cold from the rain and your body was in shock. You collapsed outside so I brought you in here to rest. Alice put you in bed; she has taken your clothes to get them dried. Would you like a glass of water? Or perhaps something stronger?"

I nodded but my head hurt.

"Water will be fine thanks." I said.

I watched as he carefully stood up and poured water from a glass jug stood on a dressing table at the far end of the room. It reminded me of a hotel, very chic, elegant, but blank. I was lying under a cream satin duvet, and the walls were painted a simple shade of magnolia. The only splashes of colour were the pillows, which were dark red, and a matching throw folded at the end of the bed. And of course

Marcus, wearing a dark red formal shirt and black trousers. He handed me the glass and I took it with a trembling hand. It took both hands to steady it and hold it to my lips. Marcus sat down again, careful not to move too quickly. I sipped carefully and the cool liquid soothed my throat, calmed my mind. I placed the glass down on the bedside cabinet and turned my attention to Marcus.

"What the hell is going on here, Marcus?" I asked in a stronger voice, "Who are you people? Am I some kind of hostage? And what happened to Jack and Danny?"

He spoke very carefully, his face blank of emotion.

"You are safe here Jessica, I assure you." he said, "I appreciate that this was not how we intended to tell you our secrets, and I apologize for that. It seems that certain events have progressed beyond our control."

Here he paused and swallowed, thinking about what he would say next.

"You are not a hostage." he continued, "But we are not human. I am a vampire, and so is Jack. What you witnessed in that bedroom was Jack saving the life of his brother. They are resting now but they will live."

The room spun around me. The faintness returned, and I fought against it and that sinking feeling in my stomach. I felt sick, swallowed carefully, and moved in the bed to try and rouse myself. I did not want to pass out again, and I did not want to be sick. But my body was tense all over, my muscles sore. I tried to relax a little to stop it hurting.

Marcus was telling the truth. Why wouldn't he? This was Jack's big secret; this was the reason for his odd behaviour. It all made perfect sense. If only I had listened to my intuition instead of to my rational mind. Memories flooded through my head; from our first night together and that mysterious love bite, to my infatuation with him, to his strange nocturnal work hours, his amazing strength, the way he wore sunglasses outside even on a dull day. My whole life had just been flipped upside down.

"You are a vampire," I said, "Jack is a vampire. Shit. I thought you guys only existed in the stories. But what I saw, it makes sense..."

I trailed off as I thought back to the last month or so. Jack had amazing strength. He never seemed to get tired. He didn't seem bothered by heat but he always wore sunglasses outside even when it wasn't sunny. And that night when I thought Marcus attacked me... I put a hand to my neck instinctively.

"You were going to suck my blood." I said.

He nodded, unsmiling.

"Yes Jessica," he said, "the first night we met I thought Jack was offering you to me as a human donor. I didn't realize that he actually had emotional feelings for you. But he does, and so does Danny," he paused, "And so do I." he added.

I cursed again and leaned back in the bed, closing my eyes as the faintness still threatened to take me. I forced myself to calm down, breathed in and out deeply, and then opened my eyes again to look at Marcus. He hadn't moved. I carefully reached for the glass of water with shaking hands, and sipped it tentatively.

"What about Danny?" I asked, "He is different I can tell."

I saw the surprise register in Marcus' expression but he quickly stifled it and answered.

"Danny is a werewolf." he said, "The brothers are something of a peculiarity in our world. Vampires and werewolves traditionally hate each other, and are always fighting for power and control. Jack and Danny share a unique bond, they are stronger than most of our kind, and they attract trouble because of it. Tonight they fought a very powerful werewolf and his bodyguards, and they almost died. But they are safe for now. Please, get some rest, we can explain more in the morning."

He stood up but I leaned forward, a hand on his arm. I drew back at the touch of his ice-cold skin, and I shivered. He looked at me with very human eyes, full of pity and sorrow.

"Please, Jessica," he said, "you must rest. Both Jack and

Danny will sleep until the morning. You have had a terrible shock tonight, your body needs to recover."

I shook my head, wide-awake now.

"No," I said vehemently, "You can't just leave me in this strange room having just informed me that vampires and werewolves exist and that you are one of them! What am I supposed to do? Am I food?"

Marcus sat on the bed beside me and reached out to touch my cheek very gently with cool fingers. I flinched but forced myself not to pull away. I would not show him my terror. He smiled softly.

"You are so very delicate, Jessica." he said, "And yet you are so strong and brave. No you are not merely food to us. Do not fear us, we will not kill you. While Jack is unconscious I promise to protect you at all cost, for my friend. He is extremely fond of you and that is precious. Jack does not give away his emotions easily."

I looked into his soft pale blue eyes, so human, so gentle, such a lie. But I felt calm suddenly, and safe. I shook my head and moved away from him as panic shot through me.

"What are you doing to me," I asked sharply, "some kind of mind game?"

Marcus looked surprised again but quickly straightened his expression.

"I was trying to soothe your mind," he said, "could you feel that?"

I replied in a moody voice. "Yes I felt it, what did you expect?"

He looked curious, intrigued.

"You are a remarkable human Jessica." he said, "It seems you have some immunity to our powers of persuasion. I was trying to soothe you so that you would sleep but you fought me, and I cannot reach into your mind."

He was trying to get into my mind.

"Do vampires read minds Marcus?" I asked.

He nodded.

"We are able to establish what a person is thinking." he said, "Some humans are easier to read than others. Some have a natural ability to block us out, like you it would seem."

He frowned as if a thought had occurred to him.

"Then again, you are not fully human yourself Jessica, are you?" he asked, "I sense something within you, something buried."

He hesitated and I realized I was holding my breath, waiting for him to say those words. He spoke again, his voice soft in wonderment.

"You are a witch Jessica," he said, "That must be why Jack was drawn to you so powerfully. You have enthralled him."

I blinked, feeling woozy suddenly, and exhausted.

"What, I'm tougher than you thought?" I said moodily, "I don't know about this witch business, I don't even understand what's happening to me. But I'm hardly going to sleep after what I just witnessed tonight. Where are Jack and Danny? Can I see them?"

Marcus nodded and half-turned, gesturing to the door but looking at me.

"They are in the next bedroom," he said, "I will take you if you like."

I pulled back the duvet and stopped as I remembered I was only wearing my bra and knickers. Marcus couldn't keep the desire off his face and I froze, staring at him. He shook himself, turned and handed me a white bathrobe that was hung on the door.

"My apologies," he said, "You are a very beautiful woman Jessica. Please follow me."

He opened the door and I followed, hastily tying the robe around me. I was confused. I suddenly saw him as an attractive man again, and that shouldn't be happening, not in the middle of this drama. But he was being very gentle, very protective, and he made me feel safe in some bizarre way. I had to remind myself about our first meeting to distract my thoughts and focus on what was happening now.

Marcus led me onto the landing and opened the door of a bedroom to my left. He stepped back and I walked in, my legs shaking, heart pounding. From the light of the landing I could see Jack lying in the bed, a duvet pulled up to his waist, his chest bare. He was on his back, very still, and someone had cleaned his wounds. In fact there was barely a scratch on him; it was amazing. He didn't seem to be breathing and his usually tanned skin was white, like marble.

I approached the bed, my nose wrinkling at the smell of cleaning products, fresh linen, and blood, and then I stopped as I saw a woman lying next to Jack, apparently naked, her body curved against Danny where he lay also on his back naked from the waist up. The woman was Sally, and I tried not to look at her. I had another shock as Simon suddenly sat up on the other side of Danny, his hair tousled with sleep, his body naked also.

"Hi, Jess are you ok?" he whispered, "I am so sorry about this. I can explain, but in the morning. Please just trust Marcus for now, he will take care of you. I know him."

I replied in a whisper.

"Simon?" I asked, "What are you? Shit I knew you were keeping something from me. Yeah we can talk tomorrow but I might go crazy first."

He nodded and lay back down again, cuddling up to Danny. I tentatively reached down and touched Jack's cheek. It was icy cold. I half expected him to wake and jump out of bed, but he didn't. I wanted to kiss his lips but I didn't dare. I let out a breath, and glanced at Danny who lay perfectly still, chest rising and falling steadily, a large square bandage covering his chest wound. He was so pale.

The whole scene was surreal and I could not understand it. I turned and walked slowly back out of the bedroom to Marcus. He closed the door and looked at me.

"Both men will be healed by morning, Jessica." he said, "Jack will wake and will need human blood, Danny will have to hunt as the wolf with his pack members." I raised my face to him as I realized the truth about my best friend.

"Simon is a wolf?" I asked.

Marcus nodded.

"Simon is second-in-command to the Redcliffe pack behind Danny," he said, "and Sally is third in line. They will help their master to heal tonight."

I nodded.

"Of course," I said in a tense, high-pitched voice, "it makes perfect sense. What that woman said about the pack, and why Simon is always following Danny, and the Ship."

I was growing hysterical as I continued.

"All those times Simon seemed different, he acted like a dog, and I never saw it," I said, "And Sally. She dotes on Danny. She follows him faithfully everywhere. Is there anyone around me who is human in this town?"

My voice grew shrill as hysteria set in. I cried out with frustration and fear, and sank to the floor against the bedroom door, head in my hands, sobbing uncontrollably. Everything was falling apart. What could I believe in now? I felt sick and agitated and so angry with everyone for keeping these secrets from me. I was so stupid; I should never have trusted them.

I jumped as Marcus very carefully slid his arm around me. He was crouched in front of me and as I looked at him all I saw was a concerned face and gentle blue eyes. I threw myself into his arms, crying. He held me, his body warm and solid, and comforting. He produced a tissue from somewhere and I took it gratefully, mopping up the seemingly never-ending tears that flowed down my face and soaked into the soft cotton of the bathrobe.

Eventually I calmed down and tried to stand but my legs wouldn't work, my body had given up on me again, muscles aching with the strain and the shock. Marcus lifted me easily into his arms and I protested but he stopped me.

"Please Jessica," he said; "you have received an enormous shock tonight. Your human body needs to rest. Allow me to carry you into your room."

28

Marcus carried me back into the guest bedroom and laid me on the bed. He pulled the duvet up over me as though I were a child. As he turned to leave I stopped him.

"Please, Marcus." I said, "I don't know what's happening, or even if I can believe all that you told me, but right now you are the only person I think I can trust. Please stay with me, I don't want to be alone."

He nodded and closed the bedroom door, then carefully lay on the bed beside me. This was so intimate suddenly; I had expected him to sit in the chair. I remembered our kiss from the other night, and the way he had stroked my hand and my leg. I remembered how I enjoyed the sensations, and how I could barely stop him from taking it further. He smiled at my expression.

"The bed is far more comfortable than the chair, Jessica." he said softly, "You must try to relax if you are to continue being friends with vampires."

I laughed without thinking, the fuzziness slowly clearing as my body relaxed. I was struck again by how handsome he was, how young he seemed, and how old all at the same time.

"How old are you Marcus, really?" I asked.

"I am around one hundred and fifty years of age," he replied, "I lose count nowadays."

I nodded, smiling.

"Of course you do," I said, "This isn't crazy in the slightest!"

Marcus smiled and gently stroked my hair, a soothing gesture that felt nice. "Yes it is 'crazy' as you put it." he said, "But you are strong Jessica, and you are handling this whole situation incredibly well."

I froze as I realized I was enjoying his caress, my body wanted him despite everything. I had been attracted to Marcus the first time we met and now I had the opportunity to do something about it. I felt a rush of shame at how easily I could consider doing this to Jack once again, especially now when he had almost died. Marcus smiled and his cool hand stroked my cheek, soothing me.

"Do not feel ashamed, Jessica." he said, "Your desire is perfectly normal. Vampires are driven by lust; it is how we attract our donors. But I will not feed from you, not without your consent."

I frowned.

"What do you mean, donors?" I asked, "Do you kill when you feed?"

"We no longer need to kill," Marcus said, "We take as much blood as we need, we use a simple mind-control technique, and our donor is none the wiser." he paused, "But a vampire will use sex as a means of gaining power," he continued, "We are Incubus and Succubus, as of the old myths. I do not deny that I find you incredibly attractive Jessica. I made that clear to you the other night."

He continued stroking my face, smoothing his hand over my hair, and then he slid his hand down my neck to my shoulder, opening the bathrobe and carefully sliding the duvet down just slightly to expose my skin. I shivered with the sensations, but enjoyed his attention even as my true love lay half-dead in the next room.

"Marcus, how can you do this," I asked quietly, "with Jack and Danny lying in the bedroom next door, half-dead? Are you even worried about them? You seem so calm."

He smiled, still stroking my skin, and still I didn't stop him. His voice was gentle as he spoke.

"I have seen Jack and Danny recover from wounds far more severe." he said, "They are warriors, they always survive. We moved swiftly and Jack was able to save his brother. All they need now is rest for their bodies to regenerate, and they will be their usual selves."

He paused and his fingers froze on my skin.

"You however have received a huge shock," he said, "and since my promise to Jack was to take care of you, I am attempting to reassure you and soothe your confused and frightened mind."

I held my breath as I looked into those pale blue eyes that seemed more silver than before. His mouth was sensual, kissable; I had a sudden urge to touch his body, to press my body against him. I forced myself to lie still.

"Can you read my thoughts right now, Marcus?" I asked.

"Yes," he murmured, "I feel your desire, I can smell it. It is perfectly natural Jessica. Do not fight it."

I sat up, pulled away.

"No!" I almost shouted, "I am with Jack! You can't do this to your friend. I can't cheat on him."

I was growing frantic, trying to push Marcus away as he sat up beside me, "You must be making me feel like this," I said, "stop it, get out of my head!" I cried out in anguish.

I wanted to hit him or push him away, anything to stop from feeling this strange sexual attraction for this man, this vampire. Instead I stumbled out of bed and across the room, grabbing the back of a chair set in front of the dressing table. I would not faint; I would not collapse in a heap again. I was still wearing the white bathrobe and I hugged it around me, covering as much of my body as possible. But Marcus' caress left an imprint on my skin, a soft memory, and I wanted more. I needed more. He was addictive, enchanting. And he was offering himself to me, completely. Who was I to resist?

Marcus sat staring at me intently. He was completely still, and completely inhuman now I knew the truth about him.

"I am not 'in your head' Jessica," he said calmly, "you block my powers remember? And you will not be 'cheating on' Jack; that is a thoroughly modern phrase and concept. He understands our primal urges; he is a vampire after all. You need to feel protected and safe after the revelations of this evening, and I need to feed from your desire. I am hungry," he said simply.

"I would leave if I knew you felt nothing for me," he continued, "but you want my body Jessica, you cannot hide from that." he blinked and showed me those enchanting silver eyes, "We have a connection you and I, an understanding. I offer myself to you now as comforter, as a friend, as support."

I hugged the bathrobe around me; my body was cold and shivering suddenly. But it wasn't enough. I needed something more to warm me, and Marcus could offer me that even with his lies and deceit. He carefully slid off the bed, so graceful, and approached me slowly and tentatively.

I stood tense and defensive as he wrapped his arms around me, and kissed the top of my head. I whimpered in spite of myself, feeling weak and pathetic but most of all, I wanted him with a raw hunger. I wanted him naked and inside of me, our bodies pressed together. I wanted to be wild. But it was wrong, so very wrong.

He lowered his face to mine and when he kissed me I didn't move away. At first I tried to resist, thinking about Jack, about how I loved him and I couldn't do this to him. Then I remembered that he was a vampire, he had kept this huge secret from me, and even now I could be in serious danger because of his actions. And I felt that anger again, that rage at being humiliated and abandoned by those who pretend to care. So I returned Marcus' kiss, hungrily, all the while screaming inside that I shouldn't be doing this, that it was wrong. He ripped open the bathrobe and slid his hands over my breasts, down my stomach, between my legs, caressing me with such tenderness, such experience, and I moaned with pleasure.

My hands tugged at his clothes, undid the buttons of his shirt and trousers. He moved enough to remove his clothes and he knelt in front of me wearing just a pair of tight black boxer shorts, his muscular youthful body firm and strong for me. His hands were soft, gentle, and cool as he stroked my skin and slid the robe off my shoulders. He carefully undid my bra and threw it to the floor but I didn't stop him. I was in a dream; I might as well enjoy myself.

He kissed and caressed my body, lifted me easily into his arms, and carried me over to the bed. I lay back and welcomed him on top of me as we stripped off our remaining underwear and made love, slowly, rising to a passionate crescendo. He was so gentle, and so tender, but seemed to know when I wanted more; he knew what I needed from our lovemaking. I needed passion and excitement, but above all I needed his comfort.

Afterwards we lay together in bed, his arms wrapped around me as I spooned against him, my body seeming to curve against his naturally. My mind was racing. What had I done? The man I loved was lying unconscious next door having nearly died and here I was having had sex with another man, his friend no less! And then I remembered, they were vampires; the rules of normal life no longer existed. I was in a strange crazy new world, stumbling around with no real clue as to what was happening or what I should do. I fell asleep.

29

I woke slowly, feeling a little groggy as though I had been drinking. My head ached and my body was sore, all of my muscles having been so tense the night before. I opened my eyes and sat up with a start when I saw Marcus facing me in bed, lying on his side. He was naked, and I struggled to understand why and what had happened. His face was serious, his piercing pale blue eyes carefully neutral of expression. "Good morning, Jessica." he said.

Memories of the previous night flooded back and I cried out, almost falling out of the bed to get away from him. I found the bathrobe on the chair and clutched it to me, pressing my back against the wall.

"What did we do?" I cried, "How could you do that to me, to your friend? How could I do that?"

I choked back the sobs and concentrated on not crying as Marcus sat up in bed, looking irresistible, his hair tousled from sleep.

"Jessica, please calm down." he said, "You did nothing wrong. We did nothing wrong. You were upset after everything that had happened, you needed comfort, and I offered that to you."

He shrugged and his eyes shone silver. I caught the glimpse of his fangs, noticed how white his face was, how pronounced his cheekbones were.

"Vampires use sex for food Jessica." he continued, "Jack will understand. Your guilt is the least of your worries."

My heart leapt into my throat as Marcus rose from the bed in one smooth movement, so graceful. I tried to keep my voice steady as I spoke.

"Are you going to kill me," I said, "and drink my blood?"

He stood in front of me, naked and beautiful. He was smiling but his expression frightened me. I suddenly felt incredibly vulnerable. When he spoke I could clearly see his fangs, and his pale blue eyes were now glowing pure silver.

"I told you before do not fear me Jessica." he said, "I have given my word to Jack that no harm will come to you in this house, and I intend to keep that promise. But you must remember you are not dealing with humans now and we react very differently to certain situations. What happened between you and me last night will stay between you and me, unless you decide otherwise."

He gestured to the floor and I glanced down and was surprised to see my overnight bag sat near the door.

"I took the liberty of sending Alice back to your house last night for some clean clothes and toiletries," he said, "I hope you don't mind."

I shook my head, confused. When Marcus spoke again his fangs has disappeared, he had some colour to his skin, and his eyes were blue again, human. "There is an en suite shower room, please help yourself." he said, "I have some business to attend to but you are welcome to anything in the kitchen and I will answer your questions when you are ready."

With that he quietly opened the door and left me alone in the room, still shaking.

I moved slowly over to my bag and was relieved to find my favourite black jeans, black vest top, and red and white checked shirt along with matching clean underwear, deodorant and body lotion. Alice had been very thorough, she must have collected things from my bathroom as well, and even my toothbrush and comb were in there. She had also packed my trainers and a pair of ankle socks; the night before I had been wearing ballerina pumps that I imagined would still be wet from the rain.

I walked into the en suite bathroom and switched on the shower, then caught sight of my reflection in the mirror above the sink. My skin was white, even more so than usual if that was possible, and I could barely even see the freckles on my face. My eyes and lips looked very dark as though I was wearing make-up, and I did not look human. I smiled wryly at the joke and then climbed carefully into the shower.

30

I don't know how long I stood beneath the powerful jet spray of the shower. The hot water seemed to cleanse my skin, and I imagined it was cleansing my body of everything that had happened. Perhaps when I went downstairs I would find Jack awake, healthy, and human. Maybe Danny hadn't nearly died. Simon couldn't possibly be a werewolf because they didn't exist. And Marcus and I had simply had sex, and now I needed to resolve my relationship with Jack and carry on a normal life. But once I walked back into the bedroom to get dressed, I knew that everything was true. The world was even more terrifying and confusing than before. I needed answers. I needed safety. But first I needed food, as my stomach rumbled loudly, empty and demanding breakfast.

I walked slowly across the landing to the stairs, clean and dressed, feeling much more refreshed but incredibly thirsty, and very hungry despite the faint nausea. I paused outside Jack's bedroom door but I couldn't just go in. I was afraid of what lay in that room. Instead I walked carefully down the sweeping staircase, hesitating at the bottom and taking a guess on which door led into the kitchen. I chose one at the rear of the house and was correct.

Marcus was seated at a square dark-wood table with a laptop in front of him and a coffee mug next to that. He was dressed in a black pinstripe business suit with white shirt and black tie. There was a flat screen television on the wall and I could see the BBC Breakfast news program. The time was 7.45am. It felt like lunchtime, I felt as though I were still in a dream. Everything was surreal, slightly foggy round the edges. Perhaps I was still in shock. I didn't know, and I didn't care.

Marcus smiled as I entered, faltering in the doorway.

"Hello Jessica." he said brightly, "Are you feeling better

now?"

I nodded and approached the table. Marcus stood up and walked over to the kitchen area, a modern set-up of stainless steel units and granite work surfaces. He poured coffee from the jug on a percolating machine, and brought it over to me with a small jug of milk and a bowl of sugar. I took it gratefully, and added two heaped teaspoons of sugar, although I usually didn't have any in my drinks, and I accepted his offer of toast. It seemed so domestic, so normal, as though we were new lovers. I was confused. Had I dreamt all that stuff about vampires and werewolves? Was that my way of justifying what I did?

The coffee was perfect, strong and smooth. Marcus put a plate of wholemeal toast in front of me, spread thickly with butter. He moved round the table and sat back down in his chair. I picked up the toast and began to eat slowly but found that I was actually very hungry, and I soon demolished it. My mind was racing with hundreds of questions and I didn't know where to start. I decided to try.

"Do you know how Jack and Danny are now," I asked, "and when they might wake up?"

Marcus leaned back in his chair.

"They are both almost healed," he said, "I checked in on them before. They should wake very soon I think. Alice has fetched clothes for them as well so they can prepare for the next meeting with Seamus and his wolves."

I nodded, sipped some more coffee, and looked at Marcus.

"So what happens now?" I asked, "Am I to wait here, go home, go with them?"

"You should wait here unless Jack decides otherwise." Marcus said, "He may take you to a police safe house but I am not sure. You cannot return home until Seamus is defeated. He is a most dangerous and powerful man and would not be above kidnapping you if he saw an advantage."

"Who exactly is this Seamus?" I asked, "All I know is that he was the bad guy they were chasing in Scotland, and apparently he is a rival werewolf to Danny? And how do you know about him anyway if you aren't connected to the police?"

I shivered as I said those words. It all seemed so unreal. Marcus nodded. "Seamus Tully is a very powerful werewolf," he said, "I know him by reputation. In our community, certain non-human creatures become infamous for their actions and behaviours. He is Irish, and has been building a network of wolf packs all around the UK. His reputation as a cruel, harsh Master precedes him, and from what Danny and Jack tell me, everything I have heard is true. Normally I wouldn't concern myself with what the wolves do, but now he is in my territory, threatening my friends, and that I cannot accept. So I will support Jack and Danny, and assist them where necessary."

I turned as Marcus looked up towards the door behind me. My skin crawled with tension as I sensed someone close by. My heart was pounding, my senses on the alert. Danny stood in the doorway, with Simon and Sally just behind him. His hair was tousled, he was wearing only boxer shorts and his chest was smooth apart from the line of a scar near his heart, where the wound had been. He grinned, winked at me, and ran a hand through his hair.

"Good morning," he said, "So our secret is out, Jess? Sorry about that."

I smiled without thinking; Danny had that way with people. My tone was friendly but wary; I wasn't ready to trust him just yet.

"Danny you seem a lot better." I said carefully, "You were almost dead when I saw you last night." I took a deep breath, "Yes it was a huge shock to find out that my closest friends are not actually human."

Here I fixed my eyes on Simon who ducked his head but said nothing. Danny nodded, his expression more serious.

"Well, I'm sorry you had to find out like this," he said, "but I assure you my enemy will pay for his crimes. Now if you will excuse us, we need to hunt."

He turned and strode away, Simon and Sally following

without a word.

I turned round to look at Marcus.

"So he is healed, just like that?" I asked, "Will he have a scar forever? What exactly happened to him and Jack last night?"

Marcus carefully closed the laptop and clasped his hands on the table.

"Danny was stabbed in the chest with a silver blade." he said, "Silver can be deadly to shape shifters; it acts like poison to their blood. Jack took the poisoned blood away and gave Danny his vampire blood to help him heal. It was their genetic link that saved his life; any other werewolf would almost certainly have died from such injuries. I believe that once he changes back from wolf form there will be no scar."

"Of course." I said flatly, "So I take it Jack is still asleep?"

We both moved as we heard Alice's voice from upstairs, low and urgent. "Marcus," she called, "I need you please."

Marcus was on his feet and up the stairs in a flash and I hurried after him without thinking. I jumped as I heard Alice scream and saw Marcus disappear into the bedroom where Jack and Danny had been. I was halfway up the stairs when Marcus came out of the bedroom carrying Alice in his arms, apparently unconscious. She was wearing a bathrobe and I saw blood on her neck.

"What happened," I asked, "is she alright?"

Marcus looked at me and then walked smoothly down the hallway towards his bedroom, saying over his shoulder, "She will live. Jack is awake; you can go and see him. It is safe now."

And with that he shut the door behind him and Alice.

31

Heart in my throat, I quietly climbed the rest of the stairs and approached the bedroom. Jack was sitting on the edge of the bed naked apart from a pair of boxer shorts. He was leaning with his head in his hands, elbows resting on his knees. Someone had opened the window and a gentle sea breeze wafted through the room, blowing away the faint scent of blood and disinfectant. The sun was shining and the air smelled fresh after last night's storm. I stood in the doorway, nervous, not daring to approach the man I loved because he was a monster, the monster who had been haunting my dreams for the past few months.

Jack raised his head slowly and stared at me from a pale face, his lips and eyes very dark against his skin. He looked ethereal, his appearance frightened me, and I gripped the door handle, my body tense. He spoke in a quiet voice, blank of emotion. "Do not fear me, Jessica," he said, "I momentarily lost control but I am back now, and you are safe. Please step into the room and I will try and explain myself to you."

I did as he asked, curiosity getting the better of me. There was a chair next to the bed much like the one in the room where I had stayed, and I walked slowly over and sat there now. My back was rigid and I tried to relax into the chair but was too afraid. Common sense told me to run, to escape from this danger, but emotion took over.

Jack's expression suddenly changed to one of sorrow, and such sheer sadness that my heart leaped and I felt tears spring to my eyes. I fought to gain control of myself. My voice was surprisingly calm.

"Well," I said, "now I know your big secret. I feel like this is some kind of crazy dream or nightmare but I know I'm awake."

Jack nodded, sitting straighter now. The muscles on his

upper body rippled deliciously and I felt the stirrings of desire even as I tried to focus on the serious issues that we were facing. Jack spoke quietly, voice gentle.

"Yes, you are awake." he said, "I am a vampire, my brother a werewolf, and your best friend a werewolf. Please do not fear me Jessica. Do not fear any of us. There have been a few complications that caused me to lose momentary control of my human sense but that will not happen again."

His voice wavered and I saw tears in his eyes.

"I cannot lose you Jessica," he said, "I love you."

My heart was pounding and the room spun around me; my head was spinning and my throat dry. He had finally said it! After so many months of us both avoiding the truth, now his secret was out, and he could finally be honest with me. I swallowed nervously and tried to speak round the lump in my throat, tears stinging my eyes.

"I don't fear you Jack." I said, "I fear the vampire. What I have seen over the last few hours…it is completely insane!"

Then I smiled and moved closer to him, but still sitting on the edge of the chair.

"I love you too Jack." I said.

Suddenly he was on his knees before me, hands either side of my face, kissing me so gently on the lips. When he drew back he was smiling.

"Thank you, Jessica," he said, "You need not fear the vampire, we are one and the same, and both under control now."

He was staring at me with those amazing bright blue eyes and I spoke in a whisper.

"Your eyes, I knew they weren't human," I said, "They look like blue flame, too intense. Everything makes sense suddenly, the strange behaviour, your strength, and your old-fashioned language. How old are you really Jack?"

He knelt before me with his youthful thirty-five year-old muscular body, and answered.

"I am around 130 years old." he said, "I became a vampire during the Great War in 1916, when I was 35. Danny and me were soldiers and were marching through France. We set up camp in a village where I fell in love with a local woman. Danny knew that she would be trouble but I wouldn't listen, I was infatuated," he paused and I nodded encouragingly.

"When the time came for us to leave she grew hysterical," he continued, "and it was only later that I discovered her true identity. Danny was attacked by a wolf one night after we were ambushed, and while I tried to save him, she appeared and bit me, and drank my blood."

Jack paused again and looked at me. I nodded for him to continue.

"She thought I would leave my brother to die and spend eternity with her but she was wrong." he said, "Nothing ever separates Danny and me, and nothing ever will. We are brothers and allies for all eternity. After he became a wolf we experimented with our abilities, shared each other's blood and consequently some of each other's abilities. It made us both more powerful and more dangerous to our kind, the non-human community. They seek to destroy us because they fear our strength. And now this renegade wolf, Seamus, is here in Redcliffe to have his revenge and take over Danny's pack. We must stop him."

He was standing over me now, intimidating and yet so attractive. I was watching his stomach muscles, his arms, and my eyes moved down his body. The heat flared in my own body and then guilt rushed over me as I remembered my infidelity last night. Jack saw my expression and crouched in front of me, taking my hands in his.

"Jessica what's wrong?" he asked, "Have I upset you? I thought you wanted to know the truth."

I shook my head and blinked away the hot tears.

"No, Jack you haven't upset me." I said shakily, "But I did a terrible thing last night and I am so stupid and you will hate me."

He kissed my hands and drew me into his arms, kissing the top of my head. "Jessica you cannot have done anything wrong." he said, "Tell me, I won't judge you, I promise."

I stood up and moved away from him, shaking my head as I paced the room. "No, Jack." I said, "While you were in here unconscious last night, I was in the room next door – with Marcus. I slept with him. I am so sorry."

And the tears poured down my cheeks, the shame and the guilt flowing out of me, sobs shaking my body. I sank to the floor on my knees, face buried in my hands.

Jack's face changed to an expression of bewilderment and then he smiled. He was kneeling in front of me in an instant, his arms around me, his soft lips kissing my cheeks, forehead, and lips.

"Oh, do not worry about a trivial thing like that," he said, "Didn't Marcus explain to you that we vampires are not so uptight about sex as humans? It means nothing; I know you are not in love with him. You were understandably confused and in need of physical comfort and he offered it to you while I was unable. I am glad it was Marcus and not a lesser vampire."

The tears were still flowing and Jack very gently wiped them away with his fingertips. He drew me to my feet and led me over to the bed, sat me down, and cuddled me against him as I cried. When I had calmed down I turned to face him. "You really are not bothered that I cheated on you?" I asked incredulously.

"No Jessica it does not bother me." he replied, "You were merely gaining comfort, nothing more. Do you have romantic feelings for Marcus?"

I shook my head.

"Then no," he said, "Do not give it another thought. He took care of you, simple as that. As long as you were willing and he didn't take undue advantage then we shall say nothing more of this."

I looked into those intense blue eyes and my heart was fluttering as I gazed at the man I loved, the vampire I was in love with. He was smiling softly but he looked ill, his skin deathly white. I broke the silence.

"You are so pale, Jack." I said, "Is that natural, do you make your skin look tanned to match Danny?"

He nodded.

"I am pale because I still need to feed," he said, "I took some blood from Alice before, but it was an instinctive reaction. I had just woken and was thirsty. I smelt human blood and I took it. But it wasn't enough, because I quickly regained control. Alice is Marcus' donor. I should not have taken advantage of her. But he stopped me in time and she will recover. When I am fully fed I have the ability to appear tanned. It is also connected to Danny's powers and our shared blood bond. Vampires are usually pale, that is how you can notice them in human society."

I was quiet for a few moments as I processed more questions in my mind.

"Do you need to take human blood or can it be animal?" I asked.

"We can drink from animals but I prefer human blood," he replied, "It is sweeter, more fulfilling, and gives me more power."

"Do you kill to feed?" I asked, "Have you killed before?"

Jack hesitated, looking down. When he looked at me again his eyes blazed.

"I have killed humans." he said quietly, "In the early days I couldn't control my hunger, and innocent people paid the price. I killed people during the wars when I was a soldier. And I still do kill people, both human and non-human, but only those who threaten me and my colleagues and friends. But I no longer kill to feed. I take just what I need and my donors are none the wiser."

This was intense. He was a killer. But this was Jack and I loved him. How should I react? Well obviously I should run away, stop seeing him, escape this corrupt life before I became too closely involved. But somehow I knew it was too late to back out, and I couldn't just leave him.

I closed my eyes, breathing in and out deeply to steady my nerves. Jack's voice was low and seductive, his Irish accent coming through stronger.

"I can hear your heart pounding, Jessica," he said, "the

blood coursing through your veins. It takes all of my self-control not to bite you now and feed on you. Since we first met I wanted to taste you but I couldn't."

My voice was husky as I spoke.

"Why couldn't you?" I asked, "Were you going to feed from me that first night in the pub?"

"Yes I wanted to." he replied, "But you are too precious Jessica. I cannot explain it but there is energy about you, a promise of something deeper, stronger. I feel you may have some ancestry of witchcraft and that is what drew us together."

Witchcraft? This was getting worse. I remembered Marcus' words from last night, and Lillian suddenly sprung to mind, and what she had told me about my heritage. How did Jack know about that? But as I opened my eyes and looked at him all I could see was the blue flame in his eyes and I wanted him so badly. I wanted him to feed from me, to see what it was like.

"You think I am a witch Jack?" I asked.

He nodded, swallowing as though he were struggling to control himself. I felt a rush of something strange, some kind of knowledge of my power over him. I enjoyed it, this potential to seduce. Was this my witch ability? Was that why Marcus had slept with me? I didn't know.

"Well I don't know about that, Jack," I said, "Maybe I should check out my family history but right now I need to deal with the fact that my boyfriend is a vampire."

I smiled but Jack was serious.

"Yes of course." he said, "I will understand if you want to leave me Jessica, but please allow me to deal with Seamus first."

"I don't want to leave you Jack." I said, "I can't leave you, especially now when there is a whole new side of you for me to properly meet. I trust that you won't harm me, at least not on purpose."

I shifted round to face him and swept my damp hair to one side, showing him the line of my neck.

"Here," I said, "You need to feed, take my blood."

He went very still, eerily so, but his eyes were glowing with that unnatural brilliance.

"Are you sure Jessica?" he asked tentatively.

"Yes I am sure." I replied, "If this is what you need then take it. I want you to."

He very gently took me in his arms and lay me down on the bed, lying on top of me. I stared into his eyes and willed myself to stay calm as he kissed my lips and then moved to my neck, licking the skin, tasting me. I caught a glimpse of his flame-blue eyes, and his sharply defined features in his white face. His body was cool on top of me.

His head reared back and he struck in a sudden quick movement. I cried out as his fangs pierced my skin and he held me tightly in his arms. My body writhed beneath him and then I lay still. The sudden sharp pain faded, replaced by something magical, beautiful. Suddenly I was flying above a vast ocean, holding Jack's hand. We were laughing and I could feel the spray of water on my face, cool and refreshing. The moon was glowing, the air was cool, and we were ecstatically happy. I came down to earth as Jack drew away from me, licking his lips, his eyes burning with intensity.

I opened my eyes sleepily and murmured, "We were flying, and it was so beautiful!"

Then I drifted into sleep as he gently stroked my hair and face.

32

When I woke Jack was standing beside the bed with a fluffy white towel wrapped around his waist, drying his hair with another one. He looked irresistible; his skin was tanned, his eyes sparkling, his muscles rippling. I sat up, felt a little woozy, and put a hand to my head. I fell back against the padded headboard, waiting for the dizziness to pass. Jack spoke quietly.

"How are you feeling, Jessica?" he asked, "Should I get you some water?"

I managed to nod but kept my eyes closed for a moment. Then I slowly opened them, looked at him and spoke in a hoarse voice.

"I'm alright thanks." I said, "You look a lot better."

Jack had produced a glass of water from somewhere, which he handed to me. I took it with shaking hands and sipped carefully. Maybe Marcus was used to having weak humans in his house. Or maybe they were just being prepared after last night. It seemed too trivial to worry about in the circumstances. My neck felt a little stiff and the tiny wound smarted as I remembered it was there. But it was only a slight pain, sort of like a shaving cut, and I soon ignored it.

Jack nodded.

"I am much better thanks to you." he said, "Your blood is sweet and nourishing. You should feel better soon, you have been asleep for twenty minutes."

I watched as he moved around the room, picked up his bag and rifled through it to see what clothes Alice had brought. He pulled out black jeans, dark grey t-shirt, boxer shorts, a belt, and deodorant. All I could do was stare at his body and he smiled, moved toward the bed and pulled off the towel so he stood naked before me. "I can smell your desire Jessica," he said, "and I can plainly see it in your face."

He knelt on the bed and kissed me gently, then grew more passionate, and when I responded hungrily he was suddenly pulling at my clothes.

This time I didn't stop him, no more questions. I just gave in and enjoyed our love making, knowing that it was precious and should not be ruined by pointless emotion and rationalizing. I loved the strength of his body, the way he took control of me and yet was gentle and intimate at the same time. I knew that somehow I had power over him even if I was human and he was a vampire. We were meant to be together. And when he moved against me, eased himself inside my body, I cried out in ecstasy, grabbing his buttocks and scratching my fingernails up and down his back. He brought me to a gasping orgasm, almost screaming until I stopped myself, biting at his neck instead.

Afterwards I lay on the bed watching him, as he got dressed. I felt lazy, contented, and just for a moment I forgot that Jack had a killer to catch and some complicated non-human politics to deal with. Then he brought me back down to earth when he looked into his bag again and drew out a gun holster and two guns. I watched as he laid them on the bedside cabinet, slipped the holster on and fastened it, then checked each gun in turn and put them in their respective places. He spoke without looking up, fiddling with straps.

"When this is over I would like you learn how to use a gun, if you are willing," he said, "It would be safer for you. There is a training centre that we use at the station, and I can sign you in as a spouse. It's a self-defence issue, you can be licensed."

My heart skipped a beat but I nodded, then I carefully slid off the bed and started to get dressed myself.

"Yes ok." I said, "It frightens me but I understand I might need them sometime in the future."

We were talking about a future together. It made me feel anxious and excited for very different reasons. I was actually making a commitment to this man. When we were both dressed we walked downstairs together and found Marcus and Alice in the kitchen. The four of us sat down at the table and drank coffee as though we were all normal humans on a normal day.

33

An hour had passed and I was reading the local newspaper that Marcus had left on the table. It was somehow important that I make some connection with the real world, outside of this house. I had stopped asking questions for the time being. There was plenty of time, and I needed to calm my mind at least for a short while. Marcus and Alice had excused themselves to go to his offices, leaving Jack in charge of locking up when we left. I got the impression that Marcus was used to sharing his house with Jack and Danny, and their associates, especially when I found out Jack had his own key.

Alice seemed perfectly calm around Jack after what he had done to her and I wondered if she regularly donated blood to him. When we first walked into the kitchen she was sitting calmly at the table with Marcus stood behind her. There was a neat, square surgical bandage on her neck, just visible under her hairline. She was a little pale but otherwise seemed calm and collected, immaculately dressed in a black skirt suit, white blouse, hair neatly blow-dried into a bob, and her face carefully made-up.

Despite my determination to be quiet for now, my mind was racing with questions. I was worrying about what was going to happen, and at the bottom of it all, I was excited. This was an adventure, a break from the norm, and it was something that I had never even imagined could happen before. I knew I shouldn't be excited. This was a dangerous situation, and Jack and Danny should not have involved me. Then again I wouldn't have given Jack up so easily. I knew that now. Somehow it felt right to be sat here in this modern kitchen, with the man I loved, drinking coffee and reading the newspapers amidst an upheaval of everything I had ever known.

Eventually my mind got the better of me and I looked at

Jack, questions ready to burst from my mouth. He smiled knowingly at my excited expression, and sat back in his chair, waiting for me to begin.

"Ok," I said, "tell me about vampires first. Are the old stories and films correct, or is it all just make-believe?"

Jack nodded, thinking about his answer before he spoke.

"The ancient myths are largely correct," he said, "Vampires seem to originate in Eastern Europe and possibly even Egypt but I have never really bothered to research it. I take it you want to know what we are capable of."

I nodded, leaning forward in my chair, playing with the mug in front of me. "Yes," I said enthusiastically, "I mean, I know that you eat human food because I've seen you, and I know you have a reflection in the mirror and that you need blood to survive. How does it all work?"

Jack exhaled and settled back in his chair before he spoke.

"It is true that early vampires killed people for food." he said, "Indeed only two hundred years ago I have been told that vampires did not eat human food or even drink water. But over the centuries our kind has evolved to better integrate with society." he gestured toward the kitchen area, "You see me eating food but I do not really enjoy it and I do not need it for sustenance. Over time vampires discovered that they only needed to take a small amount of blood from a human, but more frequently. I personally drink blood two or three times a day, more if I have been injured. But I have a personal supply from a local blood bank through a private contact. And I have regular human donors that I visit when necessary."

My body had gone cold as I processed the information, and as I realized suddenly why Jack would mysteriously disappear when we were together.

"So all those times you were working," I said, "or called away on urgent business, or sneaked out of bed at night, were you feeding?"

He nodded. I continued, speaking slowly as I thought about my words.

"So you never took my blood before today?" I asked.

He nodded again, and then leaned forward, an earnest expression on his face. "I could not take your blood lightly Jessica." he said, "To me any donor is precious but for you I needed something more. It was that which made me see that I loved you. You are beautiful and delicate and I needed you to understand what I was. I needed your consent before I fed from you."

He sat back.

"But also I see your power." he said, "You call to me from a primal place, and I know that somehow I am central to unlocking your own secrets, things that you never knew about yourself."

Now my heart was racing and I had one of those moments where the room spins, my stomach lurched, and my head seemed to move even though I was sat still. It was like being on a roller coaster, or those old fairground rides that spin you round and jerk your body, the Waltzers. It was the adrenaline in my system, that instinctive warning telling me that something wasn't right. But now I knew that it was just my body and my mind conflicting.

I heard Lillian echoing in my head, whispering that Jack was right, and that I should let him help me to unlock my own power. I should fight the fear. But I repressed her voice for now. There was too much to think about, too much else to deal with. I took a gulp of sweetened coffee, swallowed it carefully, and hesitated before I spoke again.

"So these donors," I asked, "where do you find them, who are they?"

"There are some humans who know about our kind and who offer themselves to us." Jack said, "At the Ship we have human employees who act as donors for me and other vampires. I offer them my protection from any stranger that might try to take advantage. During tourist season we see a lot of non-humans, but most of them know that Danny, Marcus and me run this town, and they respect that. Those who don't soon pay for their mistake."

He paused, thinking, then continued.

"Of course recently it has only been Marcus and Simon enforcing things, but that will change," he said, "For the humans it is a beautiful experience, a sort of exhilaration, when we feed. But I also take my food from strangers, people I meet socially or as part of my police work."

This sounded a little too gentle. Jack must have seen the cynicism on my face because he continued, face serious.

"Vampires can make the act of feeding both pleasurable and painful for humans." he said, "It is true that I have been violent and vicious with some of my donors in the past. I do not pretend to be a gentle vampire; there is no such thing. But I promise that with you I am gentle, I would never hurt you."

But he had hurt me, several times in fact. Maybe it wasn't physical, but the threat had been there. I nodded and fought to keep my body from shivering, trying to forget how close he had come to hurting me recently, and I found his words hard to believe. Yes I was afraid but I still believed what Jack said and I wanted to know more. Again I thought about how easy it was for domestic abuse to spiral out of control. I was sat here with a very violent and dangerous man, who I just happened to be in love with, and I trusted him. I would stand by him rather than escape to save myself.

Jack proceeded to explain that he could hypnotize humans before feeding from them so they were unaware of what had happened. He told me about his ability to read minds, and his enhanced speed and strength. And he told me that the old religious beliefs about vampires were simply myths created by a god-fearing society. Jack said that a wooden stake through the heart could kill a vampire; but that it was an outdated method and nowadays silver bullets could be just as deadly, as they were to werewolves. Apparently silver has some sort of poisonous component that reacts badly with a non-human body. But the blood he took from Danny was weaker which was why it didn't kill him, something to do with the brothers' natural metaphysical powers and abilities.

I was completely overwhelmed with all of these revelations. So the old stories were partially true but a bit outdated. It actually made perfect sense. I asked about werewolves and Jack said that yes, they were connected to the moon cycles through some magical way that people couldn't explain. A new werewolf would experience their first change on the next full moon after they were attacked but as they grew stronger some could control when they changed form, like Danny and Simon. The werewolf may not be immortal like the vampire but this was where Jack and Danny were different. Because of them being twins they had experimented with blood sharing rituals, and so far Danny seemed to have taken some of his brother's immortality. This was partially what upset rival wolves like Seamus, and why Jack and Danny were a target for non-humans seeking to destroy what they were unable to have for themselves.

It was such a strange feeling to think that my boyfriend was actually around 130 years old. I couldn't believe it when I saw his 35-year old face and body. But it certainly explained some of his mannerisms and the way he spoke. I asked if that was why his Irish accent was so faint. He said that was probably because he had moved around a lot and learnt to integrate himself in English society. It was the same for Danny. They had both schooled themselves to have a fairly unrecognisable accent to allow for better police investigation. They had less chance of being recognized by the criminals they were pursuing. It made even more sense now I knew his real age. But it felt strange for myself. I mean, technically he was dead, and I was having sex with him. I tried not to think about that. It was easier to just see him as a thirty-five year-old man. I could handle that.

34

Next I asked how a vampire and a werewolf came to be working for the human police. Jack explained that he and Danny were soldiers during the First World War and while they were still human had made a good impression on their commanding officers. After they were separated from their battalion and were attacked by the wolf and vampire they lived rough in the Swiss and French countryside while they adjusted to their new situation. They both fed on wild animals and lone humans to begin with, and gradually found themselves back in human civilization.

Then they were reunited with the British army and sent back to England to recuperate in a hospital. It was in the hospital where they were involved in a vicious fistfight with another soldier who accused them of leaving their regiment to die. They almost killed this man and were arrested and taken before the Court Marshall. And here the hidden authorities discovered them. The government already knew about vampires and shape shifters and subsequently offered the brothers a job with the police force, working as detectives to cover up supernatural crimes and deal with the perpetrators as appropriate. Apparently there were several other vampires and werewolves that also worked within the police force, and it was their job to follow up on non-human criminals using whatever strength was necessary. It was all kept carefully secret from the media and I was amazed at these revelations.

Jack fell quiet, watching me. I roused myself and looked around Marcus' modern 21st century kitchen to remind me of where I was. There was his laptop on the table, its charger plugged into the wall socket. The flat screen television was now silent but large on the wall, and there was an I-pod docking station on the unit in the far corner, and all of the modern kitchen gadgets glistening on the work surfaces.

"Wow, Jack," I said, "This is an incredible story! So the government has kept your secret for all these years."

"Yes," he said, "and that is why our job is so important to us. We are both very powerful supernatural beings but we wish to remain within human society and live normal lives, or as normal as possible. We have an arrangement where we move around every ten years or so, and we don't make any lasting friendships with people other than those who already know our true identities."

I felt panic rise in my throat suddenly.

"Do you mean you shouldn't have made friends with me?" I asked.

His eyes were very bright as he replied.

"Yes." he said, "We have become involved with humans in the past and it always ends badly. Danny and I are better off on our own but now we know you it is not so simple. I cannot leave you and neither can Danny. Now you must decide whether you wish to continue our friendship or not."

"Of course I do!" I cried, "What else can I do? I love you Jack, I don't care if you are a killer, I'm sure you only do it for the right reasons!"

I stopped and thought about what I had just said. Jack was a vampire, a killer, and here I was telling him it was all right. No, it wasn't right; I would never get involved with a criminal. But he wasn't a criminal; he was a police detective, a well-respected person in society. Now I was confused. He smiled grimly.

"I am not like the fictional vampires, Jessica," he said, "I do not despise what I am, I embrace it. But the simple fact about my kind is that our emotions run very deep, they drive us, and that can sometimes be our undoing. I had vowed to distance myself from the humans until you came along."

My heart was pounding and I slowly stood up and moved around the table to where Jack sat. I could see clearly in his face that he was remembering something painful and all I wanted was to heal that pain, to chase it away. In the back of my mind a voice warned me to be careful, telling me that my emotions were false, that these were all just vampire tricks. Then I remembered what Lillian had said about me trusting the Mason brothers, and that I had to believe how much they cared for me. She was telling the truth; she was my mother, and even though I didn't fully understand how she was visiting me in my dreams, I knew it was real and that she was real, and so I trusted her.

I stifled the voice of doubt, dismissing it as my rational mind. I had witnessed enough non-human activity in the last twenty-four hours to convince me of the truth. And none of that affected my true feelings for Jack. Yes he was frightening. Yes he was a killer. But I was certain that he loved me, and I loved him, and right now that was the important thing.

I put my hands on either side of his face and stared into his eyes, into that blue flame. My heart swelled with the emotion I felt for him, breath caught in my throat, and I held my body as still as possible, not wanting to break the spell. We didn't speak but somehow I heard him in my head saying "I love you Jessica" and I smiled and very gently kissed him on the lips. I knew that we had a lot of talking to do but right now he had criminals to catch and I could wait. But I knew for certain that I could not leave this man, no matter what he told me, how old he really was, what he really was, or if he was a killer. All of a sudden that cheesy power ballad song 'Love Hurts' popped into my head again!

35

The spell was broken by the sound of the front door being flung open and suddenly Danny was stood in the kitchen doorway, glowing with good health, clean and wearing fresh clothes. Apparently he had been home to shower and change after his hunt. Simon and Sally were right behind him, also freshly showered and changed. I could smell the outdoors following them in, that fresh smell of grass and plant life that you get after a storm. It was delicious, tempting, and if I weren't in the middle of a crisis I would be outside, walking along the promenade and up the cliff tops, enjoying this fresh new morning. But that would have to wait.

There was something in Danny's attitude that made me uneasy. In fact it frightened me a little. I was reminded of his power and strength and the fact that I was only a human amongst supernatural creatures.

The air was suddenly thicker in the kitchen, stifling, but I couldn't explain what it was. It was almost like when you walk into a room and know that the other person is in a bad mood, or if they are upset. But this was magnified to a frightening level, and it made me tense.

Without thinking about it I backed up to the L-shaped kitchen units until I was leaning against the solid wood and granite. Jack slowly followed me, slipped an arm around my waist, gently squeezing me against him, and I calmed down and knew that he would protect me. I looked at Danny, Simon and Sally; my friends, people whom I had trusted implicitly. They were strangers to me now. They were animals. They frightened me.

Then I had a vision of them as wolves, running through the forest, chasing deer and smaller animals. I could hear snarling and growling, tree branches snapping, the high-pitched scream of terrified prey. I sensed a wolf attacking a

LOVE HURTS

prey animal, heard tearing flesh, and then the eerie howl of the wolf in triumph over its kill.

"Jessica," Jack called as if from a distance, "Jessica. Are you with us?"

I roused from my reverie to find myself slumped on the floor by the table, lying across Jack's lap. How had I got here? What happened? Jack's face was serious, concerned. Sally appeared kneeling beside me with a glass of water and I took it with a shaking hand, sipping carefully and spilling some down my top. I managed to speak, my voice only a little hoarse.

"I'm fine, sorry." I said, "I had some sort of vision. It was weird, but it's gone now."

I tried to sit up, and saw Danny and Simon crouched nearby, not sure what to do. Jack spoke.

"What do you mean, a 'vision?'" he asked, "We thought you fainted."

I told them what I had seen, watching Danny, Simon and Sally as I spoke. They all looked momentarily shocked, and then Danny gathered himself.

"Ok," he said, "so you saw some of what we did as wolves. You must have channelled us somehow psychically. Has anything like this happened before?"

I shook my head, just as confused. Then I managed to stand up on shaky legs, feeling silly suddenly. Jack stood with me but his movement was far more graceful. I put the glass on the table and looked from Jack to Danny, shaking my head.

"I don't know," I said, "I can't remember. Maybe we should talk about this later."

Danny nodded and he, Simon and Sally all straightened up to stand before me. They were dressed in almost identical clothes it seemed. Danny looked like he had got dressed from Jack's wardrobe. He was wearing a tight black t-shirt, black jeans, and black boots, and he had a shoulder holster with guns that looked identical to those Jack carried. If Jack hadn't been wearing a grey t-shirt it would have been almost impossible to tell them apart.

My gaze moved to Simon, who looked completely different to his usual casual, relaxed self. His baggy jeans and cartoon-print t-shirt was gone. He too was wearing a black t-shirt, jeans, boots, and my heart skipped a beat as I realized he also had a gun holster. This was so unlike the best friend I knew that I was overcome by sadness suddenly. Our friendship had changed forever, and it might never be the same, now I knew the truth about him. It actually hurt that I had never even suspected he hid such a secret from me. I dismissed it as just another crisis to deal with later.

Finally my gaze moved to Sally. She was wearing a dark grey fitted t-shirt and black jeans and boots, and the shoulder holster and guns. Her fluffy blond hair was tied back in a severe ponytail, and she looked angular, dangerous, and yet still so attractive to the right person. She promised danger and violence if anyone dared cross her. But somehow I knew that she would protect me. We may not be as close as I was to Simon, but for some reason it was easier to accept Sally's secret identity. Maybe it was because I didn't know as much about her background.

I jumped as Danny spoke, obviously studying my expression.

"This is a huge shock, Jessica," he said, "I understand. You are handling it incredibly well. Please do not be afraid of us."

He paused and I nodded, lifting my head to look at his eyes, intense blue, just like Jack's. But they weren't burning with flame. They were blazing with an energy I couldn't explain, but I could see it, and I could feel it all around me. My voice was hoarse when I spoke, and I coughed to clear my throat.

"What is that energy I can feel from you, Danny?" I asked, "It's like a heat radiating from all three of you, it's stifling."

He inclined his head, frowning, and Simon and Sally both shifted uncomfortably, clearly confused about my sensitivity to them. They waited for Danny to speak.

"You can feel our energy Jessica?" he asked.

I nodded, crossing my arms in an instinctively protective gesture. I felt Jack's reassuring presence beside me, but right now it was the wolves that had my attention. Danny continued.

"Now that is interesting," he mused.

He glanced at Jack and I half turned my head to see the brothers exchange knowing looks. Danny spoke again.

"Jack said you had an ability." he said, "I felt it but it was so faint, I thought it was dormant. Yes we are building metaphysical power, drawing energy from the wolves in our pack to give us strength to defeat our enemy. That is what you can feel."

He frowned and stepped toward me, and my body stiffened instinctively so that he stopped short of touching me.

"You are not fully human yourself Jessica." Danny said, "Now I see why Jack was so infatuated with you. And Marcus. You are a witch, do you realize?"

I shook my head, then nodded, not sure what to say. Jack spoke before I could, and I was thankful.

"Danny," he said, "she has had some revelations to deal with, we should leave her to adjust to this new situation. Jessica is aware that she herself hides secrets, and when the time is right I will help her unlock them. For now let us deal with Seamus and secure the pack; that is our priority."

Danny stepped back and nodded. His gaze moved down to my neck and he tilted his head to one side.

"Jack has fed from you, Jessica," he said, "Did you allow him to?"

My hand moved instinctively to the tiny wound, which I had forgotten about. "Yes Danny." I replied, "He needed to feed and I could offer it to him. Is it a problem?"

Danny smiled and shook his head.

"No," he said, "Actually it puts us in a stronger position. You are essentially tied to Jack now. He has marked you, offered you his protection. In our community that is very important, a sacred bond between human and vampire."

I did not understand a word of what he said but I simply accepted it because it was easier. My head hurt from all the crazy thoughts crowded inside, and the fear about what lay ahead. It was time to change the subject.

"So, what happens now?" I asked all of them, looking at Danny as I spoke, "Do we wait here, do you go and meet this Seamus man somewhere?"

Again Simon and Sally were silent, watching Danny for his response as I looked from him to Jack and back again. Danny spoke. Apparently this was his mission and he was in charge, I guessed because of the werewolf connection.

"Jessica," he said, "we will take you to a safe-house in the city. I have two wolves from my pack waiting there. They will be your bodyguards. It is too dangerous to stay here, and Redcliffe is the last place you should be in while Seamus is still alive. He and his two wolves are hidden somewhere in the town and we need to track them down. They hold the upper hand at the moment because they know the location of my lair, and they can easily find me, and you."

He paused and ruffled a hand through his hair.

"Seamus wants revenge," he said, "Jack and me killed many of his wolves in Scotland, and the rest we turned in to the legal authorities to be tried and imprisoned for their criminal activity. We destroyed his power base, which is now why he wants to take mine through any means necessary."

I took in what he had said, and a light dawned in my mind. I looked at Simon in wonder.

"Your lair," I said slowly, "It's the pub, the Ship." my voice was growing shrill with excitement, "There are caves underneath, I knew you were lying!"

Simon smiled in spite of himself, and I looked at Danny again.

"That's how come you own the pub," I said, "it makes perfect sense now. You are the wolf leader; therefore you own the building that hides your lair. That's where you both were when you disappeared mysteriously. And Sally, were you really working all those shifts, or were you there?"

Sally half-smiled and spoke quietly.

"No, I don't really work all of those shifts at the hospital," she said, "That is what I tell people. I spend a lot of time with the wolves, tutoring them, offering support, managing them when they need it."

Finally that was one mystery solved, and for some reason I felt triumphant because I had figured it out after so long.

Danny cleared his throat.

"We must leave now," he said to all of us. "I must locate Seamus and formally challenge him to a duel. What he did to me last night was a blatant attempt on my life and my pack, and it must be dealt with properly."

He strode out of the kitchen with Simon and Sally following faithfully behind. I looked at Jack, heart pounding, and adrenaline pumping through me. He smiled gently. "Do not be alarmed, Jessica," he said, "I am certain that Danny can defeat Seamus, and I will be there to help him. We will resolve this situation, we will save the Redcliffe pack, and you and I can move on with our lives together."

I nodded, surprised to find tears springing to my eyes suddenly.

"I don't want to be alone with strange people in a strange house, Jack." I said, "Can't you stay with me, or Simon or Sally?"

He shook his head and gently stroked my hair.

"No Jessica," he said, "We need to stay with Danny and deal with our enemy. Simon and Sally are his lieutenants; they must fight alongside their Master when he needs them. You will be safe with the bodyguards, please trust us. I will return to you as quickly as possible."

He gently took my hand and led me out of the kitchen and across the hall to the open front door. I hesitated outside while he locked up, not sure what to do. Danny's black BMW stood on the drive. It was identical to Jack's, except for one digit on the number plate. To the untrained eye you would not tell the two cars apart, and I wondered if the men did that on purpose when they were tracking criminals. It didn't sound completely ethical to me, but who was I to judge. I was inexperienced in these situations.

Danny was in the driver's seat, Sally beside him. Jack motioned for me to climb in the back, and I sat between him and Simon. Danny drove out onto the main road in silence, but I saw that everyone was alert, looking around them, watching for danger. I looked at the normal daily scenery.

The sea seemed gentle today after last night's storm, sunlight glittering on the waves. The road was quiet. Most people were either at work or on the beach at this time of day. I glanced at the clock on the dashboard. It was early afternoon. Where had the morning gone? Oh yes, I had been learning about vampires and werewolves. Just a normal Thursday morning. Yeah right!

I wondered how Liz was doing alone in the shop. Well she wasn't completely on her own. Marie was working today, so at least I didn't have to worry about that. And I knew Rob would be checking up on them during the day. Should I have sent her a text message? No, she wouldn't worry yet. She would simply think I had stayed at Jack's house, and she would expect to see or hear from me later. Maybe I could phone her from the safe house. I had my mobile phone in the pocket of my jeans, but hadn't thought to look at it all morning. My heart sank at the prospect of being left alone with strangers. I wanted to stay with Jack, but I knew that wasn't possible, and I understood the situation.

I roused myself and looked from Jack to Simon. Jack was staring out of the passenger window, expression serious, and his features rigid and stern. Simon was looking at me with apologetic eyes as we drove along the coastal road.

"I am so sorry about all of this, Jess," he said, "I really did want to tell you the truth but it was never the right time, you know?"

I smiled and nodded.

"It's ok, Simon I understand." I said, "If you had told me I wouldn't have believed you and would probably have tried to get you to see a doctor. But it certainly explains a few things about your behaviour."

He laughed and a tension left his body. He must have been terrified about my reaction. It was absurd suddenly, a werewolf afraid of a human because she might be angry with him for keeping his secret from her!

Our attention was broken as the car suddenly swerved, and screeched to a halt as Danny slammed the brakes on. I shivered with fear as a growl emanated from Danny's throat, followed by the same from Sally and Simon.

"It's an ambush!" Jack shouted.

Then everything happened in a blur of chaos. I saw a figure standing in the road in front of the car, and then it was gone. I thought it was a woman but all I saw was a swish of dark hair as she moved. Jack shouted at me to follow him; he grabbed my arm and hauled me out of the car towards the cliff edge. Simon, Sally and Danny were out of the car in a flash and we were confronted by three people: LuAnn, Celine and Seamus. I tried to see what Seamus looked like but everything was happening too fast, and all I knew was that he was tall, muscular, and terrifying.

The wolves all flew at each other, snapping and snarling but still in human form. It was unreal, like a nightmare. Jack grabbed me and tried to move away, with me stumbling after him. But someone lunged at him, he was knocked to the floor and I fell, crying out as I hit the rough ground. I put my arms out to try and break the fall and jarred my wrists in the process, yelping with pain. I was on the grass verge but there were stones and gravel amongst the grass, and the naked skin of my hands, face and neck seemed to catch them all. I tried to scramble to my feet, ignoring the searing pains.

Then suddenly I was airborne, hauled over Seamus' shoulder. I could hear the sounds of fighting and struggle, and Jack flew at Seamus, snarling and hissing. A gunshot sounded loud and clear, cracking through the air around us. Then I heard three more shots, and a female voice screaming. Lying across Seamus' shoulder as he fought with Jack, I screamed, kicked and struggled, and Seamus lost his grip, dropping me to the ground. This time I landed on tarmac and my whole upper body took the impact. I think I cracked a rib but I wasn't sure. As I tried once again to scramble to my feet someone was in front of me. I glimpsed a blood-streaked female face before her fist slammed into me and I collapsed, unconscious. The last thing I heard was Jack shouting my name, and another high-pitched female scream of pain.

36

I woke slowly, groaning as my body cried out in pain. It felt like there was something burning in my chest. My back was in agony. My head was pounding. I groggily opened my eyes, blinking at the sunlight streaming through the window. Panic shot through me, I sat bolt upright, cried out in pain and collapsed on the bed I was lying on. Fear washed through me and my heart skipped a beat as I heard a male voice from somewhere at the foot of the bed.

Where was I? I blinked and tried to focus, concentrating on keeping my breathing calm. Do not give in to hysteria, it only makes things worse, I counselled myself. My vision slowly cleared so I could see who the man was in this room. It was Seamus, and he spoke with a far more pronounced Irish accent than either Jack or Danny. It was gruff, almost a growl.

"I wouldn't try to move if I were you," he said nastily, "That was quite a fight you put up considering you are just a human. You should rest up before the exchange this evening."

I squinted at him, trying to focus my blurry vision. The man I saw was actually handsome in a rugged distinguished sort of way. He reminded me of a James Bond baddie. He was tall, very muscular, possibly more so than Jack and Danny. His dark hair was slightly greying but it enhanced his appearance, and he had a short, neatly trimmed beard. I guessed he could be about forty. He was wearing dark blue jeans and a red button-through shirt.

Seamus was leaning against the wall by the door to the hotel room. I knew it was a hotel room because of the uniform magnolia-painted walls, the garishly patterned curtains and bedspread, and the bland furniture. And as I looked around I saw the obligatory customer information pack next to the bedside telephone. I recognized this as a local

Travelodge that Liz and me had stayed in when we were buying the bookshop.

I was back in Redcliffe at least. Things weren't all bad. My mind was racing. I was a hostage. How could I possibly escape? I tried to drag myself into a sitting position, grimacing and holding back my cries of pain as my whole body came alive with injuries. I must have cracked a rib, which was where the burning sensation was. But since I had never so much as sprained an ankle in my life I wasn't sure what had happened to me.

Seamus moved away from the door and crawled onto the bed to lie beside me, close enough to invade my personal space, making me shiver again and try to move away. He smiled and it was cruel, promising pain and unpleasant things. There was no evidence of a fight on him at all; no cuts or bruises, and his clothes were intact. Maybe he had changed.

I wondered how long I had been unconscious, but I couldn't see a clock and my watch was at home. I glanced down at my shirt, which had been torn at the hem and one sleeve, and my jeans may have survived but were streaked with dust, and were damp from the wet grass. Seamus slowly reached out a hand and touched my knee, gently squeezing my leg. I held my breath, watching what he would do next. My body was painfully tense, rigid. When I looked at his face his eyes were amber wolf eyes and the panic rose in my throat. Without thinking I scrambled off the bed towards the door, stumbling and groaning with pain, clutching at my chest where I felt the burning sensation, my left knee buckling beneath me.

To my surprise the door opened easily and I hesitated, unsure suddenly about the possibility of escape. I half-turned but Seamus was lying on the bed watching me with those frightening eyes. He didn't seem concerned. Was he playing with me? I limped out into the hallway, expecting Seamus to haul me back in, but then Celine appeared in front of me, blocking my exit. She was smiling with that arrogant expression but there was a large cut above her eye.

LOVE HURTS

It was healing fast but still evident. Her clothes did seem scuffed, but I barely had time to register that. She crossed her arms and shook her head slowly, saying something in French.

In a blur of movement she grabbed my hair with one hand, and dragged me roughly back into the room and shut the door. For a small person she had incredible strength, and her fingers dug into my arm painfully as she gripped me with her other hand. She released me so I fell to the floor in a heap, falling to my hands and knees, head smarting where she had pulled my hair, body prickling with tension and fear. I raised my head to see the two of them standing before the window, watching me. And I knew how it felt to be a helpless prey animal awaiting its fate.

37

I managed to shuffle back to sit against the wall by the door, watching the two of them. My vision was still slightly blurry after banging my head on the hard tarmac road, and the panic was rising in my throat again. It escalated as Celine slid gracefully to the floor and crawled towards me on hands and knees, her wolf eyes amber, her body still beautifully human. She was dressed in skin-tight black jeans and a very tightly fitted black and white sweater, trendy and chic. She was even wearing black spike-heel boots, which I could never even have contemplated walking in, let alone running.

Seamus mirrored her movements, looking for all the world like the proverbial wolf in human clothing. His casual clothes seemed totally appropriate and yet totally wrong all at the same time. I stiffened as they both put their faces in front of mine and gently sniffed my skin. Celine leaned closer and gently licked a wet line up my cheek, sending shudders of revulsion through my body. I jumped as Seamus once again laid a hand on me. This time I struggled to my feet, not wanting to be on the floor. I tried desperately to block out the pains. I backed up as the two of them stood slowly, enjoying the moment.

I remembered my mobile phone, and tried to find it in my pocket. I could phone Jack, tell him where I was. But the phone was gone, and I jumped as something passed me in a blur of movement. I cried out in pain as Celine grabbed me, and twisted my arms behind my back, holding me against her. She nuzzled her face against mine, and the sickly smell of her floral perfume nauseated me.

"What shall we do with her, Master?" she asked Seamus.

Again she licked my cheek, and I shuddered, wanting desperately to escape but trapped in her strong arms. I was aware of her pressing her body against me, and I realized that she was enjoying this. She was getting some sort of kick from it. I didn't even know basic self-defence, and cursed myself for never bothering to go to the gym. Now I was weak, especially when faced with two powerful werewolves.

Seamus walked slowly across the room to us, a thoughtful expression on his handsome, arrogant face. My arms were hurting from Celine's painful grasp, but I would not cry out. I would not let them see my pain. Seamus stopped in front of me, and spoke in that strange, growling voice with the broad Irish accent.

"What shall we do indeed, my love?" he replied lazily.

He smiled, but it was sinister. He touched my cheek with his fingertips, tracing the line of my face down to my neck. Then his expression grew harsh and he tilted my head to the side, looking at Jack's bite mark.

"The vampire has marked you," he said in a harsh voice, "So you truly are his blood-whore. Have you tasted the wolf yet, or are you saving him until last?"

I swallowed, not sure whether to reply, or even what to say. Seamus stepped even closer, so I could smell his aftershave, which was actually quite pleasant but would now forever remind me of fear and pain. He inhaled deeply, and exhaled, in a totally inhuman mannerism. I realized he was taking in my scent, sniffing me like a dog would. He opened his eyes and they were glowing amber, large and round. He smiled.

"The wolf has not taken you yet." he said, "You smell of vampires and sex. And not just the Mason vampire," he added, "I smell another one, very powerful. So you like the undead?"

He shook his head, and then continued.

"The wolves can offer you life, power and heat, yet you choose death, and the cold, calculating lies that they offer." he said.

I tensed, my body rigid as he touched me again, this time moving his hands down my chest, over my breasts but on top of my clothes. I was painfully aware of Celine pressing her body against me, nuzzling her face into my neck, sniffing me in much the same way as Seamus had. She was still holding me tight so there was no way of escape. I fought to remain calm. I had to distract them, but how? I tried to speak.

"I don't know what you are talking about." I said, "Jack is my partner, we are a couple. I am not his 'blood-whore,' whatever that means. He needed food and I offered it. That is what humans do for vampires isn't it?"

Seamus' arrogant expression suddenly turned harsh and feral, and my heart pounded as fear coursed through me again. I thought he would hit me, and I braced myself for the impact. Celine spoke in an excited voice, barely discernible through her thick accent and the inhuman growl.

"She is frightened, Master," she said gleefully, "she smells delicious! Please let us play."

He smiled cruelly, and I jumped as he groped me roughly.

"Well," he said, "we have time to kill before the exchange this evening. We should have a little fun. She should experience what we wolves can offer, not her precious vampire."

No! I could not allow him to rape me. I had to fight, but how?

A thought struck me, and I tried desperately to make him talk, to distract them both from their games.

"Where is LuAnn, your other mate?" I asked innocently, "She was there earlier wasn't she?"

His expression changed, became serious and angry. I felt Celine stiffen against me and Seamus answered.

"They shot her," he said, "and took her, your precious wolves. They have gained more power. I thought we had finally dispatched of Danny Mason, and that we could claim the Redcliffe pack, but we underestimated him."

Then he put his face close to mine.

"LuAnn told you to pass a message on yesterday, and you failed." he hissed, "Danny Mason brought his brother to our meeting place. That was not part of the deal. You must be punished."

Panic coursed through me. Was it only yesterday when they had come into my shop? It seemed like a lifetime ago. I fought to remain calm as I replied.

"I did not fail." I said coldly, "I gave Danny your message. Did you really expect him to see you alone, all three of you? What is this exchange tonight?"

Seamus seemed to relax slightly and stepped back again. My arms were really hurting now and I desperately needed Celine to release me. But of course she wouldn't. Seamus spoke again.

"Tonight, after nightfall, we will return to the wolves lair." he said, "That is where they have taken LuAnn. We will exchange hostages, and then I will fight Danny Mason for leadership of the Redcliffe pack."

His voice rose, as he grew excited.

"And I will defeat him, and his interfering freak of a brother. And you, and all of his wolves, will be mine, under my control."

Celine shifted against me again, and spoke in a seductive voice.

"Please, Master, let us play," she pleaded, "The afternoon is long, and we will teach them a lesson if we corrupt their innocent human."

She terrified me. What did she mean by 'play?' I had a good idea of what she meant. The way she pressed her body against me and nuzzled my face was way too close for comfort. I didn't know if it was a wolf thing or if she was gay or bisexual. All I knew was I had to stop this. They could not rape me. I could not let that happen.

Suddenly I felt a cool wave of calm wash over me. I heard Lillian in my head, her voice calm and reassuring, soothing me.

"Do not fear, child," she said, "I will deal with them. They will not harm you here."

I closed my eyes, aware of a cool breeze in the room. Celine stiffened against me, and then she stepped back, apparently confused. She hissed and growled.

"What is that?" she asked, "What are you doing?"

I opened my eyes, feeling cool, calm and collected again. My pains had dulled, and I had my arms back at my sides, mine to control. Seamus stood before me, a confused expression on his face. Lillian spoke again in my head.

"I will speak with them," she said, "Relax, my child, and allow me to step in." I did as she asked. I took a deep breath and let it out slowly, feeling my body relax. There was a tingling sensation all over me, but it was pleasant. I realized it was power, energy. It was my energy. It was the witch energy that my mother had told me about. I had finally unlocked it! I felt her shadow step into my body, and I drew myself up to stand proud before Seamus, staring into his amber eyes. Lillian spoke with my voice, using my body, and I allowed her to.

"Seamus Tully," I said, "you will leave Jessica alone. She is not yours to take, and certainly not yours to corrupt. Play games with your own pack, with your willing victims. Do not play games with Jessica. She belongs to the vampire, not to you. And I will see that you are killed if you so much as touch her improperly again."

I was aware of Seamus. It was as if I was watching from within my body, but Lillian was beside me, just not physically. I could not explain it. But I felt stronger, reassured with her presence. She would protect me. Seamus spoke in a formal tone, no longer mocking.

"Who are you?" he asked, "What are you?"

He sniffed deeply again, and Celine moved slowly to stand beside him, mirroring his actions. Then he snarled.

"You are a witch," he said, "So that's why they wanted you. You are not human at all."

And he slowly turned away, apparently in disgust. Celine followed him, and they both sat on the bed, staring at me with large wolf eyes. I was aware of Lillian stepping back again, and she spoke once again in my head.

"You are safe for now, my child," she said, "They will leave you unharmed, and tonight they will return you to the wolves' lair as promised. Please try not to worry too much. I am still here if you call."

Then I felt her leave my body, and I physically slumped, weakened after the efforts. My pains flared back to life, reminding me that I was human, and I staggered back to sit in the upholstered armchair that was by the window. Seamus stared at me, then shook his head and turned to Celine without a word.

"She will not play, my love," he said, "No matter, we have each other."

And he embraced her, crushing his lips to hers, taking her in his arms as though I wasn't there watching.

Somewhere in my befuddled mind I realized what had happened. They had wanted to 'play' with me. I had started out as prey, but they underestimated my abilities. I underestimated my abilities. And Lillian, my mother, had saved me from being raped and humiliated. I possessed my own power, my own energy, and suddenly I was excited.

Silently I cheered to myself with this little victory. It seemed as though Seamus and Celine would leave me alone for now, which gave me time to think about my situation and how to get out of it. But my injured body protested. I was still human, no matter what witch abilities I had hidden within. I ached all over, the burning sensation was still strong in my chest, my arms hurt from Celine's rough handling, my head hurt, and my knee hurt. I wanted nothing more than to curl up and sleep.

I fought the tiredness, not wanting to be unconscious in this room, but finally I succumbed and slumped back in the chair. My last conscious memory was of Seamus and Celine writhing on the bed together, snarling and growling, and moaning with half-human, half-animal voices, as they pleasured each other, ignoring me.

We were on the beach, Lillian and I. This time we stood facing each other, and the sun was beating down on us. I felt no pain, no injuries. She stood before me smiling gently, but her eyes were sad.

"I am so sorry about all of this, Jessica," she said gently, "There is only so much I can do to keep you safe. Thank you for trusting me, for allowing me access to your physical body."

I shook my head, hugging my arms around myself.

"I don't understand," I said, "How did you do that? Are you a ghost? You saved me from being raped."

There were tears on my cheeks. Lillian nodded.

"I am Spirit," she said, "I can manifest as a ghostly entity but only on occasion. It takes a lot of energy, so I must use it wisely. It was the same when I inhabited your body, possessing you if you like. I needed your trust in order to do that."

"How come you never did any of this before?" I asked, "I needed you for all those years, and you weren't there, you were dead."

Her expression was gentle, but the sadness was evident.

"I could not speak to you until you were ready to accept me, Jessica," she said, "You know nothing about our world, or at least you didn't until recently. There is much to learn, and Jack Mason can educate you. But for now you are still in danger. There is more to come, and I cannot protect you. I will not allow you to die. Your time on the Earth Plane is not over yet; you have much to accomplish. Please trust that I will do what is necessary to keep your human body alive. The pain you must deal with yourself; it is part of your great lesson."

I panicked as she stepped back and the sun faded around us.

"No!" I cried, "Lillian, come back! Please, tell me more. What danger? What will I have to deal with? No!"

I fell to my knees on the sand, crying, and fighting to keep the dream alive, to bring her back. But she was gone, and everything faded into blackness.

I woke suddenly in a panic when someone yanked my arm, dragging me to my feet. I cried out in pain and tried to lift my aching head, and saw Celine standing in front of me scowling. She was dressed again, and her expression was harsh, full of hatred. I pulled my arm back and glared at her defiantly, forcing myself to stand straight and hide the pain, and she laughed.

Seamus walked into the room from what I guessed must be the en suite bathroom. He was buttoning up his shirt, and when he spoke his voice held that rich, deep growl that made me shiver with instinctive fear.

"Leave her be, Celine," he said roughly, "I promised to return her safely and we must rescue LuAnn."

Celine stopped laughing and stepped away from me, looking subdued. Seamus stopped before me, staring at my face with interest, putting his fingers under my chin and lifting my face so that I could see those wolf eyes of his.

His voice was dangerous, gruff.

"We are going to walk out of this hotel like three friends out for a walk, understand?" he said.

I swallowed nervously and nodded once. Seamus continued.

"If you try to get the attention of anyone that we pass I will kill them, and any who interfere, and then I will kill you in front of your precious vampire. Do you believe me?"

His voice was rising as he spoke, the growl more pronounced, less human with every word, and I felt the fear chill my body, my nerves on edge. Again I swallowed and tried to speak, but my voice came out hoarse and nervous.

"Yes, I understand," I said, "I will not say a word."

He abruptly let go of me so that I staggered and almost fell back onto the chair, grabbing the arm for support, catching my breath and trying not to cry. I quickly gathered myself. I would be safe. Lillian was protecting me. She said trust the Mason brothers. They would defeat this enemy. I believed her implicitly.

Seamus led us out onto the landing, with me in the middle and Celine right behind, close enough to grab me if I tried to run. Truthfully I knew there was no escape. I was a human and they were werewolves, and I was also injured. Escape was not an option. Besides I truly believed that Seamus would kill more innocent people and at least now I knew we were going to meet Jack and Danny. I knew that it wouldn't be quite so easy but they were all I had, and I had no choice but to trust that they would save me from these monsters.

I had tried to smooth down my torn and tattered clothes to try and avoid attracting unwanted attention. I could feel a bruise forming on my cheek from where I had been hit so I ducked my head, allowing my hair to obscure my face. The shirt was torn at the hem and covered in patches of dust and mud but I had brushed the worst of it off, and my jeans were undamaged once I had dusted them down. I concentrated on walking steadily, ignoring the nausea in the pit of my stomach, and followed Seamus out into the hotel car park.

He led us to a sleek, silver Mercedes, very similar to the one Marcus used. It was not exactly the kind of car I had imagined he would drive. But then what car would a psychopathic, mafia werewolf drive? The whole idea seemed so bizarre I smiled to myself, and then quickly hid my expression in case they saw it. I did not want to be hit again. The car had tinted windows and Seamus bundled me roughly into the back seat. I suppressed my instinctive reaction to answer back, and carefully fastened my seatbelt. Seamus slid into the driver's seat with Celine next to him, and we set off. The scenery outside the windows was just so normal my heart ached as I looked out.

We drove down a familiar road towards Redcliffe town centre, approaching the harbour end. I could see the coastline on one side, fields and forests on the other. Did the wolves hunt among those trees? They must do. There was nowhere else I could think of where they could go and not be seen by humans. The sun was setting, glittering on the beautiful blue sea, casting a warm glow to the bay.

There were families and groups of friends on the beach, trouping back to their holiday apartments after a day spent building sandcastles, paddling and sunbathing. Other people were out walking without a care in the world, perhaps heading to the restaurants and pubs, or maybe the amusement arcades and fairground. I choked back the tears which reminded me that I been brutally ripped away from normal life and what lay ahead was bleak and confusing.

38

I was jolted from my reverie when we pulled up on the car park for the Ship. What were we doing here? Oh yes, it was the wolves' lair, how could I forget. My heart lurched as I dared to feel slight relief; at least I was in a familiar place. Seamus appeared beside the passenger door, opened it and dragged me roughly out so that I stumbled against the car. He kept a tight grip on my arm and I was sure it would leave a bruise.

Celine was beside him watching me closely. There was no way I could run from them. The streetlights had not yet switched on, so the car park was dark and strangely quiet. Having said that, most people would walk to the pub at this time of night, and I could hear the sounds of people in the beer garden, and I smelt the delicious scent of home-cooked food. I hadn't eaten all day, and it looked like I wasn't going to. Maybe that was why I felt so faint and why I struggled to stand up. My captors didn't notice this of course.

Seamus led us towards the rear of the building and the entrance via the decked smoking area that overlooked the beach. My heart ached to be sat in that beer garden enjoying a hearty meal, with the people I cared about. Seamus kept a rough grip on my arm and I tripped and jerked as I tried to keep up with his movement. Celine followed faithfully behind her Master. We went inside and it was cool and familiar in the hallway leading to the main bar area at the front, although the food and beer smells mingled and made me feel nauseas.

I realized I was terrified of what was about to happen, remembering Lillian's warning. But I had to let events unfold naturally, it was meant to be this way. Nobody in the beer garden had looked twice at us, and I wondered idly if anyone even saw the huge bruise that I felt swelling across my face, or if they saw my unhappy expression. We saw no customers in the hallway; they were all outside or in the bar and restaurant, and all I heard was the clink of glasses and crockery, the sounds of people laughing and talking as they enjoyed themselves.

My heart flipped as I saw Simon standing in the corridor. His face was serious, body taught. There were no guns, no shoulder holster; he was simply dressed in his black t-shirt and jeans. Perhaps they were doing things in some formal wolf-ritual. Simon looked at all three of us but focused on my face as he spoke.

"Are you alright, Jessica?" he asked.

Before I could speak Seamus yanked my arm and snarled at Simon.

"She is unharmed, as you can see." he growled, "Now take us to your Master and your precious human will be released."

Simon nodded once then turned and opened a door marked 'Private: Staff Only' which I knew led into the cellar. We followed him down the wooden stairs, Seamus holding me just slightly in front of him and Celine bringing up the rear. She carefully closed the door behind her.

Simon walked smoothly across the large room, past the store shelves full of bottles, packets and boxes of stock, and he led us to a heavy wooden door set in the back wall. This part of the cellar was dark and smelled musty and old. My heart was racing, blood pounding in my ears, as Simon opened the door and we followed him into a dimly lit corridor beyond. Again Celine closed the door behind us; I guessed that she didn't want other humans being involved after all.

I looked around me as we walked and saw that the lighting was electric if very basic; there appeared to be individual light bulbs strung across the stone wall high up, sort of like oversized Christmas tree lights. The floor was stone and earth and I sensed that we were moving deeper into the cliff face. These must be the ancient tunnels that were rumoured to be hidden beneath the town. I had heard stories of how these caves had been used by smugglers and pirates hundreds of years ago, and then by Black Market traders during the World Wars.

The corridor ended in a large square room with bare stone walls and more of the large light bulbs. The lighting seemed focused towards the middle of the room leaving lots of dark shadows around the perimeter. There were what looked like two huge animal cages in one corner and I shivered, not wanting to know what they were used for. This whole place reminded me of a dungeon and I didn't like it. I half-expected to see chains and manacles attached to the walls, but I refused to look, not wanting to see if it was true. Simon strode ahead of us to stand beside Danny. I almost ran towards him but Seamus' grip tightened on me and I bit my lip to stop from crying out. We stopped in the middle of the room.

Danny was stood with LuAnn on her knees in front of him, her hands tied behind her back and blood drying on her face. There were bloodstains on her white t-shirt, and I realized with a shock that she had been shot at least twice in her upper body. Yet she seemed angry, and not seriously hurt. Her expression was defiant and angry but she looked up at Seamus with some other emotion and I realized it was love for her partner, her mate.

Simon stood to Danny's left side, Sally to his right and I was afraid of the sheer power that seemed to flow from all three of them. Again it was stifling, like in Marcus' kitchen that morning, and I slowly became aware of other people in the room with us. They must be Danny's wolves, the Redcliffe pack. I wondered if I knew any of them, and who they might be.

My attention turned back to the important people in the room. I reminded myself that these were my friends and I trusted them to protect me. Lillian's voice echoed in my head once again.

"Heed my warning;" she said, "be prepared my child."

I nodded, and then stopped myself, not wanting to draw unwanted attention my way. Danny broke the tense silence, his voice rough, strong, and powerful, with a hint of growl.

"Seamus Tully," he said, "I admit you into the lair of The Redcliffe Pack. You will release the human as she is of no concern to our business and us. Your grievance is with me, Pack Leader. You may challenge me if you wish. I will protect my people to the death."

Seamus nodded and answered in an equally serious, gruff voice.

"Danny Mason of The Redcliffe Pack," he said, "I accept your hospitality. You will release my Mate and your human will be safe. I formally challenge you for leadership of this great and powerful pack."

Everyone was silent, watching the two men, and as I dared to glance around, I saw the people stood around the edge of the room, the Redcliffe wolves. I vaguely recognized a few of them as bar staff, and they all seemed to fidget and shuffle anxiously, awaiting the fight.

Where was Jack? He must be here somewhere. A voice in my head reminded me that this was the wolves' lair and vampires weren't welcome. It wasn't Lillian's voice, it was Jack, and I knew it. He was here, somewhere, both for me and for his brother, and he would appear when the time was right. I realized I was shivering violently, my body going into shock. It took all my concentration to remain calm and in control, trying not to attract any more unwanted attention.

Danny nodded to Simon who stepped forward and released LuAnn from her shackles. She stood slowly and moved over to us, standing beside Seamus, stretching her body and flexing her muscles. He kissed her on the lips, and she responded, pressing her body against him, then embracing Celine in the same way. She welcomed her hungrily. Danny spoke.

"Now you will release the human," he said.

I tried to step forward but Seamus suddenly grabbed me, wrapping an arm across my neck and holding me tight against his body, straining my back and legs. I cried out and then gasped as he put pressure on my throat, restricting my breathing. As he did this I heard Simon call my name but Danny held him back and stepped forward himself.

"Let her go, Seamus," he roared, "She is of no use to you now. Your battle is with me."

Seamus spoke in a snarl.

"Oh no Mason," he replied, "I know she means something to you. And to your brother and your Lieutenant it seems."

He suddenly yanked my head to one side, exposing the bite marks that Jack had given me that morning, and I cried out again.

"Please, let me go." I whimpered.

My heart was racing, I was struggling to breathe, and I could feel the adrenaline pumping through my body as it tried to decide whether to panic or fight. In my mind I called for Lillian to help, please help, like she had done earlier. But her voice drifted through my head like a faint breeze, weak and exhausted.

"I am so sorry, my child," she said, "I am weak. I can no longer help you here. You must make your own escape, and accept help from the wolves."

Seamus laughed and licked my neck in a long, wet line, making me shiver with fear, sickness rising in my gut. He spoke again with his mouth hovering over my skin and the neat bite mark.

"Mmm she smells delicious," he said, "so delicate, and so juicy. Have you not tasted her Mason? Your brother certainly has. Your power must not be as strong as it once was. Why I seem to recall my female wolves falling all over you when you first joined our pack."

He laughed and I struggled, trying to escape. Seamus held me easily in his strong arms, and I only made things worse. I stopped struggling, trying to formulate a plan, to distract him somehow. I couldn't see what Danny and Simon were doing, but I sensed movement around me as Celine and LuAnn prepared for battle. Seamus looked at Danny with a sinister grin.

"You know she is a witch, Mason," he said, "I believe that is why your brother wants her so badly. We cannot have her sharing her powers with a vampire, now can we?

She does not deserve to be the vampire's blood whore!"

And with that he struck, baring his teeth and tearing at my neck.

I heard Jack scream my name in rage and pain and anger. He flew down from somewhere high up, throwing himself at Seamus, but the damage was done. I screamed as my skin tore, blood poured out and down my body. The cave was suddenly alive with movement, screaming people as they transformed into wolves, howls and growls, and a man's voice shouting, "Jessica! No!" It was Jack, I just knew.

Seamus released me just before Jack hit him, and I crumpled and fell to the floor, barely feeling it as I hit the cold stone. I was aware of Seamus and Jack struggling, heard Seamus shout.

"Leave me, vampire, it is your brother's life I want!" he snarled.

Through half-closed eyes I saw Seamus leaping towards Danny, with Jack right behind him. Simon and Sally were fighting with LuAnn and Celine. I heard screams, cries, wolf howls, more bodies moving around, thuds and the sounds of people and animals impacting against the walls and floor.

I was clutching my wounds, and barely managed to pull off my shirt, roll it up, and hold it against my neck to try and stop the blood flow. I tried to stay on hands and knees, knowing I couldn't stand up, and watched in horror as Danny and Seamus transformed into huge, terrifying beasts. I couldn't see Simon, or Sally, but I saw Jack wrestling with another wolf.

There were beasts everywhere and I was terrified. I saw the wolves that were Danny and Seamus rear up. Seamus' fur was grey; Danny's was more silver, streaked with black. Seamus struck at Danny's throat, and Jack was suddenly there on his back, but Seamus flung him off, sending him hurtling into the stone wall with a horrendous crack of rough stone.

My vision was fading, my shirt soaked with blood. I

couldn't stay conscious, even though I fought. I saw Danny strike at Seamus, tearing his throat out in a spray of blood and thicker things. The larger wolf fell to the floor, motionless, and I heard the high-pitched screams of two women in wolf form somewhere in the room. One was silenced, and then the other. I didn't know if they were dead. The blood loss took its toll, my vision faded completely, along with my consciousness, and I blacked out.

"She is dying, Jack," a male voice said, "You must save her."

I groaned, tried to open my eyes and sit up but I couldn't move; everything was faint and blurry. My head hurt so badly I just wanted to sleep, but the pain was intense and I whimpered, not even strong enough to cry out or scream. My body felt heavy and damp, and while I struggled to move my arms and legs, nothing happened. Everything hurt.

I was pulled into someone's lap but I could barely tell whom. I think it was Danny, was vaguely aware of naked flesh streaked with blood and dirt. Someone gently pulled my hair away from my neck, and I felt coolness as they removed my blood-soaked shirt, inspecting the wound. I fluttered my eyelids trying to open them and focus.

Through half-closed eyes I saw Sally in front of me, kneeling on the dirt floor. She was naked but it barely registered in my befuddled brain. Her voice seemed to echo, and was distant to me.

"Jessica, can you hear me?" she asked.

I tried to speak but failed and all that came out was a faint whimpering noise. My throat was dry, and there was a pressure on my neck that made it impossible for me to speak. Then I heard Jack's voice above me, low and urgent, but calm.

"Jessica, its Jack," he said, "I will try to help you and we'll get you to a hospital."

I tried to nod, whimpered again, closed my eyes and waited for the blackness to envelope me. Perhaps it was my time to die…but if course it wasn't, and as I felt my body lifted into strong arms, carried through the corridors back into the pub, Lillian came back to me, speaking in my dulled mind.

"I will not allow you to die, my child," she said, "It is not your time. Sleep now, they will take care of you."

I relaxed into Jack's arms, the pains growing fainter, and blackness warm and comforting. I fell asleep.

39

I woke slowly, lying in a hospital bed. I could hear the familiar sound of people moving around talking quietly, and I could sense the bright lights even though my eyes were closed. I didn't want to open my eyes because the light would hurt. Then I heard the steady 'beep, beep, beep' of a machine next to my bed and I did open my eyes, but it took a lot of effort and I felt so weak.

As the room slowly swam into focus I saw Jack sat in a chair beside the bed, and he sat bolt upright as he watched me wake up.

"Jessica," he said, "Can you see me? Do you remember what happened?"

I attempted to smile and tried to speak, but there was a tube in my throat and I gagged, panicking. The beeping noise on the machine beside me increased, and Jack was leaning over me.

"Don't try to move," he said, "I'll get a doctor."

He jumped up and hurried away. I tried to move my head and look around but I was attached to all sorts of machines. There was the tube in my throat attached to something over my left shoulder, which I couldn't see. There was an IV in my left arm, and then the bleeping machine to my right, which I guessed, must be some sort of heart monitor. I had only ever seen these things on the TV before. My body felt strangely numb. I could feel my limbs though, and I tentatively wiggled my toes and fingers to remind me that it all still worked, but I felt groggy and lethargic. What had happened to me? I needed to remember.

Jack came back to the bed with a female doctor and a nurse. She smiled at me and spoke gently.

"Hello, Jessica," she said, "I am Doctor Warner, this is Nurse Jameson. We will remove the tube from your throat and then you can try to speak, is that alright?"

I nodded once, struggling to move my head. I lifted my right arm and felt a large padded bandage on my neck; almost like a surgical collar it was so big.

I closed my eyes as the memories flooded back, my heart sinking. It was all true. It wasn't just a nightmare. It was real. They were real, all of them, the monsters.

The nurse gently helped me into a more upright position and removed the breathing tube, helping me to take a few sips of ice-cold water. It had never tasted so good. They moved Jack out into the ward and pulled the curtain round my bed, checked my responses, and did something with the machines, then the nurse left and Doctor Warner sat on the chair beside me. She was an older woman, and her presence was safe, comforting, and reassuring. She spoke gently, her voice soft.

"Jessica," she said, "I am not sure what you remember happened to you, but you were admitted last night at around nine o'clock, with a severe stab wound to your neck. Detective Mason brought you in, he said you had witnessed something and been caught in the crossfire so to speak. Now I know he will need to question you but please try to get some rest; you are very badly hurt and I cannot risk anything upsetting you further. Do you understand?"

I swallowed as I thought about my reply. My throat was really sore. So Jack told people I had been stabbed then. When I spoke my voice was quiet and croaky from the effects of the tube. It took two attempts before I could speak coherently. Doctor Warner sat patiently, smiling gently.

"I do remember what happened," I said slowly, "Did I nearly die? Did you have to operate?"

The doctor nodded but her face was blank, professional.

"You are in the Intensive Care Unit Jessica," she said gently, "There were some complications but I am very pleased that you have woken so soon and that you seem to have retained coherent thought and brain function. I will however keep you on the heart monitor for a while longer until I am sure your body is strong enough to help itself. Do you have any family that we could call?"

LOVE HURTS

She didn't seem to know that Jack was my boyfriend and I realized I couldn't say too much until I had spoken to him.

"No I don't have any family to contact," I said, "There's just my friend Elizabeth Gormond. Can you phone her for me please? She'll be worried."

The doctor nodded and I recited Elizabeth's mobile number to her, and the one for our shop, hoping that was where she would be. I had no idea what time of day it was. The doctor seemed pleased that I could remember these numbers. Then I felt weak again and sank back against the cool, crisp pillows.

"Please could Detective Mason come back in?" I asked.

She nodded but seemed reluctant.

"Very well," she said, "but I don't want him asking you questions that will upset you. Please try to remain calm. We have repaired your neck wound as well as we can but the tissue damage is quite extensive and will take some time to heal," she paused, "There is a wound on your stomach that resembles an animal attack; although Detective Mason assures me there was no animal present. You have severe bruising across your upper body, and swelling to your left knee from where you fell. I have you on some strong painkillers and anti-inflammatory drugs at the moment but they will make you drowsy and will affect your coordination."

I nodded. That was why I felt so strange, numb, but like a lead weight at the same time.

Doctor Warner went back out into the ward and a moment later Jack slipped through the curtain and sat on the edge of the bed beside me, taking my right hand in his.

"Jessica, I am so sorry about all of this," he said, "It should never have happened."

He kissed my fingertips and I saw tears in his eyes, but I felt nothing. I knew that was the drugs. Right now I needed to speak, even though it was painful. I took my time, struggling to swallow around the lump in my throat.

"So, why haven't you told the doctor that you are my boyfriend?" I asked.

His expression was blank suddenly, and I realised this

was his professional persona. He spoke quietly, his tone bland and unemotional.

"It didn't come up," he said, "It was easier to explain that you were an injured civilian; they ask fewer questions that way. Otherwise I would have had to return during visiting hours. For now the doctors think I am here to follow up my investigation, so I can use my authority and spend more time here."

"Ok," I said, "so what do we say happened? The doctor says I have a severe knife wound in my neck; now I know that isn't true."

His expression was sad and serious, and I saw a trace of guilt in his eyes. He spoke in a voice that was now subdued, definitely more personal and intimate suddenly.

"You remember everything, Jessica?" he asked.

I nodded, struggling to manage even that slight movement around the restrictive bandage and all of my wounds.

"I remember what Seamus did, yes," I said, "Is he dead? Is everyone else alright?"

Jack slowly released my hand and I lowered it to the bed. He looked at me with a serious expression on his tanned face, his blue eyes so earnest.

"Yes Seamus is dead," he said, "Danny defeated him and saved the pack. LuAnn is also dead, killed in combat by Simon. They have Celine in confinement in the lair until we decide what to do with her. Simon and Sally were injured but have both recovered now."

I processed the information with my befuddled brain and then asked Jack how he persuaded the doctors that I was stabbed. He explained that he had used some of his mind control but that it wouldn't affect my treatment. The surgeons had attempted to stitch my wound but it was too large, so they repaired as much of the damaged tissue as possible and then covered it with the bandage. Some of my medication was designed to help the skin heal itself and stop me moving around too much and disturbing it. After a short while I felt incredibly sleepy again and was vaguely aware of Jack kissing my forehead as I fell into a deep, dreamless, drug-induced sleep.

40

When I woke again Jack was gone and the curtain had been pulled back, I guessed so the nurses could keep an eye on me from their desk at the top end of the ward. It must have been late in the evening because the lights were dimmed and everyone around me seemed to be asleep. Or were they just unconscious, in a coma? I turned my head as best I could to see where the window was but the blinds were drawn. What I could see around the edges was dark. My head felt heavy, vaguely aching but I just felt like I was in a dream. Nothing seemed real around me. Was this all some crazy nightmare? Was I about to wake up in my own bed at home having just imagined this whole tale about supernatural creatures and being captured? I heard Lillian in my head again.

"It is not a dream," she said, "Everything is true Jessica, and your ordeal is over. Now you must allow your body to heal, so that you can move on and discover your own abilities, and your true purpose."

A nurse approached the bed and I recognized Sally smiling at me. She looked completely different to her bodyguard persona of yesterday. She was warm and friendly, reassuring, dressed in her pale blue uniform, hair pinned back in a neat bun, her face clean and innocent, unblemished.

"Hi, Jessica," she said, "How are you feeling?"

She pulled the curtain round the cubicle and checked my machines and vitals, then sat on the bed beside me. I managed to speak but my throat was incredibly dry and my voice was hoarse.

"I feel like crap," I murmured, "Could you get me some water please?"

Sally nodded and picked up a jug and glass from the bedside cabinet, poured the drink, and then gently held the glass to my mouth. After I had taken a few careful sips I lay still as I felt the water slide down my throat and Sally sat quietly waiting for me to speak. She looked the picture of good health, not a scratch on her. I had to ask. "Am I dreaming?" I said, "This is all so bizarre. Jack said you were hurt but you look fine."

"No you are not dreaming, Jessica," Sally said, "I know it is crazy. When I first found out about werewolves and vampires I felt like it was some kind of nightmare. But it is real. Yes I was injured during the fight but I am strong and have healed completely. This is my first shift back at work and I managed to swap with another nurse so I could look after you. I am so sorry you had to get involved."

She then told me that it was 10:30pm and Jack had stayed by my bed until the ward sister sent him home. The human staff still didn't know that I was his girlfriend but he was using his professional influence to spend as much time as possible with me. He had told everyone that I was a very important witness and needed protection while in hospital. I was confused as to why he wouldn't tell the truth about us, but Sally explained that the doctors would see that as a conflict of professional interest and they might involve more police, which could complicate the whole situation. For now she asked me to please go along with the story, try to be vague when questioned, and just concentrate on healing enough to go home.

I asked what had happened to Seamus and LuAnn's bodies. For some reason I needed to know that all the loose ends had been tied up, I don't know why. Sally went quiet and tried to evade the question, but eventually she told me that the wolves ate the remains. Apparently it was some sort of pack ritual, a form of taking into themselves the memories of their fallen enemies. They also did this with any of their own pack that died. I shivered as I thought about it, as I imagined Sally in wolf form, eating a human body. It was too much; I had to ignore it for now. She was my friend and a nurse and right now I just had to heal. Gradually the drugs took over again and I drifted off into sleep, once again dreamless thanks to my medication.

When I woke again it was still quiet and dark in the ward. I could hear the low-level murmur of the two nurses talking at their desk, and the constant beeping of the machines around me and the other three patients in the room. I felt suddenly restless, wanting to get up and move around, but I knew that was impossible. My body was in no fit state to move anywhere, especially while I was hooked up to all sorts of machines and drips.

I closed my eyes and let out a sigh, wondering what was going to happen now. My mind refused to focus completely so everything seemed a little hazy, but I knew that my life had changed completely, and now I had to relearn who my friends were. I breathed out deeply and slowly opened my eyes again, then jumped as I saw Marcus sat in the plastic chair beside my bed. I managed to keep my voice quiet, not wanting to draw attention, and even though my heart was racing the machine hadn't seemed to pick it up.

"Marcus," I whispered, "What are you doing here? It's the middle of the night, how did you get past the nurses?"

He smiled gently and replied.

"Hello, Jessica," he said, "You forget I have the ability to slip in and out of places unnoticed. I came at this time because they wouldn't admit me during human visiting hours. You are only allowed to receive close friends and family in the high dependency unit due to the severity of your condition."

I hadn't really thought about that. The doctors and nurses kept reminding me that I was badly hurt, even though they refused to admit that I had almost died, apparently not wanting to upset me further. I just wanted to go home as soon as possible. I looked at Marcus again, feeling that rush of shame when I remembered what we had done together. He smiled.

"Do not feel shame, Jessica," he said, "You and I are friends, and I came to see you because I care, and because I had to see for myself that you really were all right. Jack and Danny told me what happened. I have visited the Ship and spoken to some of the wolves, and by all accounts it was a very vicious fight. But it is over now, and we can all move on, and you can heal and take the rest and recuperation that you need."

He stayed with me for an hour, telling me it was around 3:00am. I was surprised when the nurses walked round the ward to do their routine checks, and were completely oblivious to Marcus sat silently on the chair beside me. He must have influenced their minds somehow to make himself seem invisible; it was incredible.

I wondered where Sally was, and guessed that she had been called away to deal with another patient. The nurse who checked me seemed surprised that I was awake, and she gently said I should try and sleep; it was the best thing for me at the moment. I agreed and waited for her to leave so I could talk to Marcus.

He told me that after witnessing our fight, the Redcliffe wolves were finally prepared to accept their true Master back into the pack, and Danny had reinstated his superior position. Up until that point the wolves had treated Simon as their leader, believing that Danny had abandoned them. But now he was strong again, and would be spending more time with his wolves to strengthen the pack and bring everyone closer together.

I asked about Jack, and Marcus, and what exactly their position was in this strange new world. Marcus explained that vampires were generally solitary, and that he had also spent some time away from Redcliffe recently, but now he wanted to renew his friendship with Jack and Danny, and to help me adjust to this new society. Apparently he and Jack were very powerful vampires, and held in high esteem by younger, weaker vampires who met them. They had their allies in different places, but simply moved about in human society, leading normal lives. Finally my head hurt too much, and I knew I needed to sleep again. I was vaguely aware of Marcus leaning forward to gently kiss my forehead with cool lips as I drifted off into deep, dark sleep once again, the powerful drugs working hard within my body.

41

I awoke to a bustling ward, and movement around a bed opposite mine. The doctors must have admitted another patient; I could hear more bleeping machines and a doctor giving orders to the nurses. It occurred to me that I hadn't really thought to see who the other patients were in this ward. I had just vaguely registered that they were there, and automatically assumed they were in a worse state than me, because none of them seemed to have regained consciousness since I had been awake.

I turned my head slowly to the side and saw that there was a man in the bed on my right, apparently unconscious. His chest was rising and falling with the aid of one of those machines that look like a bellows, I think it was an incubator, and I could see scratches and cuts on his face. Maybe he had been in a car accident or something. He looked around Jack's age; well his human age anyway.

I tried to look at the bed on my other side but it was more difficult, there were shooting pains in the left side of my neck, from just under my jaw all the way down to my chest. I cried out without meaning to and the beeping of my heart monitor jumped and suddenly increased as I felt my heart racing, my body twisting as I tried to fight the pain. A doctor rushed over to my bed, a young man with blonde hair.

"Jessica," he said urgently, "Jessica. Please try to calm down."

He held my shoulders and a nurse appeared beside him, trying to soothe me as the doctor did something to the machine and the IV drip. I felt the sensation of something rushing through my veins and the pain eased, my body relaxed.

I closed my eyes for a moment, concentrating on my breathing, and when I opened my eyes I saw the doctor staring at me with serious brown eyes. He was very handsome, and I smiled instinctively. The nurse stepped back and the doctor dismissed her with a polite authoritative tone. Then he turned his attention back to me.

"Hello, Jessica," he said, "How are you feeling now?"

"I'm alright thank you," I said, "Was that pain killers you shot into me?"

He smiled and nodded.

"Yes," he said, "You have been asleep for around twelve hours now; I imagine you are hungry and ready for food."

As if by reply my stomach suddenly rumbled and I tried to nod but was restricted by the bandage.

"Yes, please Doctor that would be great," I said enthusiastically, "Is there any chance of a cup of tea?"

Doctor Arran (as he finally introduced himself) proceeded to check me over again and then handed me over to the nurse with instructions to try me with a cup of tea and some toast. She hurried away and returned with the food, helped me to sit up, and she sat with me while I hesitantly drank and ate.

It was strange; my movements seemed out of sync. When I tried to reach for the mug my hand was above it, then beside it, and eventually I managed to grab the handle but the nurse had to support the mug because I was shaking so much. It was embarrassing.

I had the same problem when I went for the toast; I managed to drop a slice just when I got it to my mouth. The nurse explained that this was a side effect of my medication and that I shouldn't worry. She said I was actually showing very good signs of recovery having only been in the hospital for just over 24 hours.

I asked how long she thought I would be in here, and she smiled gently and said it was impossible to tell at the moment. The usual procedure would be to move me to another ward once my body was able to support itself without the heart monitors and other machines. I didn't want that, I just wanted to go home. I decided to try my best to appear better so that they could simply discharge me. I would far rather rest at home, in familiar surroundings, where I could talk freely to Jack and Danny about everything.

I found out that it was almost midday on Saturday. Everything that had happened seemed light years away but it was all so recent. In the space of two days my whole world had been flipped upside down, and my friends were all strangers to me. But the emotion I expected to feel was dulled, unimportant. My body just needed to heal its wounds, and was taking everything it could from the medication the doctors were giving me.

The nurse brought me a newspaper at my request and I felt a little better after catching up on the local news. For some reason it was important to me to remember that I was human and the world was still the same as it had been on Monday. It took a while for me to focus on the newspaper, and at first the nurse sat with me, not sure if I could actually manage to read. But I forced myself to concentrate, determined to do something for myself.

I managed to stay awake for a few hours and during that time the doctor told me he was very pleased with my progress and that I appeared to be healing quite well considering the damage my body had taken. I was generally a healthy person anyway, and when I asked, the doctor said I could probably be allowed home in a few days' time. First they needed me to stay still so I could heal sufficiently. They told me that both Jack and Elizabeth had visited that morning while I was still asleep. I felt bad that I missed them. Apparently Elizabeth had promised to return during evening visiting hours. I dozed in and out of sleep for a short while, but I became restless, bored and homesick.

The doctors allowed me to get out of bed in the early afternoon and a nurse had to accompany me to the bathroom, which was a very embarrassing experience. She had to unhook me from the machines and practically hold me up because my legs were like jelly, and when I tentatively tried to stand I collapsed and staggered backwards onto the bed.

My left knee in particular was very painful; I could barely put any weight on it. The nurse had offered me a bedpan but I was determined to walk to the bathroom and take care of myself as much as possible. Privately it was more about remembering that I was human but of course I couldn't say this out loud. She was very patient, and I guessed this was everyday work for her, but I absolutely hated being so helpless and weak.

When we got back to my bed after what seemed a mammoth task, the sheets had been changed which was nice, and the nurse brought some soap, water and a flannel to my cubicle and washed me. Again I tried to do it myself but she said she had to work round my bandages. I knew about the one on my neck but it turned out there was also one on my stomach from a large scratch.

What was it Doctor Warner had said? Something about an animal wound? Ah yes, I vaguely remembered Seamus putting pressure on my belly but I never felt him actually put his claws into me. He must have done it when he ripped my neck open, and that took all my attention at the time.

The nurse asked if I remembered where the wound came from because the doctors identified it as being caused by an animal yet Detective Mason had said there were no animals present. I managed to feign innocence and pretended I couldn't remember what happened, allowing my voice to rise a little with pretended hysterics, and the nurse very tactfully changed the subject. I felt much better after she had cleaned me and put me in a fresh gown.

I asked about the possibility of wearing my own clothes if someone fetched them for me but was told that for now I had to stay in the gown. The doctors weren't convinced that I wouldn't have a relapse and need further medical treatment or even more surgery, and the gown gave easier access to my body, to the wounds and all the tubes and monitors I was attached to. The nurse did fetch me a phone so I could call Elizabeth however. I almost cried when she answered the phone and heard my voice. "Jessica," she said, "is that really you? Oh my god what happened, when can I see you?"

I could hear her sobbing and I choked back my own tears and spoke. "Elizabeth, yes it's me," I said, "Calm down, think of the baby."

"I'm sorry," she gasped, "Jack told me what happened, he said you had been stabbed. Oh my god, I thought you were dead!"

She broke down again and then immediately tried to calm herself. I felt such a rush of love for my friend that all I wanted at that moment was her arms around me. She continued talking through her sobs.

"Did the doctors tell you I visited this morning?" she said, "You were asleep. Oh Jessica, whatever happened? You look a right state, and there are machines keeping you alive."

I had to smile at her tragic tone.

"Liz calm down," I said, "Honestly I'm fine. The doctors have pumped me full of drugs, so all the pain is numbed, and I'll be out of here in no time. Well, hopefully."

I felt a pang of sadness, missing my shop suddenly. All I wanted at the moment was to be sat behind the counter with my beloved books and my best friend, drinking coffee and munching biscuits. I had taken it for granted, and now I had learned a hard lesson. I choked back the tears again, and managed to keep the self-pitying tone out of my voice.

"Liz," I asked, "could you do me a favour? Would you mind bringing me some clothes and things to the hospital? The doctors say I'll be here for at least a few more days, so I'm going to need some books or something, it's driving me insane!" She laughed at that, and promised to visit as soon as she closed the shop. She would bring gifts and things to cheer me up.

42

I had been drifting in and out of sleep for a couple of hours after my exertions with the nurse, and even my phone conversation with Liz had left me exhausted. I opened my eyes to find Danny sat beside my bed. He was reclining in the chair, watching my face, and when I opened my eyes he leaned forward and touched my hand.

"Jessica, hi." he said.

He looked perfect, not a scratch on him, his skin glowing, his bright blue eyes sparkling. It wasn't fair! How come I had to end up half dead in a hospital bed and pumped full of drugs?

"Hey, Danny," I said, "What are you doing here? What time is it?"

He smiled.

"It's nice to be welcome," he said in a tone of mock-indignation, "I'm here to see you of course. It's getting on for 6:00pm, why?"

"I feel like I'm in a time warp," I said, "like I've been here for days or weeks. Nothing seems real. And Liz is coming soon with some clothes and things for me."

Danny nodded, seeming to understand, and then spoke in a quiet voice so people around us couldn't hear.

"Sally said you felt like you were in a nightmare," he said, "Unfortunately everything you remember was real. But you are safe now and you are healing. The doctors might even let you go home on Monday."

That was a relief. I really did not like being in here and being helpless. Apparently I was showing excellent signs of recovery, and the doctors were quite surprised at how quickly I was coming round. At the time I simply thought it was because I was a generally healthy person, and because I was so determined to get home. But things are never so straightforward are they?

Danny told me that Jack was busy with a work assignment. He gave me a look when he said this, and emphasized his words. I nodded as I realized it must be a euphemism for vampire business. I said as much, keeping my voice quiet, and Danny nodded.

"Jack wanted to come and see you but I promised to pass the message on," he said, "He's worried that you'll think he doesn't care about you. He does Jessica, and so do I."

My heart flipped and I half expected the machine beside me to go crazy again but it didn't. I went hot all over, trembling, but it wasn't the drugs or my injuries. It was my reaction to what Danny had said. He really cared about me. Of course I already knew this. Even Seamus Tully had seen it during the brief time he knew me.

Up until now I had treated Danny as a friend, nothing more, but the fact that he and Jack were identical was difficult to handle. Now I was suddenly wondering again if he had romantic feelings for me, and what that would mean now I knew the truth about the brothers. I didn't understand yet just how different their attitudes and behaviours would be, and how much this would affect my relationship with both of them.

As if he could read my thoughts Danny let go of my hand and sat back.

"Sorry, Jessica," he said, "I shouldn't be confusing you while you are in this state. Look, when you are allowed home, would you please come and stay with us? You will need someone to take care of you, and Elizabeth has to run the shop. It makes sense."

I waited for my pounding heart to slow and my body to calm down before I spoke, and was pleased that my voice didn't shake.

"Um, yes I suppose I can stay with you," I said slowly, "I'm not sure if it's a good idea though. I know you and Jack mean well but we are all so different, you know what I mean?"

He knew. His expression was tragic as he realized I was trying to say that he and Jack made me nervous now. I wanted everything to be normal but that couldn't be, not for a long while. They were not human and I was, and all I wanted was to try and repair my everyday existence as much as possible. This would be tricky. When Danny left I lost myself in my thoughts.

I remembered everything from the last few days. I thought about Marcus, feeling strangely happy that he had visited me, because I genuinely did feel an attraction to him, and while I knew I should keep away and not encourage it, he was like a drug and I couldn't stop now I had had a taste. I couldn't help but feel shame about sleeping with him, even if Jack had said it didn't matter. It mattered to me. I had betrayed myself with my lack of control.

Then I remembered the sight of Jack feeding from Danny's wound, the shock when I saw Simon and Sally and realized for the first time that they weren't human. I wondered just how many non-humans lived in Redcliffe, and were there just vampires and werewolves, or were there other creatures? I supposed I would find out in time.

I remembered my time with Seamus and Celine. I did not want to face her again. She was evil. Then I thought about Lillian, who seemed to have faded into the background again. Maybe it was all the medication, confusing my psychic link with her. I was confident that she would return in time. Once my body was healed, I could work on the mental scars, and develop my abilities. Liz would be happy to know that I was finally ready to find my lost family.

After another drug-induced sleep into which I drifted from my heavy thoughts, I woke to find Liz beside my bed this time. Her face was anxious and streaked with tears, and when she saw me open my eyes she cried out and almost flung herself at me.

"Jessica," she cried, "You are alright! Well, you are not alright, but you are awake!"

I had to laugh at her confusion. Liz was the one constant in my life. I knew she was human, she was normal, and I could trust her and believe in her implicitly. She tried to hug me awkwardly around all of the machines, drips, and bandages that covered my small frame. Her voice was quiet and sad when she spoke again.

"What happened to you, Jessica?" she asked, "I thought you had stayed at Jack's house. But then you didn't return my text messages, your phone was switched off, and the hospital phoned me. Was it to do with those women who came in to the shop?"

I managed to nod at that, but told Liz that my memory was hazy and the doctors had said it was amnesia induced by the trauma and stress. I felt terrible lying to my best friend like that, and even worse when she believed me, but what else could I do? She would never believe the truth, and it wasn't fair to burden her with it. I was relieved to find that she had brought a bag of clothes and toiletries for me, and also my latest book, a couple of new magazines, and my I-pod. It was good to immerse myself in real life again, and I started to feel better.

I listened to Liz telling me about some of our regular customers from the shop, and some gossip from the hair salon next door. Then she told me how her baby had been moving around in her belly, and I managed to awkwardly reach over and put my hand on her bump, while she stood sort of leaning over my bed. I felt the little kicks through her skin and it was such an amazing sensation I almost starting crying again in my fragile state. Liz promised to visit the next day, and left after more tears, more awkward attempts to hug me, and promises to take care of me while I healed.

The next two days passed in a blur. I was deemed well enough for the machines to be taken away but the doctors wanted to keep a close watch over me. They seemed very surprised by my swift recovery. In fact they told me that it was probably only the medication that was making me drowsy and affecting my coordination. When I asked if I could stop taking it they said no because the pain would most likely be too intense.

Apparently the bite or 'knife wound' on my neck was

very deep and quite ragged and the doctors had been unable to stitch it completely. They wouldn't let me see the wound because it was still raw and might cause me to have an adverse reaction. The doctors were concerned that it might cause me to faint or have a seizure because the sight of it would be too grotesque for my brain to accept. I thought they were making a big fuss about nothing, but I accepted what they told me, knowing that they were the medical experts here. I was bored, anxious, and I didn't want to spend any more time here, even though the nurses and doctors were fantastic.

Finally, after I insisted that I was feeling much better, they agreed to let me go home. I had managed to hobble awkwardly to the bathroom, and had demonstrated that I could handle basic functions by myself. I had been able to eat and drink without throwing it all up again, and I assured the doctors that my friends would take care of me.

I was instructed to stay with a friend for at least one week and not to over exert myself. I could not return to work until a doctor signed me off, which could be for at least two weeks, maybe longer. And I was to return to the hospital outpatients department to have my wound checked after one week, and to return regularly after that for my healing to be monitored.

The doctors also prescribed me three different types of tablets, which would apparently keep me in a drowsy state, so that my body had the opportunity to heal sufficiently. They also gave me some very strong painkillers and spare bandages for when I was ready to change my dressings. As long as I was allowed home, I would take whatever medication the doctors gave me.

43

I had arranged to stay with Liz and Rob for a few days. Jack was very upset that I wouldn't stay at his house but I just felt too nervous. I mean, I had two large open wounds on my body, wouldn't that scream 'victim' to a vampire and a werewolf? No I was afraid, and I needed to be in a familiar place with familiar people. Rob was on holiday from university for the summer so he could be with me while Liz went to work, and he could even run the shop for us if need be.

Jack compromised and insisted on collecting me from the hospital. I was dressed and waiting when he arrived. He walked into the ward and I smiled to see the admiring glances from other women and even a few men. My heart flipped again and I suddenly felt like a schoolgirl with a crush on an older man. Then I realized this was probably the first time I had seen Jack without some disaster happening since I learnt the truth about him and his true age. I felt an overwhelming shyness, but fought to suppress it, and did my best to act as normal as possible.

Jack picked up my bag and offered me his arm as I stood up from the chair beside the bed. I caught my breath as the room spun, and I gripped his arm, determined not to fall back. The doctors didn't want me to leave as it was but I really needed to get home. Jack understood and he slid his arm carefully around my waist to support me.

"It's alright, Jessica I'll get you out of here." he said reassuringly.

He smiled dazzlingly at the helpful nurse who had approached us.

"Is everything all right, Jessica?" she asked, "Are you sure you are well enough to go home?"

She smiled with a motherly expression and stepped towards me. I straightened up and Jack moved away just enough to give the illusion that I was standing on my own. My smile was grateful as I answered her.

"Thank you, Julie but I feel fine, honestly," I said, "I just want to go home and sleep for a week. Jack will take care of me."

She narrowed her eyes, and I realized that the staff still thought Jack was just a police officer and not a personal friend. I glanced at him but he continued smiling as he spoke.

"Don't worry Julie," Jack said in his disarming Irish lilt, "I have offered to return Jessica home to her friend. We have a few loose ends to tie up for our paperwork, nothing too strenuous, and we are endeavouring to offer Jessica as much assistance as she needs. It is the least we can do in the circumstances."

Julie hesitated, then relaxed and smiled, saying goodbye to us as we moved towards the door. I glanced at Jack, wondering if he had used his powers of persuasion again, but it really didn't matter right now. If he helped me to get home I would be happy.

We made it outside slowly with me leaning quite heavily on Jack. I was limping from the damage to my knee after the fall and even the short walk to the lift and out to the main reception left me exhausted and with pains in my neck and stomach. Jack handed me a pair of sunglasses.

"You will need these, Jessica," he said, "The sunlight will be very dazzling."

I put them on without questioning and was glad I had when we stepped out into the bright summer sunshine. It was a beautiful hot day and yet I was cold, dressed in a purple gypsy skirt, wide necked white t-shirt and my favourite purple cable-knit cardigan. I was wearing flip-flops, nice and sensible. Liz had carefully brought me clothes that were loose and easy to pull on and off, after she had seen the extent of my injuries.

I had seen my reflection in the bathroom mirror at the hospital, and knew that I had a large purple bruise across my cheek from where Celine had hit me. I also had scratches and grazes on my face, neck, upper chest, arms and hands, so I ignored the curious and sympathetic stares from strangers as we walked out into the car park, keeping my head down and allowing my hair to obscure my face.

Jack's car was parked close to the front doors and he carefully helped me into the passenger seat. He waited until we were on the main road back to Redcliffe before he spoke.

"Jessica," he said, "I really would like you to stay with me. It's not just that I want to take care of you. You can't talk about what happened to Elizabeth and Robert."

He glanced at me and I stared straight ahead watching the traffic in front. When I spoke my tone was sullen.

"Maybe I don't want to talk about it," I said, "I just discovered that the man I love is a fucking vampire, his brother a werewolf, and then I was almost killed!" the hysteria was back again now I was away from the hospital, "I need some normality Jack." I said more quietly.

Where had that sudden rage come from? It took me by surprise. I caught my breath again as waves of pain washed over me, and I gripped the handle of the car door, trying not to double over. Yet somehow the pain soothed me because it reminded me I was still human and suddenly that was very important.

Jack swallowed and fought to keep the emotion from his face but his body went very still, so still that I actually turned to look at him to see if he was still there. It was eerie. When he replied his tone was flat, devoid of any emotion.

"I understand that you are angry about the situation," he said, "But there are things I need to explain, and I cannot do that in front of your human friends. Please Jessica, just consider it?"

I relented a little and nodded slightly, then winced as pain shot through my neck. Ok so nodding was out for a while. I spoke quietly, watching the road.

"Fair enough," I said, "but first I need to be with my friends Jack. I mean it's not just you and Danny; it's Simon as well," I continued, "I need to let everything sink in properly so I can decide what to do next, ok?"

He seemed to agree with that, and didn't try to change my mind again.

Jack left me with Liz who had just returned from work when we arrived. She took me in and made me lie on the sofa with a blanket over me and then she set about cooking me a wholesome dinner. It was wonderful.

We ate a delicious mixed vegetable stew sprinkled generously with herbs and served with warm crusty bread, thickly buttered. My appetite was ravenous, and Liz was pleased to see me eating properly. I missed my usual glass of wine but because of my medication I was on water for a few weeks. Still at least it was healthy I suppose. Rob ate with us and then went out with some friends. He was very understanding. He didn't ask awkward questions, he simply accepted that something bad had happened to me, and that I would talk when I was ready. I felt a rush of gratitude to have such a nice, uncomplicated, human friendship.

Liz and me settled down to watch a film once we were alone. But she wanted to talk.

"Jessica," she asked, "how bad is it really? You keep saying you are fine but I see your face when you get pains, and those pills the doctors prescribed are very strong, I checked them in my medical book. Please be honest with me."

I turned my body slightly so I could look at her. She was sat on the rug before the fireplace, leaning against an armchair, hugging her knees, and suddenly she looked so young and childlike despite her baby bump, or maybe I just felt old. My voice sounded tired and weak when I spoke.

"Yes," I said, "I am in pain, Liz but it will take time to heal. I really want to tell you what happened but I can't. It's too painful."

I choked back the tears that suddenly sprang to my eyes, surprised. Liz scrambled to her feet and hurried over to me, flinging her arms around me so that I cried out as her arm brushed my neck wound. She jumped back.

"Oh my god I am so sorry Jess, how clumsy," she exclaimed, "Are you ok, did I make it worse?"

I had to laugh at her stricken face and she smiled, but then my laughter turned to tears and she held me gently as I cried out all of the fear, confusion and frustration of the past week. She rubbed my back and soothed me with comforting words, and when I calmed down she knelt before me.

"Look, Jessica I don't need you to tell me anything," she said, "I know that you've been through a lot and you'll talk when you are ready. Just try to relax now so that you can heal and we can get things back to normal."

So we relaxed, and I actually almost forgot about everything as I became engrossed in the film, a good old-fashioned period drama based on a classic women's novel. It was such a simple uncomplicated story, and yet so beautiful in its simplicity, but it struck a chord with me and seemed wholly appropriate at this time.

Liz entertained me with talk about our customers in the shop, and the latest gossip from the high street. She was just so normal that my heart swelled with love for her, and I badly wanted to keep her pure and innocent amidst everything that I had learned. She was my rock, the one person that would never let me down or abandon me.

44

I woke the next day in the familiar guest bedroom at Liz's house. The bed was a single but that was fine because my movement was restricted anyway. I was snuggled under a pretty white duvet with a modern daisy print on it. Opposite the bed was a pile of bags and boxes containing baby paraphernalia that had already been delivered from the excited grandparents-to-be. I could see hand-knitted cardigans and jumpers in neutral shades of white, cream and yellow, since Liz and Rob had decided not to find out the sex of the baby.

It made me smile to think of this beautiful baby, and his or her wonderful parents, and then I felt a twinge of regret that maybe I could never experience that now. But I dismissed the idea, determined to focus on healing myself first. I shouldn't jump to conclusions without talking to Jack. Just because fictional vampires were unable to have children didn't mean real ones couldn't. Then I was struck by how ridiculous that train of thought really was.

Here was me recovering from almost-fatal injuries inflicted by a werewolf, and I was thinking about wanting to have a baby with my vampire boyfriend. One step at a time Jessica! I looked over at the quaint pine wardrobe and dressing table that Liz had found at auction a couple of years ago. She loved antique and bric-a-brac shopping, and I remembered how excited she had been that day. We should do it again sometime; it had been far too long. Surely we could make use of Rob during the summer holidays and take a day off work together.

I heard movement on the landing and then the sound of the shower, and after a few minutes Liz quietly opened the door to check on me. Seeing that I was awake and trying to move, she helped me to get out of bed and down the stairs, putting me straight on the sofa while she prepared breakfast.

The smell of toast, the delicious mug of tea I drank, and the breakfast news on television all helped me to feel more normal. Liz and Rob went through their morning ritual of bickering and teasing each other over breakfast, Rob fussing that Liz needed to fortify the baby, Liz telling him to stop worrying, it was her body and she knew how to feed it. She helped me to wash and dress in more loose clothes, and then she gave me a quick, gentle hug and promised to come straight home from work. I heard her whispering to Rob when he gave her a goodbye kiss at the front door and I knew she was telling him to take care of me. My heart ached with love for my friends and for this wonderful human existence that I had always taken for granted. Well from now on I would enjoy every moment, and cherish it all, especially this little baby.

Rob walked into the living room and stood in front of the fireplace where I could see him. He was smiling gently and he took off his glasses and carefully cleaned them on a corner of his t-shirt. I knew him well enough to see that this was a nervous trait and he was about to say something uncomfortable. He looked at me with his clear brown eyes.

"Liz said you were a little upset last night," he said slowly, "She wants me to watch you closely today in case things get too much."

I smiled, embarrassed.

"I'm fine, Rob honest," I said. "Yes I got a bit choked up but that's the effect Liz has on me, you know? And I suppose it was the first time I really had to think about what has happened to me. You don't need to spend all day with me. I'll probably just sleep anyway."

He nodded, his face serious, and as he put his glasses back on he moved to perch on the edge of the solid wood coffee table just in front of me. He opened his mouth, closed it, let out a breath and then spoke slowly, quietly, glancing down and then up, but not directly at me.

"I know the truth about Jack and Danny," He said seriously.

His expression was careful and he lifted those intelligent

eyes to face me. I frowned, feeling panic rise in my throat suddenly. I fought to remain calm. Rob was human, I was certain of that.

"What do you mean, you know the truth?" I asked tentatively.

My heart was pounding because I knew what he was about to say, and Rob continued with that calm, quiet tone.

"I know that Jack is a vampire and Danny a werewolf and I'm guessing that your injuries are a result of an enemy of theirs," he said, "And I also guess that you only discovered their true identities within the past week."

The tears sprang to my eyes again and Rob handed me a tissue without speaking. I took a few deep breaths, dabbed at my eyes, and concentrated on choking back the sobs before I tried to reply. My throat was dry and I took a sip of water from the glass that Liz had left on the table for me.

"You know about them," I said, "How?"

Rob told me that he had discovered the Masons' true identities shortly after they approached him for help with an investigation some five years ago. He had promised to keep their secret and had remained a friend but didn't want to be involved in their business. He explained that he would never tell Liz any of this because he wanted to keep her safe.

"So I understand how you feel, Jessica," he said, "She is your best friend and yet now you have this huge life-changing secret that you cannot share. It is bound to confuse you for some time while you get used to the idea. But I'm sure you will agree that Liz is safer if she doesn't know the truth about them."

Rob was right. I felt so horrible having to be secretive and this was just the beginning. Now I knew the truth about Jack and Danny I would act differently around them even if I tried not to. But Rob had been keeping this secret all along.

"How do you manage it, Rob?" I asked, "I mean, you don't seem awkward around them or anything. Aren't you worried about what might happen?"

He shook his head.

"Yes it was difficult at first Jessica," he said, "But Jack and Danny are no different in the way they feel about you as a friend."

He hesitated, glanced down shyly and added.

"And lover, in the case of Jack." he said.

I had to smile at his simple act of male embarrassment. He was right. I knew that Jack loved me and that Danny was my friend, and no matter what happened I couldn't just walk away from them. I sighed.

"You are right Rob," I said, "I won't just walk away, I can't. But I do need some time to think. Things will be different now and I have to figure out how to act around them. I suppose you know about Simon as well then?"

Rob nodded.

"You see, that is even harder to handle," I continued, "I thought me and Simon had no secrets but I know why he kept this one obviously."

I leaned my head back against the cushions, exhausted. When I closed my eyes it felt like I was spinning but that was just my injuries and the medication. Right on cue my neck spasmed with pain, I could feel the uncomfortable bandage on my abdomen, and my knee felt thick and swollen. My human body was clumsy, weak, full of pain and hurt.

I felt movement beside me and half opened my eyes to see Rob perched on the sofa. He very gently placed the back of his hand on my forehead and checked the pulse in my wrist.

"It's alright, Jessica just try to relax," he said, "All of this shock won't be helping your body and right now that has to be your priority. Try to sleep for a bit and let the medication do its job."

He stood up slowly.

"I will be in my study if you need anything," he said, "just shout."

I managed a slight nod as he left the room, and then the blackness swallowed me up, thoughts of vampires and werewolves spinning round in my head.

45

It was starting to feel like a regular pattern as I woke slowly, still feeling groggy, and I could hear voices and realized the television was still on and it was some midday soap opera. I opened my eyes and jumped when I saw a woman sitting on the armchair watching me. She was beautiful, with jet-black hair and dark eyes; in fact she looked exotic, certainly not English. She sat carefully composed, wearing a classic red dress that was chic and elegant, yet sexy at the same time, and she wore matching high-heeled shoes. Her style seemed very 1930s elegance, completely out of place in this homely living room. I sat upright and swung my legs round, not even noticing that I didn't feel any pain.

"Hello," I said politely, "Who are you? What are you doing here?"

I felt strangely calm but in the back of my mind there were alarm bells ringing. The woman sat very still but looked relaxed as she replied in a delicate French accent. "My name is Emily-Rose and I am a very old friend of Jack Mason," she said, "It is him that I have come to see. And you may assist me with the task."

She made no secret of her identity and I saw her fangs, sharp and delicate, as she spoke. He black eyes sparkled with some inhuman flame, but she seemed more frightening than Jack had been. I struggled to think how I knew her. Had he talked about her?

The uneasiness grew as realization dawned on me.

"You are the one who made him, you're a vampire!" I cried, "But how are you here, did Rob let you in?"

I looked around me and tried to make sense of the room. It all looked the same but my intuition was telling me something was wrong.

Emily-Rose was suddenly kneeling in front of me and I

jumped, surprised. Her voice was silky and dangerous, yet coaxing at the same time. She was the ultimate predator, beautiful yet deadly. Her voice was low and seductive.

"I need no invitation to see you, Jessica," she said, "your beloved has seen to that. With his blood in your body and your natural capabilities I can visit you without need of my physical form."

She leaned forward to kiss my lips and I tried to move away but was rooted to the seat. I closed my eyes and tried to scream as I felt her cool caress, her fangs against my teeth. I couldn't move; she held me firm in an icy grip. I fought to break away, calling for Lillian to help me.

I woke with a cry and sat up on the sofa, then cried out in agony as pains shot through my body. The television was switched off and there was no one in the room with me. I shivered and hugged my arms across my chest, carefully avoiding my injuries. And then I heard her laugh in my head, tinkling and sweet and extremely disturbing. I felt sick.

I remembered what she had said in what I assumed must have been a dream. Jack had given me his blood. Did that mean I was a vampire? Was that why Rob didn't want me here? And Emily-Rose had spoken of my natural capabilities. She must mean the powers that Lillian used to speak with me; she had obviously done the same. It was frightening. I had no control over my body or my mind, not even when I was asleep.

I stood carefully and walked slowly through the hallway, my legs wobbly, head spinning, holding onto the doorframe and touching the walls for support. Rob's study door was open and I stopped in the doorway, steadying myself on the frame, one hand to my head. He looked up and then jumped from his chair and hurried over to me.

"Jessica," he said anxiously, "are you alright? You shouldn't be moving around. Here take a seat."

He very carefully led me round his desk and made me sit in his large comfortable office chair. I leaned my head on the back of the seat and closed my eyes while the dizziness washed over me. When I opened them again Rob was placing a glass of water in front of me.

"Jessica do you need anything?" he asked, "Should we go back to the hospital? Or should I phone Jack?"

That got my attention. I raised my head and saw Rob stiffen at my expression. My voice was low and angry as I replied.

"Why would I want to see Jack?" I asked through clenched teeth, "It's his fault that I'm in this situation. He almost killed me, he gave me his blood, and now this woman is in my head!"

"Whoa, hang on," Rob said, "What woman, what are you talking about? And how did you know he gave you blood?"

Now I smiled but Rob looked very uncomfortable. I had never noticed before just how handsome he was. His eyes were a lovely clear brown and his hair was streaked with grey, which gave him that distinguished look that some men really do suit. Rob was one of those men. And his face was firm and square, very masculine.

I blinked and shook my head. These were not my thoughts. What was happening to me? Why was I so angry and confused? Rob's expression changed as he watched me, and then he carefully took his mobile phone out of his pocket and dialled a number.

"Jack," he said, "Yes I think you should come round straight away. Something has happened to Jessica. She knows about the blood but I don't know how. It's like she's possessed or something."

He listened for a moment and I watched him.

"Yeah ok," he said, "No problem, the door's unlocked just come in. See you in a bit."

He put the phone down and looked at me with that serious face, so careful, trying to hide his fear. But I could sense it; I could almost taste it on the air. It was delicious, and enticing. I could almost taste his skin on my tongue, and the sweet tang of his warm blood in my mouth. Again, these were not my thoughts. What was happening? Rob spoke quietly.

"So what happened, Jessica?" he asked, "Am I speaking to you now?"

I nodded and blinked slowly, trying to ignore that tinkling laughter in my head. I sipped the cold water and it helped. My voice was shaky as I spoke.

"I had a dream," I said slowly, "This woman, Emily-Rose, she was in the living room. She is the vampire that made Jack and she told me that he had invited her into my body by giving me his blood."

Tears stung my eyes and I met Rob's concerned stare.

"I don't understand, Rob," I continued, "I can hear her, it's like she is here but she's not."

The tears brimmed over and I blinked them away furiously, determined not to be weak.

Rob instinctively moved towards me and drew me into his arms, careful of my bandages.

"Shush, shush," he said gently, "it's alright Jessica. Jack will be here soon and he will know what to do. Don't worry, we will get her out of your head."

I buried my face in his soft green t-shirt, comforted by the scent of his aftershave. It reminded me of Liz and was reassuring. Then I smelt him, just him, and my body reacted so forcefully I reared back and pushed him away. He looked startled.

"Jessica?" he asked, "What's wrong?"

I felt her, Emily-Rose, in my head. It was like my experience with Lillian, but this was far more terrifying. Emily-Rose didn't ask for permission, didn't instruct me on what to do. She simply took over my body and I could see her, I could see what I was doing but it wasn't me it was her. It was as if I was behind a glass window and I couldn't break free. I screamed but Rob couldn't hear me because she was in my body. Then I blacked out.

46

"Jessica," a male voice said urgently, "Jessica can you hear me?"

I tried to speak but my voice was croaky and I couldn't move my lips properly. I opened my eyes slowly and as my senses woke up I realized I was lying on the floor. I could feel the cold laminate beneath me, and my head was in someone's lap. This was happening too often just lately. I tried to sit up but everything hurt and someone restrained me. I heard Jack's familiar voice again.

"Jessica, it's me," he said, "Please lie still for a minute. Can you open your eyes?"

I did as he asked, fluttering my eyelids with the strain. As the room swam into focus I saw his anxious face above me, and then I looked down my body and saw Danny kneeling between my legs. My t-shirt was pushed up to reveal the claw wounds, and the bandage had been taken away so I saw fresh blood. I felt a wave of nausea, and quickly choked it back. What the hell was happening here?

I tried to lift my head a little and saw Rob leaning against his desk, his face white, and his eyes wary. His clothes were ruffled and he looked dishevelled, not neat and tidy like usual. I tried to speak and managed it this time.

"What happened?" I asked croakily, "Why am I on the floor?"

Jack laughed a little shakily and kissed my forehead, and Danny sat back on his legs, relief showing plainly on his face. Rob carefully knelt beside us to look at me.

"You certainly gave me a fright, Jessica," he said, "Where did you go?"

I was confused. I had been asleep hadn't I?

Jack proceeded to explain that I hadn't been asleep. Apparently Emily-Rose had taken possession of my body and she had sent me somewhere, into some form of mental and spiritual oblivion. She had used my body to try and seduce Rob, and Jack had arrived in time to see him trying to restrain what he thought was me, but Rob knew I had been possessed. Then Emily-Rose had tried to persuade Jack to return to her, back to where her physical body was. I was shocked to find that she was actually in Italy at this time, travelling across Europe.

"Ok," I said, "but where did you come from, Danny? And why are you sat so close?"

Danny explained that Jack had phoned him after his conversation with Rob. The men both knew that I had most likely been possessed by a dangerous entity and that both vampire and werewolf powers would be stronger. As it happened Danny had used his newly strengthened status as pack leader to invoke the energy of his wolves, and he had chased Emily-Rose out of me temporarily. It would have caused some of his wolves to weaken, and maybe even transform, but he would deal with that later. Emily-Rose hated Danny with the same passion she had shown from the beginning, because he stood between her and his brother, and he would not go away. Danny continued.

"But she will return, Jessica," he said, "at least while you still carry Jack's blood. You are human but she senses something in you and she wants to know more, to see if she can use you to her advantage. I am so sorry about this."

"Why do I have Jack's blood in my body?" I asked, feeling strangely calm and detached, "Does that make me a vampire?"

I looked at Jack now, pleading with him to be honest. I was too exhausted to be angry. He spoke quietly.

"When you were dying from Seamus' attack," he said, "you had lost nearly all of your blood, and would not have made it to the hospital. I took some of the wolf poison, to try and stop you transforming, and I gave you my vampire blood to even it out. It was a dangerous thing to do. Most humans cannot survive such an attack. But you did. And there are side-effects, such as this."

He stopped, his expression full of sadness and sorrow.

He had apologized enough times; it was a futile gesture now. So I had almost become a werewolf, but now I was still human? No wonder I healed so well in the hospital! The whole revelation disturbed me, but I was at least grateful to be alive. I would handle everything else, I always did. It certainly explained a few things.

After ten minutes I felt stiff and needed to stand up. Jack helped me to my feet and I welcomed his support. I felt dizzy and my body was weak and tired. Jack explained that this was partly due to the mental strain. I had fought Emily-Rose and tried to cast her out by myself but of course she was much stronger and had overpowered me since I was inexperienced in metaphysical activities. I had frightened Rob and now I saw why I should allow Jack and Danny to take care of me. They didn't know how long Emily-Rose would try and possess me but they knew she would keep trying. And at least they were strong enough to fight her. I could not risk the lives and the innocence of my human friends and their unborn baby. So I packed my bag and Jack and Danny took me home with them.

47

Liz was very upset to find that I had left. She came round that night to find me in Jack's bed, weak and helpless. Of course I couldn't explain what had happened so I made up some story about needing to be with him. She didn't believe me but she accepted what I told her and promised to come and see me every day.

While I was lying alone in bed the reality of my situation suddenly dawned on me. I was in a house with a vampire and a werewolf. What other supposedly mythical creatures were alive and well in our world? And how could I continue my relationship with Jack knowing all this? I hated being like this; I resented Jack for putting me in this situation, and Danny for helping him to deceive me. And then there was Simon. I could not even begin to decide how I felt about him.

The bedroom door opened carefully and Jack walked quietly into the room, carrying a cup of hot chocolate. He placed it on the bedside cabinet and I struggled to move myself into a sitting position. He was suddenly there beside me, gently offering his help. I jumped involuntarily and my body instinctively froze. Jack moved back away from me, face serious, and he spoke in a quiet voice.

"It is still me, Jessica," he said, "I am still your lover, your partner. Please don't push me away."

I felt a lump rise in my throat at his heartbroken expression. There was that crazy urge to take him in my arms, to cuddle him and tell him everything would be all right. But I couldn't. Jack was different. Now I knew the truth about him and had time to digest it, I didn't know how to handle it. I fought to keep my voice from shaking as I answered.

"I know, Jack," I said, "But this is so hard. I don't know what I'm supposed to feel. I can't just accept it and move on, not this. You are a vampire. I'm in your house, I'm human, and I'm injured. What if you lose control again? You might kill me."

I broke off then, and the tears trickled out of my eyes, betraying me. Jack moved slowly toward the bed again, careful not to startle me this time. He sat down very carefully beside me and tentatively reached out to touch my face, attempting to brush away the tears. I held still, fighting not to break down. I closed my eyes as he very gently stroked my cheek, then leaned forward and brushed his cool lips against mine. He spoke quietly, his voice calm.

"I promise you Jessica," he said, "I will not kill you. This is your home just as much as it is Danny's and mine. If it is easier for you I will sleep in the guest bedroom tonight, and for as long as you need. But please do not cast me out. I need you Jessica. I love you."

When I opened my eyes he had moved back from me but was still sitting on the bed. His face was pale, his eyes that burning blue colour, so obviously not human. How did I not see this before? Because I wasn't looking for it of course. I whimpered and hunched my body as waves of pain flowed through me from my injuries. It must be time for some more medication. I gritted my teeth and waited for it to pass, then tried to speak. At first my voice was croaky but I managed, and Jack waited patiently.

"I want to believe you Jack," I said, "I really do. But this is all so bizarre. I need time to get used to the idea. To really understand that this is the reality of my life now."

He nodded and waited as I continued, my heart racing now, a combination of pain and exhilaration from what I was about to say.

"I love you too Jack," I said, "I do. And that is why I cannot leave you. Please stay in here with me tonight. I need you here for comfort. But please give me space and time to accept you properly. Can you do that?"

He nodded and I saw tears in his eyes as he very gently gathered me in his arms, kissing the top of my head and stroking my hair. I relaxed into his embrace, enjoying his warmth, his comfort, his familiar smell. I couldn't leave all of that. But it was a lie! A wicked voice in the back of my mind scolded me.

"You cannot trust him," the voice said cruelly, "He is a vampire! He would sooner kill you and drink your sweet, warm blood!"

I reared away from Jack; eyes closed tight, hands to my head.

"No!" I screamed, "Get out of my head! You are not real, go back to your own body!"

Emily-Rose laughed and the sound echoed through my mind like shards of glass. She was trying to possess me again, and she almost succeeded because I was weak and in pain. I was helpless as she looked at Jack through my eyes, and he eyed me warily, knowing what to expect. She spoke with my voice, and I couldn't stop her.

"My darling Jack," she said in my sweet voice, "why won't you return to me? Your life is miserable here. I can give you great pleasure, don't you remember? Those times we shared together, they were wonderful, weren't they?"

I had moved close to him, leaned forward to kiss his lips, but he sat like stone, cold and distant. He gripped my shoulders firmly and stared into my eyes, searching for her, to chase her out.

"Leave her alone, Emily-Rose," he said, "I did not give her my blood for you to play with her. She is hurt and she needs to heal. Leave her. I will never return to you. Our history is long gone and will never return."

That was it. I had had enough. I forced all of my energy towards her, and shoved her away with all my mental strength. I wanted her out! She laughed, but it changed, faltered as she realized that I was stronger than she thought, and suddenly she was gone, but her parting words were, 'I will return, and soon. You cannot stop me, little witch.'

Jack was still gripping my shoulders, staring at me. I slumped, exhausted, into his arms. His voice was urgent, wary.

"Jessica," he said, "Are you back?"

My voice was croaky.

"Yes it's me," I said, "I forced her out. Shit Jack, I don't know how much more of this I can take."

Jack wrapped his arms very carefully around me, and I felt drowsy, my fragile body in so much pain. He shook his head.

"I am so sorry Jessica," he said, "I never meant for her to do this."

He carefully lay me down against the heaped pillows, and pulled the duvet up over my shivering body.

"Please drink your chocolate; it might make you feel better," he said, "I'll go and get your medication and some water."

I managed a weak smile at that. I hadn't said I was in pain or that it was time for my tablets, but he knew. Through half-closed eyelids I watched him walk out of the room and my heart flipped again.

Despite everything, all of the trauma, all of this continued stress; I most certainly could not resist my love for him. It would be more painful to be without Jack than to be with him. That left me very few options, and I supposed I might as well get used to the pain for now. Emily-Rose wanted him back; she wouldn't give up that easily. But for now I could dismiss her, she wasn't important.

I carefully reached for the mug and sipped the hot chocolate. It was delicious, sweet and soothing, and was now just the right temperature for me. Jack had made it with cream and marshmallows, just the way I like it. He returned with my tablets and stayed with me, lying on the bed watching TV, cuddling and talking just like any ordinary couple. And eventually it felt right; I knew that this was where I should be. I was safe. I was home.

48

The sun was shining when I awoke, having slept deeply and with no dreams once again. A part of me was sad. I wanted to see Lillian again, and without her having to protect me or warn me, or anything serious. I just wanted to talk to her, to ask her about my heritage, and where I should go next. I didn't know what I should do. But somehow I knew that she would return. She was simply giving me space to heal my wounds, and to repair my damaged relationships with everyone.

I opened my eyes to find I was lying on my back in Jack's bed, and he was asleep next to me. I turned my head to look at him, and pain shot through me. Oh yes, I was injured. He was a vampire. This wasn't just any normal day. I managed to shift awkwardly to one side so I could see him, but it was very uncomfortable, putting pressure on my wounds.

Jack lay on his side facing me, apparently still asleep although I wasn't convinced. His skin was pale; did he need blood? I shivered at the thought. I definitely couldn't be a donor in this state. Then I thought about him taking blood from another woman. It was such an intimate act. Would he take it from her neck, or somewhere else? I had some pretty vivid memories from watching horror films, and now I wasn't sure whether they were actually partially true or not. I quickly dismissed the thoughts; now was not the time to get jealous and possessive.

Jack's face looked so young in sleep, he seemed so innocent. My heart sped up as I realized he was actually over a hundred years old. I couldn't comprehend it. No, he was thirty-five, that was much easier to accept. But maybe he could tell me a bit more about himself later, perhaps that would help me to adjust to this whole new existence.

I reached out very carefully and gently traced my fingertips across his face, from his forehead, down his cheek, to his lips and chin. He smiled and opened his eyes slowly, and I held my breath at the pure naked love in his expression. My body ached for him but I was too damaged. It was so frustrating and so upsetting.

"Good morning, darling," he said, "how are you feeling?"

His voice was low and deep, sending thrills of excitement through me again. My voice was quiet, not wanting to break the mood.

"I'm ok thanks," I said, "Still in pain but I'll get through it."

Jack fought to hide the grief on his face, because it was his fault I was in this state. We couldn't deny that. But I had to say something; I couldn't bear to see the naked pain on his face.

"Its fine Jack," I said, "You never meant for this to happen, I know that. And what is life without a few adventures anyway? I'm still here!" I forced a laugh.

We lay in bed together for a while, just talking, catching up with each other. Jack could finally be honest with me, and could fill in some of the gaps in our recent history.

I finally plucked up the courage to tell him about Lillian, but of course he already knew. She had visited him as well, and had asked him to take care of me to the best of his ability. And she had instructed him to direct me to a witch who could tutor me, when I was ready. Apparently he had a female friend who would be my mentor if I wanted. I agreed that it seemed a good idea, but only when I was properly healed from my injuries. I could take it one step at a time.

Jack gently stroked my skin, tracing his fingers across my shoulders, my chest, and my stomach, all the while carefully avoiding the bandages. We managed to cuddle after manoeuvring me very gently to try and avoid jarring anything. I felt so clumsy, so helpless, and I hated it. But at the same time it was nice to have him taking care of me.

He brought me breakfast in bed, telling me I should rest while I could. It was a hearty fry-up with hash browns, beans, fried and scrambled eggs, tomatoes and mushrooms. Jack didn't have any of the food but told me that Danny was eating the leftovers downstairs. He explained that he was taking some time off work to care for me. When I objected he said it wasn't a problem, they owed him a lot of annual leave, and Danny as well, so both brothers would be at my disposal. I couldn't help but feel flattered that they both wanted to take care of me so badly.

After breakfast Jack gently explained that he needed to go out, he had to feed. I nodded, not sure what to say. He went into his en-suite bathroom for a shower, and while he was gone I slowly started to move around a bit. I wanted to look at my wounds properly. It seemed as though I hadn't had time up until now, because people had been fussing around me, and then there were those metaphysical distractions.

I shakily stood and walked slowly across the landing to the shared bathroom, resting my hands against the walls and doorframes for support. My head was still spinning and I had to move very slowly and carefully in case I lost my balance. But I had taken some pills with my breakfast and they were already taking effect, so the pain was dulled.

I could hear music playing on the radio downstairs and guessed Danny must still be in. I heard the sounds of Jack in the shower coming from his bedroom, and I badly wanted to join him, to see his naked body, and to enjoy it. Then I shuddered as I remembered how close I had come to being raped by Seamus Tully, and my body went cold, my heart racing. It was all right. I was safe now, and he was dead. He could never hurt me again.

I jumped as Danny suddenly appeared in the bathroom doorway, looking so gorgeous with a black fluffy towel wrapped round his waist that I could barely contain myself. It chased all thoughts of Seamus Tully far from my mind. Danny laughed at my expression, as I struggled to suppress my feelings for him. His voice was deep and sexy when he spoke.

"Jessica, your emotions betray you," he said, "I can see,

no I can feel, what you are thinking about me right now. I like it!"

He hesitated, his expression growing serious suddenly.

"Sorry," he said soberly, "You were thinking about Jack weren't you?"

I blinked; confused, and then I nodded. My voice was rough when I managed to speak.

"Danny you confuse me," I said, "What am I supposed to do? You and he are identical, I can't deny that, but I don't know how to act with you, especially when you flirt and torment me."

Danny nodded, all humour gone.

"I cannot deny my feelings for you, Jessica," he said, "Now you know the truth about us I was hoping we could change things a little more. You see Jack and I are extremely close. We share many things besides our looks. Do you follow me?"

My heart was racing, blood pounding in my ears, and I felt embarrassed suddenly as I realized what he meant. He was talking about sex. I swallowed nervously, half expecting Jack to come running out of the bedroom and shout at me, or Danny. Then I remembered his reaction to my infidelity with Marcus. What would he say if I suggested being intimate with Danny, his own brother? I jumped as Jack spoke from behind me on the landing.

"It is your decision, Jessica," he said, "Although I am sorry that my brother chose such an inopportune time to confront you with this. It is true we share an unusually close relationship because of what we are. There are some women in the past who have been willing to share themselves with us. But it is entirely your choice, and we will not put pressure on you either way."

I turned to look at him. He was stood wrapped in a black fluffy towel also, but his skin was white where Danny's was tanned. He gave his brother a stern look, warning him to be careful.

I turned back to face Danny, not sure what to say. My body felt weak, completely helpless, and I staggered, trying to grab the doorframe.

"Jessica!" both men yelled in unison.

Danny had caught me before Jack got there. He carefully carried me back into the bedroom, cradling me in his arms. He was so warm, and so safe. For a moment I forgot myself, and snuggled in his arms. I vaguely heard Jack speaking, and then Danny's reply rumbling through his chest.

"You should not have said that, Danny," Jack said, "She is not ready; she needs to heal. Look at her!"

"I am sorry Jack," Danny replied, "She surprised me at the bathroom door, and she was thinking about you when she saw me. Now she knows our secrets I cannot continue to play human, and neither can you."

I struggled to rouse myself, when all I wanted to do was sleep. Danny's arms tightened around me, and I realized he didn't want to let me go. But I pushed at him, and he very gently placed me on the bed beside him. This must be the medication, and my injuries. I was over-exerting myself again, and would end up back in hospital if I wasn't careful.

I opened my eyes to find Jack sat one side of me, and Danny the other. They mirrored each other. One was warm and full of life; the other was cold and dead. And I was in love with the dead one. That thought alone sent fear coursing through me, and I sat bolt upright, then cried out as I pulled at my wounds.

"Shit," I said sharply, "Fuck that hurts."

Jack carefully pushed me back to lie against the pillows, and I let him. Of course he wasn't dead, what was I thinking? This was Jack. Yes he was a vampire, but look at him. He was alive. I had to stop thinking about the old stories, and all those horror films.

Danny didn't want to leave us, I could tell. And for some reason I didn't want him to. For once I had control over my own mind. Emily-Rose seemed to have left for the time being, and Lillian was giving me some space. So what did I really want? That was simple. I wanted both of them. But surely I couldn't have that. It wasn't right. It wasn't natural.

I shivered, and both men moved in unison to pull the duvet over me, very gently, so caring. I opened my eyes and looked at them both, speaking in a voice that was growing stronger again.

"What am I supposed to say?" I asked them both, "I am with Jack; I should only be with Jack. That's how it works. And aren't you with Sally?" I looked at Danny accusingly.

Danny glanced at his brother, whose face was carefully neutral. Then he looked back at me.

"I am not in a relationship with Sally," he said, "She is my third in command. When I order her to, she gives me what I need, anything I need. And she is devoted to me; I know that. Of course I am fond of her, but we do not practice monogamy in the wolf pack. I am free to sleep with any of the wolves under my control. And I am free to be with anybody else who is willing."

I remembered that night in the Ship only recently, and stared at Danny again. "And what about Simon?" I asked him, "I saw the two of you, in your office at the pub, and you looked pretty damn close to me."

Danny actually smiled, embarrassed, and ducked his head.

"Simon and I share a very special relationship," he said calmly, "I am generally attracted only to women, but he has an unusual appeal to me. I felt a strange fondness for him when we first met, and while we do not openly show our relationship, we are close in our private quarters. My wolves know about this of course. They appreciate that it is part of what makes us a strong team, a family that will protect them."

I closed my eyes again, feeling tears welling up, but they were tears of confusion. I spoke with my eyes closed.

"Jack," I said, "what do you think about this? Be honest."

Jack's voice was strong and clear, devoid of emotion.

"I am willing to share you with my brother if that is your wish," he said, "You and I are in love Jessica, that is enough for now. But I cannot ignore your sexual desire for Danny. It is clearly obvious, and it is only your human inhibitions that hold you back. We vampires value the freedom to share ourselves with many partners. But I have remained monogamous to you because you are human, and that is how you have been raised."

I nodded, processing the information. My head hurt. My body ached. But I still felt that desire, and it terrified me, and confused me at the same time. Another thought struck me, and I spoke again, this time opening my eyes and looking from Jack to Danny.

"Do you have some sort of power that makes another person feel this desire?" I asked, "Because that's what I'm struggling with. I mean, yeah, I enjoy sex, of course I do. But it's supposed to be special, between two people, isn't it? And instead I'm going crazy. I slept with Marcus. I want to sleep with Danny. And it's driving me insane."

Both men stared at me with their brilliant blue eyes, so still, so wary. And there they sat, wearing nothing but bath towels, and making me talk about sex, to both of them. This was so not normal. Then I laughed scornfully. Nothing was normal any more, had I not figured that out yet?

Danny finally answered.

"Non-humans can possess the ability to seduce," he said carefully, "It is stronger in vampires; they use it for food. But I am certain that what you feel Jessica, is your own desire. We have not influenced you or your desires in any supernatural way."

He stood up slowly, reluctantly.

"You are tired and in pain," he continued, "Please rest. Jack will go out and feed. If you can rest your body, then you can make a conscious decision. Do not feel forced into anything you are not comfortable with."

He hesitated, glanced at Jack, and then he leaned forward and very gently kissed me on the lips, tender and soft. I jumped, but I enjoyed the sensation. I wanted to return the kiss but my inhibition held me back. Danny drew away, smiling now.

"I will be downstairs if you need me." he said.

And he left. Jack moved over and kissed me as well, in

much the same way, but for him I responded. I parted my lips and welcomed him, wanting more but my damaged body could not physically take it. He pulled away with huge effort and I watched as he fought to regain his human composure, trying to hide his fangs and his glowing silver eyes.

"Sorry," he said in a gruff voice, "I must go and feed. You are so enticing, so delicious. Please rest, and please, trust Danny to take care of you while I am gone."

I closed my eyes and snuggled under the duvet, as Jack quietly got dressed. He left me with another kiss and a promise to return quickly. I drifted into sleep, confused, bewildered, and exhausted.

49

I didn't sleep for long, maybe half an hour. I felt restless, wanting desperately to get up and go downstairs, but when I tried to sit up the room swam around me and I felt nauseas and disorientated. This wasn't good. Was I having a relapse? Maybe the effects of Jack's vampire blood were wearing off. I needed a drink but my water glass was empty.

Jack had left the door ajar, so I decided to call Danny. My voice wasn't very loud, and I didn't have the energy to shout, but he heard me straight away and I could hear him running up the stairs. He walked into the room looking more like his usual self, dressed in green baggy skate shorts and a pale yellow t-shirt with a cartoon print motif on it. He smiled.

"Are you alright, Jessica?" he asked, "Do you need a drink?"

He took my glass and disappeared, returning after a few minutes. He helped me to sit more upright, plumping up the pillows behind me. I hated being so helpless and vulnerable, and Danny knew that.

"Please Jessica," he said, "Let me help you. It is my fault you are in this situation; the least I can do is tend to your needs and help you heal as quickly as possible."

When he finished, he waited while I carefully sipped at the ice-cold water, holding the glass with both hands to try and keep it steady. Then he turned to leave but I stopped him.

"Danny, are you busy?" I asked.

He turned back to me, smiling.

"No," he said, "do you want me to sit with you for a while?"

I nodded carefully, learning how to do it without jarring my neck.

Danny sat on the bed beside me, careful not to get too

close. He was obviously aware of how awkward I felt after our last conversation, and didn't want to make the situation worse. I broke the silence.

"Do you know where Jack went to feed?" I asked.

Danny nodded.

"Yes," he said, "Today he went to the Ship. There is a willing human donor working behind the bar."

He hesitated, and then continued.

"She is young, and she enjoys Jack's company, but she is only food, and nothing more."

I nodded carefully again, trying to keep my heart from pounding. I couldn't help but imagine Jack in a romantic embrace with some young, attractive woman, while I lay here battered and broken. But I knew I was being silly, so I changed the subject.

"Tell me about your wolf pack, Danny," I said, "How does it all work, being a werewolf?"

Danny smiled, and moved up to sit beside me, leaning against the headboard. His presence was comforting, reassuring, but I didn't feel stifled by the sexual tension that we felt earlier. I enjoyed the sound of his voice, with that attractive accent, as he told me some of his secrets.

"Well," he said, "our bodies are tied to the moon cycles. The legends are correct in that most wolves only transform on the night of a full moon. Any newly turned wolf will not transform until that time."

He paused and I waited for him to continue.

"There are more powerful wolves," he said, "those with a natural super-strength, even among our kind. Those are ones like myself and Simon, and Sally. We have the ability to transform into wolves whenever we choose, and we can draw power from our pack to help us if we are injured or facing a dangerous enemy."

He paused again and looked at me, apparently unsure how to continue. I waited patiently, just wanting to hear whatever he was going to say. I didn't know what to ask, and supposed that the questions would come naturally in time, but at least now I could learn a little more about my friends. They still were my friends after all.

After a minute Danny continued.

"I know you were wondering how I came to own the Ship," he said, "The simple truth is that I defeated and killed the previous pack leader of the Redcliffe wolves. Her name was Marie, and she was strong. She was a good leader for many years, and welcomed me into the pack when Jack and I moved down here. Of course ours was a slightly more complicated situation since she had to accept Jack, even though she hated vampires. But she tolerated him for my sake."

"Why exactly do vampires and werewolves hate each other Danny?" I asked curiously.

He was quiet for a minute, thinking about it. I wondered what was going through his mind, what memories and experiences he was remembering. Then he answered.

"I think it is the ultimate need for power and control," he said finally, "Werewolves are very much like the pure animals that we resemble, but we have the difficulty of dealing with human ego and emotions at the same time. So we hunt in packs, we stick together; we claim our territory and guard it fiercely, reacting violently to anyone or anything that dares to disturb our peace. Vampires are much more solitary. Occasionally you find them hunting in pairs, but usually they are individual, they are loners. They seem to consider themselves a higher power, a more intellectual and metaphysical superior to wolves, and that is why we dislike each other. Of course I personally am more tolerant because of my brother and Marcus, but most vampires despise me for what I am, and naturally I respond in the same way."

It was my turn to be quiet and thoughtful. I supposed this all made sense really. I mean people, humans, are always struggling for power and dominance over each other. Look at me now; I absolutely hated being stuck in this helpless situation, my human body so damaged that all I could do was lie in bed and wait for it to heal. It made me feel vulnerable and weak, when I should be able to take care of myself.

So it seemed that these creatures, these vampires and werewolves, were simply fighting for power over each other. But they were stronger, and their fights were far more vicious and deadly. At least they were to my mind anyway. It would take me a while to fully understand their ways, I knew that, but at least it explained a lot of the strange behaviour I had seen from Simon over the years, and the way Sally was so in awe of Danny, and even the way Jack and Danny acted when they were being forceful, or when they just did not act human, which actually seemed blatantly obvious now that I knew the truth.

I realized that Danny was sitting quietly beside me, just watching my face, and his body was eerily still. My heart skipped a beat and started pounding as I thought about my attraction for this man, and what had happened that morning. Was this all a part of their not being human? Or was it simply a twin thing? I wanted to ask, but I was embarrassed and I felt awkward and silly. Maybe it had nothing to do with Jack and Danny, and was simply something that I was creating, another drama, and another traumatic situation.

I shifted my position in bed, my body starting to feel numb from sitting in the same place for too long. My legs were restless and I so badly wanted to stand up and move around. Perhaps I could just make it to the bathroom, and have a look at these wounds. Suddenly it seemed very important. I tried to manoeuvre myself to the edge of the bed, and Danny was there, his strong arms supporting me.

"Jessica what are you doing?" he asked, "You need to rest."

"I know, Danny," I replied, "but I really want to have a look at these wounds, and have a good wash, my body feels filthy and hot, and I'm fed up with it."

He didn't argue. Danny simply helped me to stand, shakily, and he kept his arms around me, carefully avoiding the bandages and bruises. We both shuffled awkwardly to the door of the en suite bathroom, and I had to hold on to Danny as the room swam around me. But I would not give up. I had to do something; I was sick and tired of lying helplessly in bed. At the very least I could clean myself up and change my clothes, perhaps then I could clear my head a little.

50

Once in the bathroom I sort of fell down to sit on the lid of the toilet. Danny managed to support me enough so that I didn't hurt myself, and then he crouched beside me, waiting while I closed my eyes and breathed in and out steadily, waiting for my heart to stop racing. I slowly opened my eyes to find his bright blue ones staring right at me, and there were those butterflies in my stomach again, but I stifled the feelings, ignoring them.

After a few minutes I stood on shaky legs, holding on to the sink for support, and turned round to face the mirror above it. I looked at my reflection, concentrating carefully, vaguely aware of Danny standing behind me. My face was white, eyes and lips very dark. I didn't look human, and that was suddenly very funny. I smiled wryly at the joke. Danny moved closer to me, concerned.

"Are you alright, Jessica?" he asked gently.

I laughed then, and it sounded desperate and crazed.

"Yes I'm fine, Danny," I said in a high-pitched voice, "My boyfriend is a vampire, my best friend is a werewolf, you are a werewolf, and I almost died last week. Why shouldn't I be fine?"

I bit my lip then to stop those hot tears that sprang to my eyes. It sobered me, and calmed my mind. I had suddenly had enough of feeling sorry for myself. This had happened; it was time to accept it. Get over it, move on, and learn about these people, my friends, who just happened to be non-human. So the world was even more of a crazy, mixed up place than I previously thought. So what? It was all the more interesting and exciting, that was all.

I jumped as Jack appeared in the doorway behind Danny. I hadn't heard him return, and now his skin was tanned and as I looked at the two brothers reflected in the mirror, the metaphor hit me very clearly. They were identical. Yet they were so different.

Jack stood there dressed in black jeans and black t-shirt, all dark, brooding sexual energy. Danny stood dressed in his lighter clothes, cheerful, playful, and mischievous, yet still incredibly sexual. And I had to find a way to deal with this, to understand how to handle them both. Because that was the simple truth.

I had to figure out how I really felt about Danny, and what I was prepared to do. They had told me a bit about how they felt. And while Jack and Danny obviously had years of experience in the handling of human emotions, and they must have shared partners in the past, it was new to me, and very frightening and confusing.

Jack moved slowly to stand behind me, next to his brother, and he slipped his hands around my waist. He very gently kissed my head and whispered in my ear. "You are extremely brave, my darling," he said softly, "Most humans could not handle this. It is all right to let go, if you want to. I am here to support you, and so is Danny, and Simon."

I closed my eyes and breathed deeply, fighting back the nausea that overcame me suddenly. Jack stayed where he was, pressing his body against me, and somehow it was cool and soothing.

After a few minutes I felt calmer and opened my eyes. I awkwardly turned round in his arms, but kept him at a distance. Danny stayed where he was, waiting to see what I wanted. I looked at his face, then at Jack.

"I really need a wash, Jack," I said, "And I want to inspect my wounds, I need to see them."

He stepped back, face serious, and a concerned tone in his voice.

"Is that a good idea Jessica?" he asked, "It is perhaps too early to see. The doctors did say there was extensive tissue damage and you might need plastic surgery on your neck once it has healed sufficiently."

I nodded slowly, carefully, gripping the edge of the sink behind me, but I was determined.

"I know, Jack and that's why I need to see," I said, "I

want to see what damage this psychopath did to me. It's important. But first I need a wash, since I can't have a shower or a bath."

Jack glanced at Danny, who remained still, not offering any opinion or advice. Then Jack nodded once, took the hint, and both men turned and walked quietly out of the bathroom, pulling the door shut behind them.

I turned slowly back to the sink and turned the taps on, putting the plug in and watching the white ceramic bowl fill with clean, hot water. My toiletries were already in here, the spare ones I had started to leave behind when I spent more time at the brothers' house.

I picked up a comb and carefully pulled it through my hair. It needed washing but I couldn't do that myself. Liz would help me to do that later. For now I secured it with a hair bobble, just to keep it out of my face and off my neck. I awkwardly managed to remove my pyjama shorts and vest top, leaving them on the floor, and I stood naked in front of the sink. I strained to hear sounds of Jack or Danny in the bedroom, but all I heard was a faint murmur of voices, and knew that they were both waiting in case I needed them.

The huge bandage on my neck looked grotesque, heavy and uncomfortable. There were scratches on my face, a bruise on my cheek. There were more bruises all over my body, some of which I could see, some that I could only feel. My white skin was covered with purple, black and red blotches, and a few more scratches and grazes.

The sink was almost full so I turned the taps off, checking the water temperature. Finally it was time to inspect my wounds. My medical bag was on top of the low shelving unit next to the sink. The hospital nurses had given me spare bandages, antiseptic wipes and cream, with instructions on how to change the dressing. They had asked me to see a nurse to do it but I wanted to help myself, so they had warned me to be careful, and had said I shouldn't do it alone, because my body's instinctive reaction might cause me to faint. Of course I had nodded, agreeing with them, but I hadn't thought much of it. Now I was beginning to see what they meant, and was glad to have Jack and Danny waiting in the bedroom beyond.

I took a deep breath, and then heard Danny's voice outside the bathroom door. "Jessica, are you alright?" he asked, "It might be better if you at least let Jack in to help you. Or me, if you are worried about his reaction to the blood. Please, trust us. We are concerned about you."

Again the tears sprang to my eyes, knowing that both these men cared about me so much. I kept my voice steady, which was an achievement.

"I'm fine, thanks Danny," I said, "Just about to change the bandages now."

This was it. I carefully peeled back the bandage on my stomach. There was blood on it, since the incident yesterday at Liz and Rob's house. I had seen this wound but it was still a shock to properly inspect it. There were four clear claw marks gouged into my skin. The doctors had stitched them, but they were weeping and tender. I didn't know if they would scar, and at first I was afraid to touch them, since the skin around them was so red and damaged.

I carefully cleaned the wound, wincing at the stinging pains, and then I applied a fresh dressing and bandage. Again I steadied myself against the sink, feeling light headed and dizzy, my body temperature burning up and then cooling down alternately. Danny's voice came through the door again.

"Jessica, please let me in," he said, "I am concerned that you might faint with shock when you see the damage. I can smell the blood from the claw marks. Please, do not be stubborn."

I stared into the mirror again. Should I let him in? And where was Jack, why was he so quiet? I had a vision of him salivating over the fresh blood on my skin, his eyes glowing silver and his skin white, and I shivered and went cold all over. No, I could not allow him in here, not right now. Then I remembered Danny in wolf form, even though it was hazy. He was terrifying, and I wasn't convinced it would be wise to allow him into this small confined space either. Plus I was naked, and I really didn't want to give him the wrong idea.

My voice was shaking just a little, and I was gasping from my exertions, but I managed to reply.

"I'm fine, Danny, honest," I said, "Please, just wait there. I'm nervous about what you might do."

He seemed to understand and I heard movement in the bedroom, as though he had sat on the floor.

"Where's Jack, is he there?" I asked.

Jack's voice came through the door.

"Yes I am here, Jessica," he said, "You need not fear me because of your wounds. I am fully fed, and completely in control. If you need assistance, I will be very careful with you."

I momentarily wondered about letting him in. But my fear stopped me. No, I was way too vulnerable here, even if this was the man I loved. I would handle it. If I fainted, then they could come and rescue me, but not before.

I turned my attention back to the wounds. The bandage on my stomach felt better now, and while I was tending the wound I had used a flannel with soap and water to clean myself up. My body was starting to feel more refreshed, clean and cool. My heart was thumping. Now it was time to inspect the big one on my neck, the worst wound. I could feel Seamus tearing at my neck as memories flooded back. I swallowed, forcing the memory out of my head, and then I lifted the edge of the surgical tape, and carefully removed the bandage. It came away slowly, and I saw in the mirror that there was fluid and blood on it. I rolled it up quickly and dropped it in the bin, closing my eyes to try and chase away the nausea that suddenly enveloped me. But as the air hit the open wound, I started to feel faint, and gripped the sink tightly, hoping the cold, solid ceramic would help steady me. After breathing deeply several times, I slowly opened my eyes, and forced myself to look.

My neck was a raw mess. There were some stitches, at the top and bottom edges of the wound, where the doctors had attempted to close it up. And there were traces of that brown substance that surgeons use, was it iodine or something? I wasn't sure. But there was a hole in my neck, and it was red, raw and bloody. As soon as the warm air in the bathroom hit it I lost control. The nausea took over and I barely managed to lift the toilet lid and turn myself towards it, as I was violently sick.

I fell to my knees, crying as I vomited. I tried to stand, holding on to the toilet, the sink, anything, but my body had given up and it just wanted to fall to the floor. I cried out in frustration and fear, my voice shrill but shaky with tears.

I vaguely heard Jack and Danny shout my name, heard the door bang open, and felt somebody's arms around me. It was Danny who caught me, but I could see Jack just behind him. I vaguely saw his eyes shining silver and I thought, 'It's the blood; he wants it. That's why he won't come near me.' Then I tried to focus on Danny, but my eyes were rolling in my head, my body not sure whether to feel pain or numbness, hot or cold.

Danny laid me on the floor, hurriedly putting a towel under my head, and he propped my legs up on the edge of the bath. I tried to speak, to focus on him. My voice sounded pitiful and helpless.

"Danny it's a mess," I said feebly, "It's horrible. He did that to me. Why?" Danny gently stroked my hair back, soothing me, and deftly grabbed a fresh dressing to apply. He spoke as he worked, cleaning the edges of the wound before fixing the new bandage in place.

"He wanted to kill you, Jessica, but he failed," he said, "I am so sorry. Please rest, and allow your body to heal. There are no further explanations we can give." Somewhere in my confusion I realized I was still naked but was too weak to feel embarrassed or self-conscious. I was glad when Jack moved closer to me; his eyes back to their usual blue colour. He carefully wrapped a large bath towel around my body just under my arms, tucking it into place, and I managed a weak smile.

After a few minutes Danny carefully scooped me into his arms and carried me back into Jack's bedroom, placing me on the bed. I was so weak, my body limp, I couldn't move if I wanted to. Jack brought me a fresh cold glass of water, and held it to my lips as I tried to sip it, putting an arm around me so I was cradled against his body. He seemed so warm and comforting. I just wanted him to hold me, to soothe me and tell me everything would be all right.

I felt the bed move as Danny sat the other side of me, and I was aware of him gently stroking my hair, looking at his brother. It didn't feel awkward. I was overcome by a feeling of gratitude that I at least had love and attention from these two men. They would do their best to protect me, to comfort me while I healed. I could learn about them, I could really get to know them both, properly at last. But I had to remember that they weren't human, and I had to start making allowances for that. Jack roused me enough to make me swallow a few more of my tablets, and then he lay beside me on the bed, Danny lying the other side. Their bodies were warm and comforting, and eventually I sank into sleep, exhausted and overcome with the strain of everything. There were no more questions, my mind needed to be quiet, and the last voice I heard was my mother's, gently telling me that everything would be alright and that I was finally in the place I belonged.

EPILOGUE

Emily-Rose haunted my dreams for the next week but we discovered that while Danny was around me she couldn't do very much. She had wanted the werewolf dead for more than one reason. Because Danny was Jack's twin he carried an extra metaphysical connection to his brother that was established long before they met her. And because of this connection Danny was able to break her hold over Jack. Subsequently he could keep her away from me but only if he was nearby. I struggled with the strange intimacy we had to forge but I kept reminding myself that this was what happened with non-humans. I had to learn to deal with it and accept it, for my own safety. Besides Danny was very well behaved, knowing when to stop being playful and when a serious attitude was required.

During that first week my wounds continued to heal slowly, and painfully, and my dreams were vivid and frightening. At first I relived the terror of when Seamus had attacked me, waking in the night screaming and in pain. Jack would comfort me, cuddling me his arms, kissing me, reassuring me that Seamus was dead and would never hurt me again. One night when I woke Jack wasn't there, he had gone away to feed, but Danny ran into the room and took me in his arms instead. I had to let him comfort me or I would have gone insane, so I fought back that niggling voice of reason, telling myself there were more important things to worry about.

Emily-Rose possessed me three times while I still carried Jack's blood, but she grew weaker as her metaphysical connection faded. The first possession happened when Jack was at home. I blacked out again and when I woke I was in bed and he was watching me from the chair, his body still and his face serious. He told me that Emily-Rose had again tried to tempt him away. He couldn't force her out of me but she lost her connection for some reason and while she was distracted he managed to revive me.

The second occasion was when Jack had gone out to feed and Danny was watching over me. Again he had to call his powers as pack leader to bring me back and this time I woke on the kitchen floor with blood seeping from both my wounds. Danny explained that the blood and the raw flesh helped him to bring what he called his beast to the fore, strengthening him against her. It frightened me, not just because of the blood but because I was so deeply unconscious that anything could have happened to me and I would never have known.

The third occasion was with Simon. He had come to see me and I was sitting out in the garden on a deckchair, enjoying the sunshine. It was later in the week and I was slowly starting to process everything that had happened so that I could make sense of it all. Simon had sat beside me on the grass and one minute we were in mid-conversation as he explained how he became a werewolf and the next I woke lying on the grass with Simon crouched above me. His eyes were amber, his face distorted, and his voice a growl as he spoke.

"It was her: that vampire bitch," he said gruffly, "I managed to chase her out at the expense of some pack wolves but you are safe for now. She is getting weaker." Simon told me that he had called forth some of the power from the other wolves by using his strength as Danny's lieutenant. But a few of the weaker wolves would have transformed as a result and they would need to hunt before returning to human form. He had left soon after, leaving me alone with Jack while he and Danny went to take care of their pack, and to explain to the submissive wolves what had happened.

Everything was so frightening. My emotions ran from hurt and pain, to anger and frustration, and finally to a grudging acceptance of all of these strange people and this confusing new life I was discovering. But the only way I could handle it was to focus on healing my body and getting my life back to normal. If I could just return to my bookshop, spend some time with Liz, and remember that I was still human, and then I wouldn't go insane. So that became my focus.

I had to seriously think about whether I could stay in a relationship with Jack, knowing now what he truly was. But the answer to that proved very simple indeed. I couldn't leave Jack, my heart made that perfectly clear even though my head complained. I didn't want to leave Jack. I was sure of his love for me and of mine for him, and with that certainty came the strength to deal with these revelations.

It was clear that I had matured; I had finally accepted that sometimes we have to let down our defences in order to experience real life. We cannot drift along in a tightly woven bubble of self-preservation; humans are not designed for that. We must explore our emotions, our anxieties, our actions, and our feelings for other people, no matter whether they are human or not. Otherwise we might as well be dead.

It was hard keeping secrets from Liz but I knew it was for the best. She was human and pregnant, and she had enough to deal with. Rob didn't want her to know the truth because he was worried about dragging her into trouble. I knew that there would be more enemies for Jack and Danny to face, and while I worried for my own safety, at least I had some way of dealing with it.

Once I was properly healed Jack promised to train me in self-defence and how to use a gun. At least then I wouldn't be so helpless. But he said that my biggest asset was my newfound witch heritage. I had to learn more about it, and about what I was capable of. Jack said I had the potential to be very powerful in my own way, if I was only willing to learn and explore my abilities. That prospect both excited and frightened me, but Lillian came back into my dreams and promised that now was the time and that if I would only trust Jack, I would finally learn to be at peace with myself. So he arranged to introduce me to a friend of his who was a practicing witch and could make a start on bringing out my true abilities and teaching me how to use magic as self-defence against non-humans.

Again it all depended on me healing my physical wounds, which turned out to be a slow process. It was frustrating, but I gradually began to feel excited about the new adventures that lay ahead, and in the meantime I requested some books from the local library that might offer me an insight. Jack dutifully supplied everything I needed, encouraging me to explore the legends, and bringing me some texts from Marcus' own personal library that proved very interesting indeed.

Another week after I had discharged myself from hospital I felt that Emily-Rose had left me. Her laughter was gone from my head and I stopped blacking out. Jack said it meant that I was fully human again, no more vampire blood, and that brought relief. It also brought more pain, and I was intensely grateful for modern medicine.

Now I had to adjust to living with a vampire and a werewolf. Not a problem. After being kidnapped and almost raped by a werewolf, nearly dying, and then being possessed by a vengeful vampire, life was suddenly a lot easier to handle.

Love hurts, yes, but it brings far greater rewards and experiences that make life worth living. Maybe my experience was slightly more intense and dramatic than most, but everybody has the potential to truly appreciate real love if they are willing to open up to it. It had taken a while for me to realize this, but now I had matured and discovered that love is complicated and means different things to different people. But ultimately it is a wild ride of emotional highs and lows, and incredible sensual, sexual, and spiritual experiences. And that is what I received from Jack Mason. He is my lover, my vampire, and my soul mate.